5-19

WITHDRAWN

TIPTON CO. LIBRARY
TIPTON, INDIANA

THE UNQUIET HEART

Also by Kaite Welsh:

The Wages of Sin

THE UNQUIET HEART

KAITE WELSH

PEGASUS CRIME
NEW YORK LONDON

THE UNQUIET HEART

Pegasus Crime is an imprint of
Pegasus Books, Ltd.
148 West 37th Street, 13th Floor
New York, NY 10018

Copyright © 2019 by Kaite Welsh

First Pegasus Books hardcover edition February 2019

All rights reserved. No part of this book may be reproduced in whole or in part without written permission from the publisher, except by reviewers who may quote brief excerpts in connection with a review in a newspaper, magazine, or electronic publication; nor may any part of this book be reproduced, stored in a retrieval system, or transmitted in any form or by any means electronic, mechanical, photocopying, recording, or other, without written permission from the publisher.

ISBN: 978-1-68177-749-8

10 9 8 7 6 5 4 3 2 1

Printed in the United States of America
Distributed by W. W. Norton & Company, Inc.

For Lola, with all my love.

Chapter 1

The grey stone archway loomed overhead as I dashed through the puddles from my carriage, cursing under my breath.

Julia Latymer was huddled by the wall, sheltering from the rain and smoking. She glanced up at me and nodded.

'Gilchrist.'

'Have they gone up yet?'

She rolled her eyes, shivering. 'Would I be standing out here in the rain if they had?'

'You could always wait indoors. Thornhill is.' I looked towards the building, where Alison Thornhill stood in the glare of the electric light, looking every bit as anxious as I felt.

'Tried that. She kept blabbering on at me. I'm waiting for Edith.' Julia shot me a glance, as if daring me to say something.

'I don't know what you're worried about,' I grumbled. 'You know you're top of our class. You're just standing out here to torment the rest of us into feeling even more anxious.'

'I'm worried about the same thing as you are,' Julia snapped. 'Failing my first year and being sent home in disgrace. Except it wouldn't be disgrace, because our mothers would be delighted and start casting around for the first suitable bachelor to marry us off to and that would be it. No more lectures, no more exams, no glittering surgical career. Just a husband and a household to manage and the hope that whatever remains of my brains gets passed on to the next generation.'

I stamped my feet, trying to block out both the cold and the grim reality that Julia painted – one that was far closer to my future than to hers. A gust of wet wind battered us. Was that rain or sleet? Perhaps it would snow and we'd be stranded in the medical school and I wouldn't have to go home to dress for the dreaded evening that awaited us.

'It doesn't matter,' I told her stubbornly, believing it because I needed to. 'We'll both have passed. We're just as good at medicine as the men are – better in some cases. Ross might have been able to grow a very fine moustache over the Christmas vac, but he couldn't diagnose a cold if he was sneezing into his handkerchief.' Still, I couldn't help but suspect that when it came down to it, the moustache would be judged as more important even if he scraped an acceptable mark in the examinations and I passed with flying colours.

I should have. All I had ever wanted was to be a doctor, and last autumn I had found myself studying at the University of Edinburgh, which boasted one of the most august medical schools in the world. Nothing should have distracted me from the hours of lectures and dissections, and for the first few months I had lost myself in what felt like a dream world – one of anatomy sketches and chemical formulae, of science and knowledge and finally being treated as though my intelligence was important and not an embarrassing inconvenience. A world in which I was no longer the oddity in the drawing room, trying to discuss education and women's suffrage, but one of a like-minded group of women who shared my purpose and ambition.

And yet I had found kinship not with my classmates but with a woman I had been meant to cut up as she lay on the dissection table. I had recognised her – recognised myself in her – and found myself stumbling into a world that turned everything I thought I knew on its head.

All of which was cold comfort when I realised how little time I had spent studying in the end, and how much it meant to me when it was about to be ripped away.

'You look like you're going to be sick,' Julia said dispassionately. 'Cigarette? Calms the nerves.'

I looked at her fingers clenching her own cigarette, white-knuckled from more than just the cold, and wondered if it was working. I wondered if Professor Merchiston would let us into the medicine cabinet so that I could take a long, soothing swig from the laudanum bottle – and then just as quickly forced my thoughts away from him. The memory of stumbling through my *materia medica* oral examination, frantically scrounging up everything I knew about compounds, dosage and poison as he watched me with an unreadable expression for the best part of an hour was not one I wanted to revisit.

'I'm going inside,' I muttered. Who knew how many more days I had ahead of me of loitering in university corridors. I should enjoy it while I could. Truth be told, it wasn't that much warmer indoors, but Alison Thornhill's delighted embrace took some of the chill out of my bones.

'I thought you were going to stand out there for ever. It's cold enough without Julia Latymer taking the temperature down a few degrees with all that icy disapproval.'

'She offered me a cigarette,' I said hopefully. 'That's the friendliest she's been all year. I think I'm making progress.'

Alison looked at me pityingly. 'Gilchrist, it's January.'

Before I could think of a suitably cutting retort, our conversation was interrupted by excited whoops from a gaggle of the men, and I saw the Dean of Medicine sweep through the corridor carrying a sheaf of papers, which his clerk affixed to the noticeboard as he watched. They fluttered in the breeze as the men crowded around, all as anxious as we were.

'At this rate, we won't get through that throng until next Christmas. Do you think if I poke one of them in the kidneys with my umbrella, they'll move?'

'I don't think we'll have to,' I said with a sinking heart. A shorter list had also been pinned up, and there were no students fighting to see who ranked where on that. Our names, I realised.

I eased us past the group – some cheering, some looking like they wanted to cry. We should have been there, I thought, anger curdling inside me. My name should have been sandwiched between Alexander Gibson and Malcolm Hughes. We had sat the same exams and yet my name was an afterthought, an embarrassment, shunted off to the side to let the real medical students shine.

'Is that us?' Julia marched up to the list with a bravery I didn't possess. 'Oh Chri— Ah, *cripes*, sorry, Mrs Elphinstone.' The chaperone glowered at her.

'What's the matter? Did you fail?' Much as I hadn't liked Julia last year, I would never wish for her to fail. I had wished that she would magically disappear, that someone would plant spiders in her bag or that circumstances would somehow conspire so that she lost all her luxurious chestnut hair, but I had never wanted something truly bad to happen.

'Not exactly,' she managed, pointing at the marks.

One hundred per cent. In everything. I glanced quickly down to mine, which weren't as spectacular as Julia's but were solid enough to prove that I hadn't sabotaged myself. Nothing below seventy-two but nothing above eighty-nine. It could have been better – should have been – but it was enough to keep me in class and that was good enough for me. I felt my knees buckle with relief.

'If this is the future of medicine, then God help your

patients.' The rowdy cheers died down and I turned to face Gregory Merchiston, looking distinctly unimpressed at our achievements. I avoided his eyes, and not just because we both knew that my mark in his class should have been higher.

It was hard to imagine that he was the same man who had broken down in front of me in Elisabeth Chalmers' drawing room, raw and exposed as I had never seen him before, his voice thick with emotion, tired eyes shining with tears he was too proud to shed. That his pale, gaunt face had worn stubble that rasped my cheeks, warm breath ghosting across my skin and his mouth finally brushing mine after a moment of delicious agony that seemed to last a lifetime. Had our lips really touched? I wasn't sure. I could no longer distinguish between reality and the way I had replayed it in my mind again and again in the weeks that followed – including during my examination, where the only sound in the room came from my stammered answers and the rhythmic clicking of the chaperone's knitting needles as she sat watching us, unaware that she was too late to prevent anything improper from passing between us.

There was nothing of that raw, exposed emotion present in Professor Merchiston today. He stood, his posture taut and his expression forbidding, as his gaze raked over us before finally coming to rest on me.

In the dim light, his eyes looked black as coal but lacking its warmth. He turned away and my heart sank.

This wouldn't have happened had I been a man. Probably not, I amended privately, remembering Julia and Edith and the strange embrace I had once caught them in. That was the real reason behind Julia's civility, I knew, not friendship at all. For once, it wasn't me whose secrets would see her pilloried at best, expelled at worst. I glanced at my peers, in their sober dresses and neat hair, desperate to avoid any trappings of femininity lest it remind people that their proper place was elsewhere. How many of them were hiding secrets we would do anything to protect? Even now, Julia mistrusted me. It wasn't as though I was going to stand up one day and announce to the entire lecture theatre that she and Edith were inverts, committing unnatural acts behind closed doors. Frankly, I wasn't entirely certain what said unnatural acts involved, although I doubted it was any worse than the lurid and frankly anatomically improbable entertainments the male students boasted of.

But none of it mattered, not now I had incontrovertible proof that I could do this. My love for medicine was requited and nothing else mattered. Not Merchiston, not the tragic events of the previous autumn and certainly not the contents of the box buried deep in my reticule. The sharp smell of formaldehyde and the rich tang of ink reached my nostrils as I entered the lecture theatre, and I felt all my worries fall away.

It was inevitable that even with our brief moment of comradeship, it would be Julia who shattered it.

Still giddy with the high of coming top of the class – perhaps even the year – I don't think she meant to be cruel when she called out, 'That's two pieces of good news this week for you, Gilchrist, you dark horse! Wasn't it your name I spied in the engagement notices of *The Times* the other day?'

My cheeks burned with shame at the revelation, but it was nothing to what came next.

'I didn't know you were engaged.'

Alison wouldn't meet my eyes. For a while she had been the closest thing to a friend I had, and even if she hadn't always championed me in front of a mocking crowd, she had at least always tried to buck me up in private. I should have shared this with her.

'Of course you were always going to be the first to drop out.' Moira Owen smirked, as though reading my thoughts.

'You probably only matriculated in the hopes of meeting a nice would-be doctor to marry.'

'Don't be beastly,' Julia said. 'Women can marry and work – you should know; isn't your mother a washerwoman?'

Moira flinched. I had been on the receiving end of Julia's taunts often enough to know that they stung.

One of my favourite things about the new world I had found myself in was just how divorced it was from the humdrum banality of home life. I might not have shared the late-night studying sessions over cocoa and crumpets that the students in boarding houses enjoyed, but in the quad I still felt part of things, as though I had sloughed off my old skin and was a new sort of girl. Having my engagement brought out into the open felt like being stripped down to my underthings in public. I felt exposed, embarrassed as though I had been caught in a particularly private moment. Having my name attached to a murder was hardly going to endear me to all the people who had already dismissed me as a loose woman, but I wasn't ashamed of the scandal. I was ashamed of the engagement and all it represented.

'Delightful as this tea party is, ladies, I thought you had come here intending to learn,' Merchiston drawled. 'Miss Gilchrist, there is an equation on the blackboard for correctly calculating a dosage. Kindly come up and solve it – unless you're too busy planning your trousseau.'

'Was Professor Chalmers this distracted when he married, Professor?' I snapped. 'Or do you think all women have their heads full of feathers and fripperies the moment they're handed a ring?'

His eyes grew stormy. 'Much as I hate to involve myself in the personal affairs of students, I find myself agreeing with Miss Owen. You may well fit your studies around the preparations for your wedding. You may even graduate with a ring on your finger. But I find it hard to believe that your future husband, infatuated as I'm sure he is, will ever let you practise medicine. As it stands, you are wasting your time – I will not permit you to waste mine. Now will you solve the bloody equation?'

I picked up the chalk with trembling hands, fighting the urge to throw it at him. He knew how to throw his punches, that much I'd give him. He had homed in on my biggest fear about this whole catastrophe and lanced it in public like a boil. It was unjustified, I fumed, as I solved his damn equation and made my way back to my seat.

I caught his eye for a fleeting moment and, rather than the scorn I expected to see, he looked terribly sad. When he cancelled the rest of our *materia medica* lecture, claiming a migraine, I felt guiltily relieved that I wouldn't have to face him.

By the end of the day I was exhausted, emotional and covered in stains I couldn't – and frankly didn't want to – identify. Normally all I would want would be a substantial meal and a hot bath, but if I could have stayed out in the drizzle on Teviot Place all night rather than climbing into my uncle's carriage, I would have done it and gladly.

I had seen police carriages stuffed with prisoners, all violent or drunk or both but all looking out through the window with the same expressions of fierce panic, knowing what they were headed towards but with no way of changing their fate. I had faced horrors that a few years ago I had not imagined even existed. I had walked, head held high, into a roomful of men who thought me weak and stupid and proved that I was just as capable as any of them even as my hands trembled at my sides. I had faced ridicule, scorn and sheer cruelty but I had never before wanted to run away quite as much as I did in that moment. Once I stepped into that carriage, my freedom was no longer my own – perhaps for ever.

But not yet. I would rebel against my family's wishes one

last time, and clear the air with the one person I both wanted to and could not avoid.

I rapped sharply on the roof of the cab. 'Calhoun? Take me to Newington first. I have a call to pay.'

Chapter 2

In a quiet street in south Edinburgh, I stood in front of a front door painted in glossy forest green, wondering if I was doing the right thing.

I ran my fingertips over the shiny brass plaque advertising the services of Gregory Merchiston, MD. I hadn't realised he saw private patients and I was struck again at how little I knew of the man who had appointed himself my mentor.

Summoning all my courage, I knocked on the door.

Mrs Logan, his redoubtable housekeeper, of whom Elisabeth had once confessed she was terrified, opened it with a look of distant politeness on her face.

'Is Professor Merchiston at home?' God knew where I would find him if he were elsewhere – a drinking den, the boxing ring?

Her face softened. 'It's Miss Gilchrist, isn't it? I'm afraid the doctor isn't in a fit state to receive visitors today.'

I winced. 'He's that bad?'

'Well, he's no' ready to be seen in polite company, that's for certain. Can I take a message?'

I paused. 'It's rather . . . private.' Her eyebrow rose disapprovingly, but she stepped aside. 'I can't promise he'll see you, but there's no sense you standing on the doorstep in this weather. I'll put the kettle on the hob and you can help me make up his tray. Not that the daft bugger will eat anything, if you'll excuse my language.'

'I've called him worse.'

For a bachelor's abode, it was surprisingly cosy, if somewhat out of date. I realised with a pang that this used to be a family home – what had it looked like when his wife and child were alive? I imagined light and life, a tousle-haired little boy with his father's eyes running rampant, trailed by his adoring Aunt Lucy . . .

But now it was only home to one occupant, a man grieving his sister, who had been murdered by a woman I once called a friend and whose throat, in a blaze of grief and rage and a desire to protect me, he had slit in a freezing makeshift operating theatre two months ago.

Mrs Logan led me to the kitchen, where, true to her word, she made me a cup of strong tea and handed me a generous slice of caraway cake.

'You may as well have it. Lord knows he won't. I've tried every recipe my dear mother passed on to me, rest her soul, and he won't touch more than a few bites. The birds have been eating well this winter, let me tell you.'

'He looks terrible. Is it the same every night?' I regretted the question immediately. I didn't want to know how often he spent his nights elsewhere.

'He eats here more than he used to. Time was he took all his meals with the Chalmerses.'

The same place I was nearly every evening. I felt a pang of guilt at having intruded on his one sanctuary.

She carved some slices of cold pork and added potatoes, carrots and a jug of apple sauce. It was a dismal dinner, but I suspected she had tired of making elaborate dishes that her employer wouldn't touch.

'No sense giving him soup, it'll only go cold,' she tutted,

more to herself than me. 'At least this he can eat hot or cold.'

I wolfed down my tea and cake, realising just how ravenous I was. By the time I was finished, Merchiston's dinner tray was ready – the meat and potatoes, a generous slice of cake and a pot of coffee that I suspected he sorely needed.

'You can help me with this, and we'll see if he can manage a wee talk. I wouldn't hold out for civilised conversation, mind you.'

I had no doubt that she could manage the tray herself, but I took the invitation and let her direct me upstairs to a room at the back of the house.

She paused outside the door. 'Can I trust you to be alone with him? You seem a sensible sort, but girls these days . . . Well, we were never so forward. He's in a dark place, and when he's there he doesnae always remember he's a gentleman.'

I blushed at the insinuation, but nodded. 'I promise – I'm here as a friend, nothing more.'

'Well he could use one of those, right enough.' She patted my arm. 'Good luck. See if you can get him to eat something.'

I took a deep breath and pushed the door open, not sure what to expect.

I had been inside his rooms at the university, and I had always thought they held the essence of him. More bottles of tonics and medicines and poisons than an apothecary, a stuffed crocodile on a shelf that seemed to do nothing but gather dust, and something floating in a jar I had never been brave enough to investigate. But if that was his soul, then this study was his brain writ large.

There was barely an inch of wallpaper to be seen beneath the diagrams and notes scrawled in a familiar handwriting. In one corner of the room an experiment bubbled and smoked, leaving the room smelling faintly of sulphur mingled with tobacco, stale coffee and sweat. The curtains were drawn, but from the way even they had sheaves of papers pinned to them,

I suspected they hadn't been opened for some time. I wondered if Mrs Logan was allowed to clean in here – there was hardly an inch free of debris to dust. Bookshelves lined two walls from floor to ceiling, and my fingers itched to explore their contents.

The room was dominated by the large desk, at which the man himself sat. He was lost in thought, but the light must have been too dim for him to read by. The room was lit by the warm, flickering light of the fire and the lamps had been turned down low. I wondered if he had been sitting here all day, lost in permanent night. Above the desk was a calendar of his lectures – dated three years ago. It was obscured by a yellowing headline pinned to it by a hatpin covered in what I hoped was rust.

Sensing a presence behind him, he sighed but didn't turn around. 'Mrs Logan, I said I wanted to be left alone. Now either obey or bring me another bottle before I'm forced to drink straight ether.'

I pushed the pot of coffee across the desk. 'This might be a better choice.'

He started at my voice and then snorted without looking up. 'Come to reject me again, Miss Gilchrist? Or are you here in your official capacity, the plucky young lady sleuth with her head full of detective stories, thinking she knows better than the polis? Tell me, what do you deduce from this scene?'

My heart ached for him. 'That you might be better off leaving the whisky for another night if you want to be in a fit state to lecture in the morning.'

He grunted. 'I have half a dozen young whelps who barely need to shave to escort around the Royal Infirmary tomorrow morning. Rest assured, they'll be as hung-over as I am.'

'And with such a fine mentor, who can blame them?'

He turned to me then, and I saw his eyes were bloodshot and swollen.

'And you'd know all about mentors, wouldn't you? At least I won't lure them to a dilapidated slum and pour a bottle of laudanum down their throats.'

How was it that he could talk about the most intimate thing we shared and yet feel so distant?

'If you're going to stand in judgement, you may as well join me in finishing the dregs of this bottle.' He picked up his half-empty glass and glanced around his desk until his eyes lit on a skull – dear God, I prayed, let it be a wax model – with the parietal bones removed. He squinted inside, upended it, shaking the detritus out, and offered it to me. 'Sorry, I don't have another glass.' I demurred, and he shrugged. 'Suit yourself. You might be better off; I think there were mouse droppings in there.'

He took a long draught, then looked at me, his eyes focusing properly for the first time.

'How the hell do you sleep? You were minutes from death at the hands of a madwoman, you've gone through God knows what with that bastard Beresford and yet somehow you're still there in the front row every morning, raising your hand before I can even finish a question, fresh as a daisy and a thorn in my side.'

'You work us too hard.' I smiled gently, hoping to lighten his mood. 'I'm asleep before my head hits the pillow most nights.'

He gave me a strange, long look and I regretted the image my words conjured.

When he spoke, his voice was roughened from more than just the drink. 'Every time I close my eyes, I see her in your place. What she went through . . . I should have been there. Instead, she died alone and frightened in that stinking back alley. Her corpse was in my university and I didn't even know she was dead until you stormed into my room with your theories and accusations.'

'I'm so sorry, Professor. If I'd known . . .' I would have done things so differently. Made him a friend instead of an enemy. Stopped Fiona before she could descend any further into the madness to which an uncaring world had driven her.

'What are you here for, anyway? I assume you didn't come to harangue me about my drinking.'

'Or about how little you're eating.'

'You've been listening to that mother hen in the kitchen. She'd have me fattened up like a goose for Christmas if I let her.'

'Avian analogies aside, she has a point. You might be able to teach a group of undergraduates with nothing in your system but Scotch, but I won't be the cause of it.'

He grimaced. 'You seem to forget that it was me who saved your life last autumn. Only to watch you throw it away on some chinless second son. That's the young for you, I suppose. No gratitude.'

'I came here because I was concerned for you.'

'Oh, don't you lecture me.' It was getting harder to ignore the way his words slurred, and I wondered just how much he had had to drink. 'You're not a detective, Sarah. You're not even a doctor. What you are is a first-year medical student with an unwanted fiancé, a steady hand and a talent for getting herself in trouble.'

'Better a medical student with ideas above her station than a bitter old drunk.'

The words were out before I could stop them, but by God I meant them.

He nodded grimly, as though I had said exactly what he suspected I would. 'Aye. Well if you think you can do better, lassie, please – be my guest. Save the whole fucking world and then when you realise that the human race is too stubborn and foolhardy to stay saved for long, come back and I'll pour you a drink.' He squinted into the bottle. 'But I'd advise you to hurry up, or there'll be none left.'

I put my hand on his arm without thinking. Beneath the rage and the drink, there was so much pain in his eyes. He flinched, as though my touch had scalded him, and I realised that he had his shirtsleeves rolled up and my palm was resting on his bare muscled forearm. I felt his pulse throb strong, steady and just a little too fast in his radial artery, and my fingers longed to trace the crease of his inner elbow.

When he pulled me to him, I wasn't surprised.

His breath was warm on my cheek, his face so close I could taste the whisky. The jackhammer beat of my heart quickened until I thought I could feel it slamming against my ribcage, and the whole world shrank to nothing but his nearness and the searing sensation of his hand on my wrist. I thought for one stupid, foolish moment that he was going to kiss me.

Instead, he whispered into my ear, 'I saved the wrong woman.'

He pushed me away savagely, without taking his gaze from mine. He was savouring the hurt in my eyes, and I wouldn't give him the satisfaction of seeing the tears that built hotly in my eyes.

Staggering away as though I were the one who were drunk, I yanked the door open and stumbled into the hallway and the waiting figure of Mrs Logan.

'He's a beast when he's had too much.' She looked me over, frowning. 'He didnae hurt you, did he? I've never known him to be a bad man, not in that way, but if he laid a finger on you . . .'

My wrist was sore from where he had grabbed me, but I knew without a doubt that he would have gone no further.

Banishing my doubts, I shook my head. 'I won't say that he was a perfect gentleman, but he wasn't . . . that is, he didn't . . .'

She looked at my wrist, the sleeve pushed up slightly and my skin red.

'You're missing a button,' she said. 'They're devils if you

don't use hard-wearing thread. You wait for me in the kitchen and get another pot of tea on; I'll fetch my sewing kit and see if it fell off in the master's study.'

I lingered on the stairs for a moment, listening to her raised voice, before hurrying downstairs, determined to make Mrs Logan the best damned cup of tea she had drunk in her life.

When she emerged, she gave me a swift nod as if to say that the matter had been dealt with.

'He's a good man, but a proud one. And make no mistake, he's had a harder time than most. He's hurting right now, but that's no excuse to take it out on someone who's only trying to be a friend to him.'

'Lucy,' I whispered.

She shook her head sadly. 'She was a wild one, that girl. Full of life. It's a terrible thing to lose someone you love.' Her words were heavy, and I wondered what loss had brought Mrs Logan into Gregory Merchiston's employ. 'He's been drinking himself to sleep and propping himself up with God only knows what concoctions ever since she disappeared. I thought being able to grieve her might give him some sort of peace, but he's been in a foul mood for weeks.'

Ever since I got engaged. I didn't doubt that our mutual friends the Chalmerses had shared the news with him, even if they didn't mention just how bitterly and fruitlessly I opposed it.

'You know, there's not many who'd brave the lion in his den, much less a young lady. But you lassies have more courage than men twice your age. Going into the university like that and demanding to be treated the same – if you ask me, it's the Lord's work, although there's not many who'll say it.'

I smiled, and meant it. 'Mrs Logan, you are a jewel among housekeepers. I'm tempted to steal you away myself if I didn't think that your employer would chase me down the street with half the Edinburgh police force in tow.'

'He's loyal to those who earn his trust, that's for certain. You're in that number, though God knows he didn't show it tonight. You'd best be getting back – you don't want your family to start asking questions.'

As she saw me into the cab, I yanked off my gloves, rubbing my cold hands together, and fumbled through my reticule to find the hated object that I had stuffed in there as soon as I had left the house that morning. The diamond sparkled in the light from the gas lamps we passed. Even in my bag, the silver had chilled and it burned with cold as I slid it onto my finger. As we clattered across the cobblestones, I forced a demure smile onto my face and prepared to meet my future husband.

Chapter 3

The stomach lining shone dully pearlescent under the glaring electric light, bulging hideously with flesh and sticky lumps of fat. The thought of sliding my knife through the glutinous mess made me feel queasy. If this had been an examination I would have failed it, and gladly. Instead, it was dinner.

I had survived half a year in Scotland without being compelled to eat haggis, but this was the one night of the year when patriotism won over gastronomy. Outside, the January night was bitter and dreich, sleet falling from dark, swollen clouds and leaving the cobbles slick and dangerous. Inside, there was poetry. I wasn't sure which was worse.

The university was holding a grand cèilidh tonight, where the guests would work off their neeps and tatties in frenetic whirling across the ballroom floor. I felt a pang of envy, even though any attempts my friend Elisabeth had made to teach me the steps to the Gay Gordons had ended in tangled limbs and cursing.

I wouldn't be displaying my dancing abilities tonight, however, even if my aunt had permitted it; she had reminded me as I was cinched into my corset, 'You do not have a history of comporting yourself well at parties, Sarah.' In any case, we had received a far more impressive invitation, celebrating the *deus ex machina* of Aunt Emily and Aurora Greene, each finding in the other an equally unmarriageable ward.

The reason I was here was currently stammering his way through Robert Burns' 'Address to a Haggis', although personally I thought a eulogy might have been more apt for whatever animal had sacrificed its life for such an inglorious end.

Miles Greene, younger son of Colonel Cuthbert Greene, would hardly have been my choice for a husband. In fact, I was prepared to do without the ghastly institution of marriage altogether in favour of my medical studies – not, as Aunt Emily had pointed out on more than a few occasions, that I exactly had a queue of suitors breathlessly awaiting my decision. Greene Minor himself was neither handsome nor, as far as I could tell, particularly intelligent, and if he had a sense of humour, it was one I didn't share. What he did have was money and a respectable family as eager to marry him off as mine was to get rid of me.

I kept my eyes focused on him, but my mind was wandering anywhere it could – the previous day's lectures, my less-than-impressive results from the Christmas examinations, the fact that my mother would be arriving in a few days. That my own parents were not attending my engagement party would have been cause for comment had the happy couple been anyone else. As it was, I half expected someone to check my teeth as though I were a horse Uncle Hugh was selling – for quite the bargain price.

My fiancé's family was better represented – Colonel Greene was ramrod straight and mouthing the words along with his son in patriotic fervour, and his wife Aurora was the picture of beaming maternal pride. Both her sons were in attendance tonight: the younger, Miles, who had finally found a bride even if she was a bluestocking of questionable virtue; and the elder, Alisdair. The heir to the Greene family's title and fortunes – comfortably married off and with a child on the way at his estate in the Borders – was so like and yet not like his brother that Miles looked even more lacking in comparison. With a sandy shock of hair and a firm mouth, he was like a charcoal sketch, all defined lines and shadowed planes. Miles was more like pointillism – acceptable from a distance and then worse the closer you got.

Perhaps age would improve him, I thought without much hope. We – or rather I – had agreed on a long engagement; enough time for me to finish my studies and, as my uncle said, 'get "this nonsense" out of my head once and for all'. In the likely event that Miles at twenty-seven was no better candidate than Miles at twenty-three, it still gave me four years to find a way out of the damned situation, or at the very least find a hospital willing to accept a female doctor.

'Aurora, your hair looks wonderful tonight. Is that a new style from Paris?' Aunt Emily smiled unctuously.

My future mother-in-law sighed. 'Sadly not. I'm afraid that this is hair *à la Blackwell* – our housemaid. My lady's maid, Wilson, has done a midnight flit at the worst possible time. Run off with some man, no doubt.'

'Did she leave a note?' I asked.

'You would have thought,' Aurora sniffed. 'After years of service – where she was rather generously recompensed, I don't mind telling you – she vanished without a word.'

She seemed very unruffled about the disappearance of a woman from under her roof.

'Have you called the police?'

'My dear, if one called the police about every absconding servant . . . You'll learn all this when you have a household of your own to manage, of course.'

'Enough of this gossip,' the colonel groused. 'Miles, finish addressing the damn haggis so we can eat.'

From the unholy looks of the thing, I wouldn't have been surprised if it had answered back.

The knife glinted in the candlelight and trembled in Miles' hand. He sharpened it as he spoke and, muttering something in broad Scots about gushing entrails – perhaps I had better give this Burns fellow a second chance – plunged it into the stomach.

The smell from the plate was appalling, but that wasn't what made bile rise in my throat.

'Forgive me,' I murmured, and fled the room.

I brought up what little dinner I had managed – in the face of the haggis, it wasn't much – and splashed some water on my face. Away from the table, any semblance of putting a brave face on it crumbled like ash, and I rested my head against the cool porcelain of the sink, trying to get my anger and my shaking hands under control.

I caught a glimpse of myself in the glass and it was like seeing a ghost. I could have been the Sarah Gilchrist from a year ago, the girl with a burning passion to study medicine and an unshakeable belief that the world would grant her wish, parental disapproval be damned. I wasn't her, but nor was I the frail, wretched creature from months later, who had been abandoned with her relatives and told to make her own way in the world.

The girl in the mirror met my guarded gaze. This, then, was one of the inaugural class of young ladies who had gained entrance into the hallowed halls of Edinburgh's medical school. The satirists, even the ones scribbling for a better class of newspaper, liked to paint us alternately as monstrous spinsters with brains bulging out of our heads and hairs sticking out of our chins, and swooning girls with eighteen-inch waists and an eye on a doctor for a husband. They had, needless to say, never attempted to meet with the subjects of their pens, and I wasn't sure what they'd make of me if they did. Certainly the glittering diamond on my finger – I'd have to remove that before Tuesday's anatomy lecture lest it disappear into some half-dissected chest cavity – suggested I was more interested in having letters before my name than after, but no doe-eyed maid looked this tired or resigned to her fate.

The powder my aunt's lady's maid had dusted lightly across my face and the smudge of rouge she had rubbed roughly onto my lips felt like a mask. I was no blushing bride-to-be, a maiden in her first flush of youth gazing starry-eyed at her beloved. I wasn't even the ruined girl my family thought I was, patched up almost as good as new if you didn't look too closely at the seams. The cloud of scent she had sprinkled over me couldn't hide the stench of death that followed me everywhere I went.

My short time in Edinburgh had been marked by murder – first of a young prostitute, then of her killer as Gregory Merchiston took a life to save mine, only to see me throw it away on humdrum conventionality. No wonder he was angry with me.

Much as I wanted to dwell on my fate – or slip through the front door into the street and run as though my life depended on it – even I had to concede that the time to break things off was perhaps not the night of my engagement party. All I had to do tonight was survive, and I had proved rather good at that of late.

Retracing my steps, I heard muffled voices from the rooms above. While the supposed end of my unladylike professional fortunes was being celebrated in the dining room, there were women working all around the house, an unseen hive of activity on which this household – and mine, and countless others – ran. Knowing I had delayed my return for as long as I could, I pushed open the dining room door with what I hoped was an expression of serene joy – and just in time.

'Sarah, we were waiting for you.' Aunt Emily's tone was light, but there was a warning in her eyes.

I couldn't afford to displease her; it wouldn't get me the result I wanted, and I was more likely to end up barred from attending lectures for a week than receive any sympathy.

'It's your turn now.' Miles smiled shyly.

Ah, yes. The one point of the evening I was dreading even more than simpering across the table in the direction of my betrothed.

I lifted my glass and recited the only scrap of Burns I had been able to stomach – an unfortunate pun under the circumstances – or understand.

'While Europe's eye is fix'd on mighty things,
The fate of Empires and the fall of Kings;
While quacks of State must each produce his plan,
And even children lisp the Rights of Man;
Amid this mighty fuss just let me mention,
The Rights of Woman merit some attention.'

I heard Aunt Emily's intake of breath across the table. This was not the sweet speech I had practised in front of her, but in the face of a captive audience, most of whom would rather see me dead in childbirth than studying medicine, I was not going to let this one rare opportunity to have my say slip through my fingers.

Miles watched me in that unsettling way of his, a gaze that never left my face. An eternity of his basset hound adoration loomed before me as I stumbled to an end.

Colonel Greene smiled indulgently, as though I were a small child imitating the adults. I knew his type. He might have disagreed with what newspaper opinion writers called 'the woman question', but he enjoyed the cut and thrust of the debate, of a woman at least trying to match him wit for wit. There were students like that at the medical school, and privately I always suspected them of being little more than overgrown schoolboys dipping a girl's pigtails in an inkwell to get her attention, as through frustration were on a par with attraction when it came to arousing emotion in a woman.

I would have to be on my guard with my new father-in-law.

'A toast to the happy couple,' came a warm voice to my right. At least I had friends here – Elisabeth Chalmers and her husband Randall, he a medical man and she one of the chaperones who accompanied the female students to lectures lest one of us lose our virtue during a dissection.

'Miles, you are very lucky. Sarah is one of the kindest, most selfless women I know. She will make you a very happy man – and you had better make her a happy woman, or you shall have me to contend with!'

The room broke into laughter – being threatened by Elisabeth was rather like being threatened by a kitten. She might have sharp claws, but she was so pretty and gentle that even her warning swipes seemed playful. I had witnessed her wind even the most unreformed woman-hater around her little finger, whereas all I managed to do was scratch.

'In the words of Burns' – good God, how much poetry had the man written? – '"But to see her was to love her. Love but her, and love forever."'

I felt sick from more than just the haggis. But whatever fulsome praise Miles was on the verge of spouting never materialised as a bloodcurdling scream sounded from outside.

Chapter 4

We sat in the parlour, all thoughts of dinner forgotten. The screams had alerted an on-duty constable, who, on coming to investigate, found an amorous pair of sweethearts whose evening plans had been abruptly called to a halt on the discovery of a dead body in the bushes. They would normally have been taken to the station for breaking into the street's private gardens, but under the circumstances they were cautioned and sent to the kitchen – considerably more befitting their station than a locked New Town shrubbery – while we waited for the constable's colleagues to arrive.

All this was explained by a uniformed man who looked barely older than Miles and had clearly not been expecting anything so dramatic during a night's patrol in one of the wealthier parts of Edinburgh.

His ears all but pricked up at the mention of the maid's disappearance, and Alisdair was dispatched to identify the body. Colonel Greene could barely be torn away from his wife's side, glowering at the whole room as though the perpetrator were among our company. It was, I realised with a shiver, a distinct possibility.

He turned to Randall.

'Chalmers, you're a medical man. Could I prevail upon you . . . ?'

Randall nodded, and followed Alisdair out.

A sickly silence settled on the room – even Aunt Emily, who was able to conjure small talk out of the most awkward situation, was at a loss for words. It felt like for ever until Alisdair returned, but the clock suggested it was a little less than ten minutes.

'It's Wilson.' Alisdair stood in the doorway, swaying slightly. 'She was hit on the back of the head. She must have been there since last night.' He turned to Aurora. 'Mother, I'm so very sorry to have to tell you this, but she had one of your earrings in her pocket.'

The room exploded into uproar.

'You mean to tell me that some madman has attacked your mother's maid after she stole from us?' The colonel was apoplectic.

Miles tried to speak, but all that came out was a series of stammered vowels, the earlier composure he had been clinging to utterly vanished. Alisdair rested a reassuring hand on his brother's shoulder. I could see in that moment years of interpreting what Miles was trying to say, interceding perhaps on his younger brother's behalf.

Uncle Hugh put his arm protectively around my aunt, as though the murderer might not only be in the very room but would somehow be prevented from claiming a second victim by the gesture.

'Emily, perhaps the carriage—'

'Won't be possible, I'm afraid,' Randall interjected. 'The police . . .'

'Surely that can't be necessary?'

'A woman has been murdered!' It was a moment before I realised the furious voice was mine. 'Of course the police will have questions.'

'Now we don't know that—'

'She can't have bashed her own skull in!'

The room fell silent and I felt eight pairs of wide eyes on me. Uncle Hugh had turned puce with rage.

'You must be in shock, Sarah.' Aunt Emily gave me a significant look. 'Perhaps some smelling salts – or brandy?'

'I'm sure you're right,' I agreed, dabbing at my dry eyes with a handkerchief. I paused. 'What was her first name?'

Alisdair looked blank. 'I have no idea. Mother only ever called her Wilson.'

'Clara,' Miles said. 'H-her name was Clara.'

I doubt the family could tell me her age or where she was from, her likes and dislikes, whether or not she had a sweetheart. But at least the poor creature outside had a name now.

'We won't know the cause of death until someone has examined her,' Randall reminded us. 'I have a friend – a medical man – who assists the police with their investigations. His discretion can be relied on.'

Colonel Greene nodded. 'Thank you, Chalmers,' he said with relief. 'Christ, Alisdair, sit down and have a drink before you faint like a woman.'

In the hallway, I heard Randall give a name and address to the footman and my heart sank. I had, somewhere between the maid taking our coats and the poetry, thought that tonight couldn't get any worse. I felt Elisabeth's gaze on me and studiously avoided it.

Aunt Emily, shaken as she was, sprang into action and dragged me along with her. By the time the doorbell rang, everyone had tea – liberally spiked – and Aurora had a blanket wrapped around her as though she had been the one lying outside in the frost-rimed grass.

A trembling maid stood in the doorway, jolting me out of my reverie. This must be Blackwell, the makeshift lady's maid who had arranged Aurora's hair for tonight. With a pang, I realised that she would have known the dead girl, perhaps even been friends with her.

'The police doctor is here.'

I felt myself exhale a breath I hadn't realised I'd been holding. Help was at hand.

I had thought I was used to the sight of Professor Gregory Merchiston holding forth in front of an audience – it was a thrice-weekly occurrence in my lectures. And although I had seen him once before in his role as police surgeon, his lanky figure – rail-thin next to Colonel Greene's robust frame; he'd lost weight and I hated that I knew his physique well enough to be bothered – looked out of place here, a horrible reminder that a tragedy had occurred. It was a wonder he wasn't wearing a black hood and carrying a scythe.

'Constable Niven has sent for some more officers. In the meantime, I'll need to speak to each of you in private.'

'You can't mean to implicate us!' Colonel Greene looked outraged.

'Not at all, sir. It's simply procedure. The ladies, of course, may have someone present – I believe that Mrs Chalmers acts as a chaperone at the university.'

He wasn't a policeman and he had no jurisdiction to question any of us. He wanted to speak to me, I realised with a thrill I tried to suppress.

'Since the lady of the house has had such a terrible shock, we'll let you rest for a while. Perhaps the gentlemen followed by you, madam' – this to Aunt Emily – 'and then the young lady last?' He looked at me solicitously, as though we had never met, much less argued earlier that day.

'You must be so distressed.' I felt Miles' hand on my arm, patting it damply as he realised belatedly that he should offer some comfort to his beloved. Professor Merchiston would never be so gauche as to smirk during a murder investigation, but I suspected that he dearly wanted to.

The fire grew low in the grate and Alisdair stoked it, his expression grim.

'I barely knew the girl, but she always seemed nice enough. I assume she came with good references?'

'Excellent ones,' Aurora managed. I wished he would leave her alone; she looked on the verge of swooning.

'Probably some man,' the colonel huffed. 'Girls have their heads turned so easily.'

'I can't bear to think that she stole from me,' Aurora said shakily. 'I couldn't find my carnelian earrings the other day – I suppose she pocketed them as well.'

Alisdair poured her another cup of tea, discreetly sloshing some more brandy into it. If he wasn't careful, she would give her account half-cut.

Finally, it was my turn.

Elisabeth followed us into the dining room and wandered over to pour herself a glass of champagne. It was probably flat by now and I doubted she would actually drink it, but the illusion of privacy was appreciated.

'A charming start to an engagement. You know, when Randall summoned me, I thought you'd taken matters into your own hands.' His smile was lazy, a familiarity glinting in his eyes that even our unconventional friendship did not afford. In fact, I realised, all his movements tonight had been indolent, slower than normal. Aurora, it seemed, was not the only one who had imbibed a little too much that night.

'Professor, you're still drunk!'

He shrugged, and I could see it in the looseness of his limbs, all his customary tension gone. 'A little whisky after you left. Randall interrupted me before I could really make a night of it.'

'I'm sorry we interfered with your plans. If you'd prefer, we could call for the official police surgeon, rather than a lecturer who gets involved when his own curiosity is provoked.'

'Dismiss me if you wish, Miss Gilchrist. But do you really think that Littlejohn would give a young lady – medical student though she may be – a front-row seat to the examination of the body?'

It was the first good news I'd had all night. My face lit up, and he laughed. 'You're a morbid thing. I should tell you to get back to your fiancé.'

I looked at him in the flickering candlelight.

'But you won't.' My voice came out lower than I intended, but neither of us seemed to mind.

Whatever fragile spell was between us, it was entirely broken by Aunt Emily's entrance.

'Have you finished with my niece yet, Professor?'

They had met once before over another dead body, and Merchiston's association with criminality clearly did not endear him to her, even if he was ostensibly on the opposite side.

'Of course.' He followed us through to the parlour and hovered in the drawing room doorway. It was the first time I had ever seen him look uncertain.

'I could do with an artist to capture the poor girl as she is before the police stretcher arrives. We have a photographer at the station, of course, but in this light I'm afraid he won't get much. Mrs Chalmers, Miss Gilchrist, could I prevail upon either of you?'

Randall looked appalled. 'I am not putting Elisabeth through such a gruesome scene!'

His wife shuddered. 'Thank you, darling. Much as I want to be of assistance, I don't think I could step a foot in front of a dead body without fainting.'

'Then Miss Gilchrist will have to be my able assistant. I hear that you have some medical expertise.' He might as well have winked at me – this was not likely to look good to my future relatives, nor my current ones.

Luckily, Aunt Emily was so outraged at the suggestion, she entirely missed the look behind it.

'Under no circumstances! Sarah, your fascination with this ghastly business is quite out of place – and on the evening of your engagement party, no less!'

'Ah, yes,' Merchiston interjected with a Cheshire cat smile. 'Allow me to extend my congratulations to the happy couple.'

'Thank you, Professor,' I said through gritted teeth.

'In that case, perhaps you would be so kind, Randall old chap? I doubt that even Mrs Fitzherbert here could object to that.'

The 'old chap' in question glared at his friend, but acquiesced. 'And then the ladies can go home, if you have no further need for them?'

'Thank God,' Uncle Hugh muttered.

As Miles helped me into my coat – a task that I, as a grown woman with all my limbs, naturally relied upon him to undertake – I realised that Merchiston was still standing there.

'Miss Gilchrist?'

I turned. He was looking at me, his hand outstretched.

'Thank you for your assistance tonight.' He shook my hand firmly, before turning to Miles. 'Felicitations, sir. I hope you will have many happy years together.'

I couldn't tell if it was meant as a taunt or whether it was entirely genuine. The odd pang I felt at his words was irritation, that was all. Damn the blasted man. And damn poor Wilson for having the misfortune to be left to his tender mercies.

'Mr Fitzherbert, could I prevail upon you to take my wife home?' Randall kissed Elisabeth's cheek tenderly. 'Don't wait for me, Lizzie. If we're as late as I suspect we will be, I'll sleep at the club and see you tomorrow for dinner.'

Elisabeth masked her disappointment with a sweet smile and took my arm.

Was this what marriage was? Concealing one's real feelings and being abandoned in favour of a masculine sanctuary where no one cared how late you went to bed? I had, of course, observed that my aunt and uncle slept in separate bedrooms, but separate buildings? Then again, if I did find myself yoked to Miles, then I might well persuade Randall to make him a member of his club.

It was ghoulish of me, but I didn't want to leave. Whatever secrets Randall and Merchiston were uncovering, I wanted to witness them. I had seen first-hand how an enemy could disguise themselves as a friend, how evil could lurk beneath the most seemingly charming surface. I wasn't some little girl to be sent off to bed while the adults talked, and I knew the Greene residence a damn sight better than either of the gentlemen did. Had I been a man, marrying Mary Greene instead of Miles, I didn't doubt that they would have allowed me to stay and observe – help, even. Had I been a man, my medical studies would be the object of praise rather than disgust. It was unfair that Miles, who practically fainted at the sight of blood, was permitted to remain while someone of stout stomach and enquiring mind was shuffled off home simply because she – because I – happened to be a woman.

I stewed for most of the journey, and if either Elisabeth or Aunt Emily understood the reason for my silence, they chose to ignore it.

'Sarah, you will join me for tea tomorrow afternoon, won't you?' I glanced at Aunt Emily and she nodded wordlessly. I suspected I knew what was behind Elisabeth's invitation – even if Randall could not be prevailed upon to tell us what had happened, Merchiston might.

'I'd love to. I'm sure I'll need the distraction, after such a terrible shock.' My voice sounded grating and false to my ears, but Uncle Hugh nodded approvingly.

'Now, get some sleep,' she said in a warning tone as she kissed me goodbye. She knew that I would be up half the night puzzling over the evening's strange events, and I knew that she would be chastising me for yawning through the next morning's lectures when I failed to take her advice. It was, I felt, solid ground for a friendship.

'I can't think why they live here,' Aunt Emily sighed as we left. 'Somewhere in the New Town would be so much more pleasant, and far more fitted to Mrs Chalmers' standing.'

'Randall likes to be near the university. And Elisabeth says it's livelier.'

Aunt Emily's lips were pinched. 'Perhaps you ought to confine your social activities to a more respectable area from now on.'

'Perhaps she shouldn't leave the house at all, with a madman on the loose.' Uncle Hugh's earlier boisterous air was gone and he looked like a sulky child kept too late after his bedtime.

Aunt Emily, however, had more pressing concerns.

'Your mother,' she sighed. 'What on earth are we going to tell your mother? I told her the Greenes were a good family!'

A woman was dead, Aurora Greene was half mad with shock and their genteel home was crawling with policemen. But in the chilly carriage, my mother's disapproval loomed large, more immediate and therefore far more terrifying than some murderer straight out of the pages of a penny dreadful.

'Some silly girl got herself killed,' Uncle Hugh snapped. 'I hardly see how that reflects badly on the Greenes. Probably had a lover, or a debt. For heaven's sake, don't rabbit on at your sister about it when she comes. There's more at stake here than just a wedding, you know.'

If there was, that was the first I had heard of it. Aunt Emily shot him a warning look, and returned to the subject at hand.

'And how horrid that the girl stole from Aurora,' she sighed. 'The thought of some common thief rummaging through her things . . .' She shuddered. 'Well, best put it out of our thoughts.'

But try as I might, I couldn't shake off a looming sense of

dread that what we had witnessed tonight was only the beginning of something terrible.

Aunt Emily was restless too. As I was getting ready for bed, she knocked on my door with a worried look on her face. Dismissing Agnes with a jerk of her head, she met my gaze with a querying one of her own.

'That professor of yours . . .' she said.

'Elisabeth was there,' I said defensively. 'We weren't alone.' Elisabeth had been examining a potted plant in the corner and I now realised with a hot flush of shame that she hadn't just been giving us privacy to discuss a murder.

'The last thing you want is Miles being jealous of a perfectly innocent acquaintance.' The tone of her voice warned me that Merchiston had better be an innocent acquaintance – or else. 'I heard he caught that terrible man who killed Miss Hartigan. I'm sure he'll find whoever did that horrible thing to Aurora's girl, but that doesn't mean I want you speaking to him alone.'

Even in death, it seemed that a maid didn't warrant a name. Wilson to the household, she would have been known by the family's surname when they travelled, and even now her identity was erased.

'Her name was Clara,' I whispered. 'Not "Aurora's girl". Not "Wilson". Clara.'

Aunt Emily took my hand in her chilly one. Poor circulation, she always said. I suspected it was more to do with not having a heart at all.

'Don't you see, Sarah? This is what a husband can protect you from.'

'Aurora and Colonel Greene are married, yet they still had a murderer on their doorstep.'

'I don't mean that, you silly girl. Clara Wilson's fate could be yours more easily than you realise. Those degenerates the clinic treats – what would stop one of them from getting violent?'

'They're poor, not degenerate!' Aunt Emily's expression suggested that if she was aware of the distinction, it wasn't a big one.

'You see a woman's sphere as confining, limiting. But better a life that occasionally leans towards tedium than one that comes to such a terrible end.'

'You find domesticity tedious?' Aunt Emily's hidden depths grew deeper by the day.

She scowled. 'Of course not. But I can see that for a woman of your intellect, the benefits might not seem so obvious at first.'

She hugged me, a quick, tight squeeze that felt all the more affectionate for how uncharacteristic it was.

'I'm so glad you've found a man to take care of you.' She pressed the lightest of kisses on my forehead and left me to my night-time ablutions. Her parting words raised my hackles and gave me a pang of guilt at the same time. How could I hate her when she was so truly happy for me?

As Agnes undressed me, I retrieved the folded piece of paper I had found discreetly pressed into my hand as I left the Greenes' house that night, and once she was gone, I examined it. It was a scrap of paper torn from a notebook. On one side was a scribbled chemical equation and on the other, in Gregory Merchiston's handwriting, an address, a date and a time.

It seemed my assistance was needed after all.

Chapter 5

I walked through freezing fog up to Princes Street, where I would be able to hail a cab in relative anonymity. Already the smell of hops hung in the air, thick and yeasty. I used to hate the scent, the constant reminder of my uncle's breweries and his omnipresent reach. Now it was a welcome reminder that I was out of the house, no matter the weather or the circumstance.

A hansom slowed to a halt on Frederick Street and I clambered in. If my destination was unusual, then my coin was as good as any respectable woman's, and the carriage clattered through the waking streets towards the City Chambers, where Professor Merchiston was waiting for me outside the police mortuary.

He was leaning in the doorway as I arrived, watching the street with an unreadable expression. Outside was still black as night, with only the flickering gas lamps to illuminate the gloom, but the city was teeming with life, not all of it reputable.

His clothes were crumpled and I doubted if he had slept since I last saw him, but he was wide awake, his eyes bloodshot but alert. The thrill of the case must have made him jittery, because I had never seen him so animated. I barely had time to remove my coat before he was talking, leading me through the rabbit warren that housed the Edinburgh City Police.

We paused at a kitchen. 'Here.' He passed me a mug. 'Coffee. At this hour, you'll need it. Have you eaten?' His hand lingered over the biscuit tin.

'Yes, my aunt had the kitchen prepare me a slap-up breakfast before I slipped out at five o'clock in the morning to examine a corpse.'

He narrowed his eyes at my sarcasm, but didn't rise to the bait. 'You'll be grateful for an empty stomach once you're down there.'

'It's hardly my first autopsy, Professor,' I reminded him.

He snorted. 'I've seen coppers twice your age swoon like debutantes. If the innards don't get you, the claustrophobia will. Now, follow me – and stay close.'

The morgue was buried in the bowels of the building, and as Merchiston led me through a maze of hallways and staircases, I realised I could not find my way back if I tried. At such an early hour, the place was quiet and dark and it was easy to believe that if I got lost, I might never be found.

'Did you know there's a whole city down here? They call it the Vaults. Miles and miles of streets and tunnels twenty feet below the ground. Edinburgh was expanding faster than the town planners could accommodate, so they dug into the rock and carved out a whole new city. Tradesmen used to sell their goods there for a time; it was a thriving hub of activity, all taking place beneath the cobbles. Then they moved above ground and the only people who plied their trade down there weren't ones you'd like to meet in a tunnel on a dark night.' He smiled, but in the gloom all I could see was teeth. 'Tell me, Miss Gilchrist, do you believe in ghosts?'

I shook my head, hoping he couldn't see me shiver. 'I've seen enough evil done by the living not to worry about the dead.'

'Aye, me too. Me too.'

He stopped abruptly and pushed open a door. With the flick of a switch, the room was flooded with harsh electric light, and I blinked, dazzled for a moment.

It was chilly, with no natural light and not even a grate to provide warmth. I regretted leaving my coat upstairs.

'You'll warm up once we get started,' Merchiston promised, moving quickly to tidy up some apparatus – a needle and a vial, although what use his patients down here would have for drugs was another matter. 'Nothing like a post-mortem to get the blood pumping.'

My glance flickered to the table, where the distinct outline of a body lay beneath a sheet. Clara Wilson. No more beating heart for her, no sense of cold or heat. No kisses or tears or laughter; just a wooden box and the cool earth of the graveyard.

And yet she had secrets, and if her mouth could not whisper confessions, then maybe her body would.

Merchiston looked at me. 'You feel it too.' He ran his hand down the slab. 'All that possibility. So much information, hidden in one package of flesh and hair and nails. Our bodies tell stories, Miss Gilchrist. The language may be foreign to most, but learn to translate it and you will be privy to all the secrets of our species, living or dead.'

I wondered what stories my body would tell on this cold January morning, alone in a room with a man who had not given me the shiny bauble on my finger. I twisted it off violently and tossed it onto the table. Yet the indentation remained, a band of depressed flesh that revealed what I wanted most to forget.

'They found a note on her.'

'From her killer?' What sort of person would leave an explanation on the body of his victim?

'We think so. It looks like someone was blackmailing her – or she was blackmailing them. Either way, it gives us a motive.'

He pulled the sheet down, revealing bruising on her sternum. 'Whoever killed her was stronger, but she was a slight wee thing so that's not surprising. There were scraps of debris on her coat and skirt – looked like rubbish. I think she'd been attacked somewhere else and then hidden in the bushes. That bruising suggests she might still have been alive when she was carried.'

I shuddered.

'There's no sign of . . .' He broke off, glancing at me. 'That is to say, she wasn't . . .'

'Raped?' I supplied. 'Well, there's that at least.' It was cold comfort under the circumstances, but I was glad she had been spared that.

He nodded. 'Sadly, the killer didn't leave any stray hairs behind to give us a nice obvious clue. But we'll see if there's anything else to be found. "There's no art to find the mind's construction in the face",' he quoted. 'What's beneath the skin, though – that's another matter.'

He took Clara's hand gently in his. 'See that, under the nails? Arsenic, I'd bet money on it.'

I frowned. 'But she wasn't poisoned.'

'She didn't die from poison,' he corrected. 'The symptoms of arsenic poisoning in its early stages, provided the eventual murderer is slow and methodical rather than slapdash and eager, can be confused with an unpleasant stomach complaint. Perhaps she was being dosed by someone who grew impatient.'

I scraped the residue from beneath her nails, dropping it into the vial Merchiston had provided. I held her hand for a moment, chilly and limp in mine. The backs of her hands were smooth, but the fingertips were calloused – she would have taken charge of mending all Aurora's clothes, and although a lady's maid would never demean herself by blacking the grate or sweeping the floor, she still did more manual work in a day than her mistress would in a year. But presentation was important, and she would have scrubbed her nails assiduously – a woman unkempt in her personal appearance could never be trusted to look after a household or its occupants. There were countless ways she could have come into contact with arsenic – in her food, in her face cream (or in Aurora's face cream, if she was the type of maid to enjoy her employer's personal possessions once in a while). She could be a glutton or a thief, but she would never be messy.

'Perhaps she wasn't the victim,' I murmured.

Merchiston lifted an eyebrow – he looked impressed, and I tried to ignore the warmth that suffused me.

'There's only one way to find out. Hand me that scalpel.'

He pulled the sheet away, settling it neatly just below the pubic bone. I felt my face flush as we stood before Clara Wilson's still form – her dark hair still pinned above her head, eyes open but unseeing, unaware that her unclothed body was on display before two strangers. He nodded at my sleeves, 'Can you roll those up?'

My fingers, still numb with cold, fumbled with the tiny mother-of-pearl buttons until I could push the fabric up to my elbows. Next to his forearms, taut and sinewy, I looked absurdly out of place: delicate – fragile, even. And that was one thing I had sworn never to be again. His gaze fell on the silvery scar that snaked across the inside of my wrist. It was little more than an inch, but somehow I knew that he recognised it for what it was. I wondered if his forensic knowledge could tell that it had been a hairpin, abandoned in my sheets by a careless sanatorium nurse who was later sacked for her negligence in leaving a sharp object with a woman who had been diagnosed with hysteria. I stole a glance at his face, and instead of pity saw understanding. I wondered if he himself had ever found existence so terrible that oblivion was preferable. No wonder he, too, preferred to keep company with the dead.

He picked up the scalpel and made the first incision,

pressing hard to cut through muscle and tissue. He drew it slowly, gently across her left breast and I shuddered as the mottled flesh opened in the blade's wake. He paused at the centre of the breastbone and looked at me as the cut began to ooze fluid.

'Would you like to do the right-hand side, Miss Gilchrist?'

I nodded mutely and took the scalpel, warm from his grasp. As I cut into the firm, cold flesh, I felt my nerves dissipate. I moved the knife through sinew stiffened by rigor mortis.

'What are you doing?' Merchiston's voice was cool and clinical.

'I'm cutting from the clavicular head through the pectoralis major, severing the lateral and median pectoral nerves.'

'Why?'

'So that once we've cut down the linea alba to the pubic symphysis, we can pull back the flesh from her sternum and crack open her ribs. Then we can remove the organs.' I drew the scalpel back when my incision met his.

'Nicely done. Steady hand, clean cut. We'll make a surgeon of you yet.' Glowing with praise, I went to hand him the scalpel. 'No, no. You finish this one.'

It was easier the second time, the body already cut open. All I had to do was lean into it and draw the blade through flesh.

Whatever echoes of life had lingered around her were banished now. Clara Wilson was meat and muscle, a subject rather than a person. It was a grisly spell to perform and yet I felt my own pulse quicken as I surveyed the effects of my handiwork.

'So much mess beneath such a pristine surface,' Merchiston murmured. 'We like to think that we're civilised, superior beings, but we're just bags of blood and bone like any other creature. All impulse and survival instinct.' He stroked her cheek. 'Shame that instinct isn't always enough.'

He moved to his tray of instruments and pulled out a bone saw, nodding to the desk in the corner.

'Take a seat; we'll be here a while. There's a pen and paper, so make yourself useful. Label each jar with the date, the name of the organ and the weight once I've lifted them out. This way the writing might be legible for a change.'

The pen lay untouched as I watched him retract the flesh and expose the ribcage, white bone stained reddish pink and shrouded beneath scraps of wet flesh. He leaned on it hard, and I heard a sickening crack before he lifted the saw. I was on my feet before I knew what I was doing.

I placed my hand on his as it rested on the saw. 'May I?'

His skin was so warm – the only warm thing in the room. In that moment, it felt as though we were the only living people in the city, and blood pulsed quickly, our hands pressed so close together that I couldn't tell whose heartbeat I was feeling.

'Morbid girl,' he murmured softly, and I didn't argue with him.

He moved to stand behind me, guiding my hand, and I dragged the saw through bone.

'It's going to resist you. The body never wants to give up its secrets.'

As I cut, Clara Wilson jerked back and forth as though animated. I felt my stomach begin to curdle and focused on keeping my grip steady.

My arm ached and my hands were cramping but I refused to stop. I put my whole weight into it, but it wasn't enough and the saw slipped from my grasp.

I swore, and Merchiston laughed.

'Spoken like a true doctor. There,' he said gently, taking the bone saw from me. 'I'll do the rest.'

'It's physical work,' he said quietly as he resumed. 'There's no shame in not being able to do it single-handedly. Plenty of students have that problem – you all spend too much time cloistered indoors with your books and not enough time getting exercise. You did well, considering.'

'I need to do better,' I replied mulishly.

'Boxing helps. And lifting crates for Mrs Logan because she doesn't trust the delivery boys not to steal the silver.'

'I doubt my aunt would let me help the servants,' I pointed out. 'So that just leaves boxing. I don't suppose . . .'

He paused in his macabre efforts to look at me in surprise. 'You want to learn how to fight?'

'I want to learn how to protect myself,' I corrected. 'I'm sick of being told that women are weak – too weak for surgery, too weak for intellectual thought.' Too weak to fight a man off when he tried to take advantage. 'I can't always rely on you to swoop in and save me. I'm not a damsel in distress and I don't intend to become a corpse either.'

'And how often do you intend to be locked in a room with a murderer? Fiona Leadbetter was an anomaly, it's hardly on the syllabus.'

I looked down pointedly at the dead woman we were cutting up.

'You're assisting a professor. As a medical student, that isn't beyond the realms of possibility. That's not the same as investigating a murder.'

'I was in the house when it happened! I know the family better than you do. If it hadn't been for Randall's personal recommendation, you wouldn't have even been allowed through the door. You can't do this without me, Professor. Wouldn't it be an advantage to have someone to ask questions who doesn't have to come in via the servants' entrance?'

'So high and mighty when she thinks she has the upper hand,' Merchiston commented drily. 'What would your fiancé think of it?'

'Exactly the same as he'd think about my being shut in a

room with a man and no chaperone in the early hours of the morning,' I fired back. 'Absolutely nothing, because he's not going to find out.'

He flushed in the dim light, and I realised that reminding him of the impropriety of the situation was a mistake. He could escort me out now, avoid being alone with me ever again, and this odd, tenuous partnership would be at an end.

But all he did was avoid my gaze and resume hacking away at Clara Wilson's exposed skeleton. I returned to my original task of writing up the labels to go with the organs we would preserve, and for a while the only sounds in the room were the scratch of pen against paper, the scrape of blade against bone and the less than steady breathing of two people who were trying to ignore each other.

When he had finished, he was flushed and sweating.

'Now for the organs. Whoever said the eyes are the windows to the soul never saw a perfectly dissected kidney. Let's do the stomach together. Then I'll take the bowel. It's slippery, and the last thing we want to do is cut it at this point. It doesn't matter how long it's been since you've eaten, you'll want to throw up.'

It felt like scooping out a deflating balloon that had been filled with water. Once we had lifted the organ out, he took it in his hands and scrutinised it.

'Reasonably good health. She had a nutritious diet, and all that running around after Mrs Greene kept her heart in good condition. Better than most doctors I know.'

He placed it gently on the scale and nodded before moving to a contraption of copper and glass. 'The Marsh test. If there's arsenic in her stomach, we'll find it here. It will take a while, though – best go and get yourself some breakfast before lectures.'

Grisly as it was, I was loath to leave him. 'Are you sure there's nothing more I can do?'

He waved the scattered sheets he had been scribbling on at me and I frowned. I had hoped for something a little more useful than transcription.

'Could you write these up for me? Your handwriting is neater. Mine looks like a spider fell in some ink and ambled across the page.'

'And whilst I'm acting as your secretary, you'll be doing what precisely?'

He frowned. 'This will go faster for both of us if the notes are legible.'

'You don't see me as your equal.'

He frowned. 'Well of course I don't! Oh Christ, not because you're a woman – don't look at me like that. You're a first-year medical student! In the university hierarchy, you're the lowest of the low. I don't doubt your potential, but experience and wisdom are on my side.'

'Along with arrogance!'

He gave me a lopsided smile. 'I'm a doctor. We're supposed to be arrogant. Wait a few years and it'll be part of your studies – how to enrage the general populace and still keep your calm and your professional reputation.'

God, he could be charming when he wanted. I was used to him mercurial and brooding, all gallows humour and a wry smirk. The twinkle in his eye unnerved me.

A professional reputation was all I would have left once I had finished disentangling myself from Miles. A woman minus her virginity who had called off the engagement meant to restore her facade of respectability? I wouldn't get a second chance at marriage.

He gave me a long, searching look.

'Is this really what you think you want?'

'Are you implying that I don't know my own mind, Professor?'

'I'm saying that live patients are generally more interesting than dead ones. And no police force is going to allow a woman as their surgeon, though if it were up to me, you ladies could have your fill of the poisoned, bludgeoned and drowned. I just don't want you to look back on your studies and feel that you've wasted your time. That you've allowed me to distract you from your chosen field because of my selfishness.'

'You're not selfish.'

He looked away, a colour rising in his cheeks.

'I like the company. Enough to drag you from your bed at some godforsaken hour just to help me crack open a woman's chest.'

'Precisely. You didn't interrupt my studying or pull me out of a lecture – I'm doing this in my own time and of my own free will.'

'Either way, there's nothing more you can do here. I'll take you upstairs – God knows you'll never find your way back without a guide.'

We must have made an odd pair, moving through the corridors stinking of chemicals and dead flesh. Merchiston's once pristine apron was covered in blood smears and damp patches where unmentionable fluid had splashed him.

'I can think of better places to bring your sweetheart, Merchiston.'

I almost screamed, and hated myself for it. A young constable, the first living person I had seen here today aside from the professor, was smirking at us from an office. My cheeks burned.

'Miss Gilchrist is my assistant,' Merchiston ground out.

'Aye? Dr Littlejohn approve that, did he?' A muscle in Merchiston's jaw twitched. 'Thought not. Your secret's safe with me, Professor.' The constable gave me an unpleasant smile. 'Consider it a favour to a friend.'

Once the door shut behind him, the professor swore.

'Christ. I'd rather not be indebted to him of all people. Crooked as they come and slippery with it.'

'I'm sorry.' Ever since I had met the man, I had done nothing but bring trouble to his door. And yet I couldn't feel too guilty – he had invited me here knowing how it might look to his colleagues.

'You're not in charge of my reputation, lass.' True – I was barely in charge of my own. But there was no denying that even the breath of rumour would see him censured and me sent down, yet another black mark against the entirety of the female sex within the walls of the university. Although I knew that each woman was seen as carrying the flag for our sex, representing the virtue of every female student present and future was somewhat tiring.

The truth was, I would rather spend a day in the morgue with Professor Merchiston than an evening in the company of my intended, and I didn't want to parse too deeply into what that meant.

'You've been a great help, Miss Gilchrist. Now go and get a cup of tea and some toast; I expect you to be wide awake and fresh as a daisy at eleven.' He paused. 'You might want to reread the chapter on potassium sulphate. Don't think your assistance here gets you out of me calling on you in class.'

I took the money awkwardly but with gratitude – my purse was empty and I hadn't thought beyond getting out of the house unnoticed.

When I saw him again, he was marching briskly down the street as though he had just awoken, and as I sipped my tea I couldn't help but wonder if I had dreamed the entire strange event. The only proof that I had spent the early hours of the morning accompanying him in an autopsy and murder investigation was the sharp chemical smell that clung to my skin, and beneath it the sweet stench of death.

Chapter 6

So much for Merchiston's much-vaunted discretion. The murder had made the newspapers before I even reached the university – not the better papers, not yet, but the ones hawked by grubby boys on street corners with grubbier headlines printed in ink so fresh it was damp to the touch.

HOUSEMAID MURDERED!

I had been the subject of gossip before, but nothing as public as this.

Even Alison was curious, although her cool manner reminded me that I had hurt her dreadfully. I should have invited her to the engagement party – although perhaps in retrospect it was better that I hadn't.

'And I thought your engagement would be the scandal of the term!' said Caroline Carstairs. 'Who cares about a man when you witnessed a murder!'

'I didn't witness a murder,' I sighed. Or at least, I hadn't witnessed this one. 'It all happened outside.'

'But you must have passed her on your way to dinner. Imagine getting so close to a murdered body! I would have fainted on the spot!'

'You pushed your way to the front row at Professor Williamson's public lobotomy last week and didn't blink.'

There was laughter. 'The sound of that saw! I still hear it in my nightmares.'

'It's just a bone saw, Carstairs. You've seen them before.'

'But it's different when it's the skull. I don't know why, it just *is*.'

I hadn't attended the public surgery. Instead, I had been at a dress fitting, my aunt's modiste grumbling in a bad attempt at a French accent that I had put on weight. I felt the same pressure now, like the muscle memory of my thoracic tissue compressing as Madame Leroux – Marie Lennox on her birth certificate – cinched the corset tighter. It was happening already, I realised. While the others were gobbling up any scrap of knowledge they could, I was falling behind. The memory of my marks in the winter examinations surged sickeningly and I forced it back down. This new life I had fought so hard for was already slipping through my fingers.

I slid into the lecture theatre seat moments before Professor Merchiston began to speak. His fervour had worn off, and he looked tired.

'Ah, Miss Gilchrist. How kind of you to join us. Late night?'

'She witnessed a murder!' Caroline piped up excitedly.

'Did she indeed? Well, I trust this morning's lecture won't be too tedious in comparison.' He paused, a dark twinkle in his eyes that I didn't trust for a moment. 'I recall Mrs Chalmers saying it was your engagement party. I do hope your future groom is unharmed.'

'He's perfectly well,' I said through gritted teeth. 'Please don't let me distract you from your lecture.'

'The whole university is talking about it,' Moira Owen said afterwards, a hint of chastisement in her voice. 'Honestly, Gilchrist, could you avoid miring us in scandal for five minutes? No wonder your first term marks were so dire.'

I flinched.

Julia rolled her eyes. 'It's hardly her fault some poor servant got murdered.'

Moira glanced at her sharply, knowing that she and I were hardly bosom companions.

'I didn't see anything,' I lied. 'I simply spoke to a policeman and then we all went home. It was quite undramatic.' I squeezed Alison's arm. 'You didn't miss a thing, I promise.'

She shook off my hand without looking at me.

The rest of the day dragged on painfully – I had done exactly what Elisabeth had warned me not to do and barely slept a wink, and just as she had predicted, I was no good for anything. There were not many young ladies in my social circle – or anyone's, I imagined – capable of falling asleep while listening to a graphic description of varying shades of sputum associated with tuberculosis, but as I stifled a yawn during Randall Chalmers' spirited, if disgusting, presentation, I thought I might join their ranks.

Adrenaline had helped me through my morning lectures and a cup of coffee through the first one of the afternoon, but now my eyes were starting to feel gritty and even my bones were heavy. I wondered if Randall would mind if I took a nap while he talked. His voice was so very soothing. A sharp kick to my right ankle from his wife woke me up – had I been snoring? – and I realised I was being addressed.

'Miss Gilchrist, the slides?'

I looked at the microscope on the table in front of him and made a quick deduction. There were two small vials of revolting-looking effluence next to it, each with a pipette.

I made my way to the front of the class, hoping my expression conveyed academic interest rather than exhaustion, and picked up the glass containing a rust-coloured mucus.

Randall cleared his throat and jerked his head to the other vial. This was going well already.

I sucked up a few drops from the pipette and squeezed them out onto the small glass rectangle.

'From the colour, what would you diagnose?'

It was a rather unpleasant yellow-green – I was struck with a sudden desire to burn my chartreuse gown when I got home – with brown streaks.

'Extrapulmonary tuberculosis.'

'Well done. Now take a look and let us know what you see.'

As soon as I was finished, the others crowded around the table, eager for their turn. Sketches were made, the slides were labelled and all in all we had rather more fun examining bodily fluids than might be thought proper. The penultimate lecture of the day, it went quickly – although the essay Randall set and the mountain of reading he recommended would keep me studying until the wee hours.

'Don't forget that if you wish to use the equipment outside of class you may, but make sure you book it with the faculty administrator first,' he reminded us as we exited the room noisily.

'Will you be home in time for dinner?' Elisabeth asked her husband.

'It won't be late – I'm ravenous. Tell Cook to set an extra place. Gregory will be joining us.'

'I'll let her know. Remember, Sarah is eating with us tonight too.'

'Damn – sorry, my love. It's hardly proper—'

'Neither was elbowing your way into a murder investigation last night, but the three of you weren't worrying about etiquette then,' she noted tartly. 'It's an informal tea, and Sarah needs to take her mind off all this ghastliness.'

'You mean you want to gossip about her fiancé's family,' he commented wryly.

'Why is it that when you and Gregory are discussing a case it's medical business, but when Sarah and I do, it's gossip?'

'I just don't want you getting dragged into something so ugly, darling.'

Elisabeth frowned, and I cleared my throat pointedly. Much as I agreed with her, I didn't want to play audience to a marital tiff – especially not one that could see me banned from the investigation.

I took her arm. 'We'll talk about nothing but dresses and parties, I promise,' I assured Randall.

Splashing my face and hands with cold water in the small room allocated to the female students as a cloakroom – we were not considered sufficient in number or stature to warrant giving over one of the men's dressing areas – I tried desperately to wake myself up for the final lecture of the day.

I found myself paired with Julia on a man's partially dissected leg, alternating between completing the dissection and sketching the gruesome result.

'Right before dinner,' she grumbled. 'I don't know how Williamson can stand it.'

'He's not flesh and blood, he's an automaton.' I smiled.

'No, that's Merchiston,' she snorted.

I looked away, hoping my cheeks weren't as red as they felt. I had touched his flesh, wiped away his blood. Gregory Merchiston might be the oddest man I had ever met, but he was undeniably human.

'He's far too dissolute to be an automaton,' Edith sniffed. 'The other day, I swear he hadn't shaved. And neither cologne nor formaldehyde can mask the smell of ale. I don't know why they allow him to teach.'

I had seen Merchiston suffering from overindulgence before, but it hadn't occurred to me that it could be a regular event. If his movements were slow sometimes, I had always attributed it to tiredness, or the after-effects of too much time spent in the boxing ring. Certainly the man with whom I had cut open Clara Wilson's body that morning hadn't been under the weather as one might expect – rather, he had been animated and full of vitality. A fine doctor I'd make if I couldn't even recognise the symptoms of a hangover.

Two hours later, I stretched out on the floor before Elisabeth's fireplace. It wasn't exactly the most ladylike of positions, but neither of us cared much about that.

'Is it drying?' she asked through a mouthful of crumpet.

I fingered the damp locks reaching down to my waist. 'Not really. But the warmth is divine. I might stay here all night.'

'What on earth possessed you to come out without a hat?'

'Left it in the chemistry lab. I was in such a bad mood after that practical, it's a miracle I managed to remember my coat.' I rubbed the burn on the metacarpophalangeal joint of my index finger, courtesy of being paired with a jittery Edith, who was mimicking her friend's – lover's? – attempts at friendship with considerably less conviction.

I had paid for my carelessness when the wild flurries of sleet had hit my skin like a slap, but by that point I was so desperate to leave the university buildings that I didn't bother retrieving my lost property. I had run through the Meadows, my head bowed against the inclement weather, and announced my presence on my best friend's doorstep by sneezing three times. My boots and stockings had been whipped away by the housekeeper to be dried off somewhere more private, and I dug my toes into the deep rug with a happy sigh.

'I'm surprised that you even made it out of the house this morning, after such a shock last night.'

I grimaced. 'Aunt Emily would keep me under lock and key if she could at the best of times, but with Colonel Greene so determined to act as though nothing were wrong, she didn't have much choice.'

'I'm sure the police will find the murderer soon,' Elisabeth mused. 'Randall said that Gregory was discussing all sorts of possibilities with them after we left.'

'I don't suppose he shared them with you?' I asked hopefully.

She swatted me. 'You're so morbid, Sarah. I admit, I'm intrigued, but you'd be out there walking the streets with the sergeants and constables if you could.'

'Aunt Emily would have kittens! She was unhappy enough about letting me speak to Merchiston directly, and at least he's in a respectable profession.' I smiled mirthlessly. 'For a man, at any rate.'

'You were discussing a murder together, not having an assignation.' Elisabeth was silent for a moment. 'Had you been alone with Gregory since . . . ?' I shook my head. I had been alone with the professor on far more occasions than was good for even my reputation, but not since the night he had saved my life. Or rather, the morning afterwards, when we had shared breakfast and secrets and his mouth had been so close to mine . . .

The door slammed and I nearly leapt out of my skin.

As if on cue, Randall's voice sounded in the hall, and the ruddy-cheeked lecturer entered, beaming at his wife. Behind him, shaking the snow off his hat, was Merchiston. I was uncomfortably aware of my bare feet and loose hair, and scrambled around for the pins I had pulled out and tossed carelessly on the floor. Elisabeth plaited my hair swiftly as her husband greeted us and Merchiston looked everywhere but at me.

With the exception of our sleuthing partnership, outside the university our paths rarely crossed. Although he and I were both friends of the Chalmerses, ever since we had almost kissed, he contrived to be working late whenever I was expected at dinner, and when *he* was expected, I found myself needed urgently at home by my aunt.

'Miss Gilchrist.' He nodded.

'Professor,' I replied awkwardly. How was it that this

morning we had been *simpatico*, and now we could hardly look at each other? Maybe, I thought glumly, I was only capable of polite social interaction with a man when in the presence of a dead body. Well, that would enliven my sure-to-be dull marriage.

Dinner was stilted – Randall refused point-blank to allow us to discuss murder, medicine or politics over our meal and I realised anew how limited my conversational skills had become since moving to this freezing ice block of a city.

Even Elisabeth was on edge. 'Do you have to call them both "Professor" while we're around the dinner table?' she grumbled. 'It's so starchy. It's like sitting in an examination.'

'Except if we were in an examination, Miss Gilchrist would at least be quiet.' Merchiston grinned. There was no warmth in it.

I felt my fists clench next to my plate.

She frowned. 'I thought the students were tested verbally?'

His smile was wintry. 'That's what I meant.'

I had choked in the Christmas exams, I knew I had. Too little sleep and too much worrying – over the exams, over my engagement, over the unspeakably rotten year I had endured – and by the time I was standing in front of Professor Merchiston, all I could remember was the look in his eyes as he stood before *me*, spattered with the blood of my friend and mentor.

He had passed me anyway – with a mark just shy of being insulting – and we had never spoken about it until now.

'That doesn't sound like Sarah.' Elisabeth shot me a concerned glance. Her look was already more interest in how I had got on than my aunt and uncle had shown.

'I was as surprised as you, believe me. But there was no sharp retort or know-it-all rejoinder to be found. Pity, I'd been looking forward to an argument over potassium solutions.'

I bit my tongue so hard it bled. I wanted to tell him he was an ass; that I had performed exceptionally in every essay I handed in, every test he set. That standing in front of him with Mrs Mitchell – a widowed schoolteacher with a sour expression and bad breath – eyeing us suspiciously had made all my words evaporate. That I had spent most of my first term convinced he was a murderer and I had realised in that moment I had been right all along. I would have liked to see *him* rattle off equations and dosages and medicinal properties under those conditions.

Randall and Elisabeth watched me carefully, waiting for my explosion. Instead, I concentrated on cutting my chicken into smaller and smaller pieces until it was practically minced.

'I do hope it isn't your forthcoming nuptials that have you so distracted?' Merchiston asked, tone dripping with feigned concern.

'I believe my last essay proves that my mind is on my studies, nowhere else.'

He snorted. 'Poor chap.'

The man I had spent several companionable hours with that morning was gone, and so were whatever small shoots of friendship had started to emerge.

'You're in a filthy mood. We'll take our dessert into the parlour once we're finished here. You may join us when you've decided to be civilised.'

Merchiston winced – Elisabeth's gentle temper made those times when she was angry all the worse.

'I'm sorry, ladies. I have a rotten headache and it's making me irritable. I should have dined at home tonight.'

'But then we wouldn't hear what the police have to say about that poor girl's death,' she reminded him sweetly.

'Really, Lizzie, that is hardly dinner-time conversation,' Randall grumbled. 'Or appropriate conversation for ladies at all.'

He wasn't looking at me, but I knew where his comment was directed. I felt a pang of guilt that I was corrupting my friend with my ghoulish fancies – but why shouldn't Elisabeth take an interest? She had been there as well, and she was hardly a simpleton.

Still, she kissed him on the cheek, wagged a warning finger at Merchiston and, as our plates were taken away, practically dragged me into the parlour.

'What on earth was that all about?'

'He's a beast,' I muttered. 'He wasn't doubting my competence when I was slicing open Clara Wilson's torso this morning.'

Damn. Merchiston hadn't said it in so many words, but I suspected he meant for me to keep our grisly labour a secret.

Elisabeth's eyes were like saucers, and she pushed away her chocolate torte.

'*What?*'

I cleared my throat awkwardly. 'The, ah, professor allowed me to assist on the autopsy.'

'And you didn't think to tell me?' Her eyes shone with hurt. 'Sarah – were the two of you alone?'

'No.' It wasn't entirely a lie.

'Allow me to rephrase,' she interjected crisply, lips pinched in fury. 'Were the two of you alone aside from the dead body of your future mother-in-law's maid?'

I nodded reluctantly.

'You could be sent down for something like that! Not to mention what would happen if your aunt found out. And now you're having dinner together – if anyone heard, they'd think I was facilitating an assignation. I'd lose my position, Randall would be in danger of losing his . . . Sarah, do you have any idea how reckless you're being?'

I hadn't thought of it like that. As usual, I had only thought of myself and my own insatiable curiosity.

She closed her eyes for a moment, looking pained. 'As your friend, I have to ask. Has anything improper occurred between the two of you?'

I had accused him of murder, seen him shirtless and brawling, watched as he killed a woman and saved my life and then come within half a breath of having his mouth on mine. 'Improper' didn't come close, and yet I knew what Elisabeth meant. She wanted to know if we had kissed, truly and incontrovertibly. If this morning's post-mortem was merely an excuse for him to get me alone and his behaviour this evening a smokescreen for his feelings. She didn't mean the unsettling bloom of fondness I couldn't quite quash even when I wanted to hurl my plate at him; she was concerned about furtive meetings and dishevelled clothing.

I shifted uncomfortably in my seat at the thought.

'I promise, nothing of that nature has happened. And it won't – he's my professor, nothing more.'

If it was a lie, I didn't know what could disprove it, what words could be found to capture this fragile camaraderie he kept dashing.

'You took her to the bloody morgue?' Randall's voice boomed out. I winced.

'I needed an assistant and she's perfectly capable when she isn't panicking in an exam or getting herself into trouble.'

Perhaps he didn't think I was a complete idiot after all.

Randall stormed through, a black expression on his face. 'I should have sent you all home immediately. I don't know what I was thinking, treating you like you were—'

'A man? You have no problem with my studying to be a doctor,' I snapped, stung. 'It's a little late to worry about my fragile feminine emotions now!'

'This is murder, Sarah,' he sighed. 'Not a class test or a penny dreadful. A woman has been killed and you're treating it like an academic exercise.'

'I'm already involved,' I argued. 'It happened while I was in the house, I know these people better than any of you. Just let me be useful.'

'Useful doesn't mean locking yourself away with a man while you dissect a cadaver unchaperoned. The dead may tell no tales, but all it takes is one living person to start a rumour that could end both of you. Despite what you think, Sarah, I don't see you as weak or fragile – I'd like to see you finish your studies and practise medicine, and that won't happen if you're sent down for immoral behaviour.'

'You're wrong.' Merchiston had been silent, staring into the fire as we argued, but now he was looking up at us. 'The dead have an awful lot to say, and Miss Gilchrist was invaluable in helping me translate. More than I had expected – I can show you, if you think you can keep down that marvellous dinner we just enjoyed.'

I met his gaze. 'I've dissected an arm less than an hour after lunch and I didn't so much as heave. Show me, Professor.'

Randall moved to protest, but Elisabeth gave him a warning glance and he settled in a chair by the fire with a resigned grumble.

Merchiston placed a series of photographs on the table in front of me. Whatever nerve my brain thought it possessed, the rest of me violently disagreed. Somehow it was worse seeing it in reproduction. Up close, I could get a sense of the living, breathing woman that Clara had once been. Here, in smudgy sepia, it felt voyeuristic. I wasn't examining her in the pursuit of scientific knowledge; I was just satisfying my idle curiosity. I had no right to stare at the wound on her head the way one might examine a painting, taking in each brushstroke and striation. And yet I couldn't look away. Somewhere here was the answer to the puzzle.

'Look here, at the bruising around her mouth. And her eyes were bloodshot when I removed them.'

He looked at me as though this were another examination.

'Suffocation,' I whispered. It was a horrible thought.

'As I suspected, when whoever attacked her hid her body,

she wasn't dead. She must have come to, and he – or she – panicked. I've spoken to the other servants, but they didn't see anything.' He glanced up at me. 'They're all rather fascinated by you. Not only are you that rare butterfly, a lady doctor in training, but you've consented to marry the family dunce. I think they're more shocked by that than by the murder.'

I scowled. I might not want to marry Miles – I might not even like him – but Merchiston's needling made me feel oddly defensive. The instinct would have boded well for a life together, were it not for the fact that I had no intention of becoming the poor man's wife.

'You know, you won't even have to change your monogram,' Merchiston said cheerfully. 'All those handkerchiefs you have with SG embroidered on will serve you till the end of your days. Steamer trunks, letter-openers – all that nonsense women like to scribble their initials on will work just as well for Sarah Greene as for Sarah Gilchrist.'

I wondered if it was in poor taste under the circumstances to imagine stabbing Gregory Merchiston with said monogrammed letter-opener before stuffing his body into an equally monogrammed steamer trunk and packing it off to America. I wasn't sure I minded.

I smiled slowly as a thought occurred to me. Merchiston, I noticed, looked rather frightened.

'You know, my engagement may be the talk of the servants' quarters across the New Town, but there's one advantage I have that you can't possibly compete with.' He raised a sceptical eyebrow. 'None of them dare talk to you or the police, but they're all dying to meet me.'

I rose, and left him with his grisly portraits. I had plans with the living.

Chapter 7

I arrived at the Greenes' residence the next day unsure what I would find.

A murdered servant didn't exactly require mourning, but it felt wrong to turn up at a house that had so recently seen a tragedy in bright colours. I wore a mauve dress tailored so that it almost looked like a riding habit – Aunt Emily had deemed it 'masculine', which only gave me greater delight in wearing it – with a matching coat, plumed hat and mink stole. Beneath my pristine gloves, my fingers were stained with ink and face powder. I had been in my bedroom trying to work out a method of making myself look both ladylike – so that my appearance wouldn't shock the Greenes – and like the radical bluestocking the below-stairs staff were expecting.

If Aurora thought it odd that I wanted to give my condolences in person to those who had worked with her maid, she let it slide and waved me in the general direction of the kitchen. I wondered if she was still drugged – it would explain her unnaturally calm demeanour.

The servants were anything but calm. As I sat at the kitchen table, the housemaid, Blackwell, tried unsuccessfully to hold back her sobs and I found myself consoling her.

'Clara was so young. And so pretty . . . Really, it was a tragedy. Did she have a family?'

Blackwell nodded, wiping her eyes with the back of her hand. I passed her a handkerchief and her eyes widened. 'Miss, I couldn't! It's too nice for me to rub my face on.' It was one of a dozen in my dresser, and I felt an ugly stab of guilt over something I was as likely as not to lose within the week.

'Please. I insist. Clara deserves more than crying into a tea towel.'

She smiled, dabbed her eyes gingerly and tucked the handkerchief into her sleeve.

'She was the eldest of six. Her mother died and her father's health is bad – he was a miner up north, and it broke him. She and her sister raised the bairns – all of them in service except the sister, who nurses after her pa.' She looked up. 'You'll know all about that, miss, with your doctoring.'

I imagined raising four siblings only to find myself, instead of enjoying a blooming womanhood with all the suitors and frivolities that should come with it, looking after a parent and trapped in the same cramped, grubby house I was born in. My studies and all that would hopefully come after were nothing to that.

'Will you no' gi' the doctorin' up when you're married to Master Miles?'

I sighed. 'I suppose that's up to him.' I realised that Clara was not the only one the girl had information on. 'Do you like working for him? Please, answer honestly; I'd like to get a sense of who he really is.'

'Nicest of the family, if you ask me.' I suspected that wasn't difficult. Still, it was promising. 'He doesnae mind if I make a clatter when I'm blacking the grate. Sometimes I catch myself humming a song if I've been at the music hall.'

At least he wouldn't be one of those fractious men who complained endlessly of their nerves and demanded complete silence. Not that I could imagine what we would talk about.

'Did Clara like him?'

'There was nothing like that goin' on, miss, I swear. Clara was a good girl, church every Sunday and not one of those who only mouths the words. And I've never heard anything said against Master Miles, not by any of the girls.'

Her words were telling. 'What about Colonel Greene?'

'Him neither, miss.'

'I suppose Clara would have known more about that, as Mrs Greene's maid.'

'She wasnae one to tattle, I'll tell you that. Always very close when it came to the family. Said she wouldn't betray a confidence for a king's ransom, she thought that much of her job.'

Her job, not her employers. And why say that if there were no secrets to tell? A king's ransom was one thing, but a genuine chance for money to buy her family's way out of poverty – that would be harder to turn down. And knowledge held only by one person could command a much higher price than backstairs gossip.

'She doesn't sound like the kind of woman to steal from her employer.'

The girl shook her head violently. 'I'd never have thought it of her. But Mrs Greene did have jewellery going missing. She said it was carelessness, didn't want us to report it to the polis or mention it to Colonel Greene. Clara looked as shocked as anyone about it.'

Either she was a better actor than she was a thief, or there was more to Clara Wilson's pockets full of jewels than met the eye.

I changed tactics before the maid could question my motives for being below stairs.

'I must say, my future mother-in-law looks as immaculate as always. Has she hired a new maid?'

Blackwell blushed. 'She asked me to help her. I'm no'

trained, but I've been working here a time and she says she trusts me.'

'I'd much rather have a maid I knew attend to me than a perfect stranger,' I agreed. 'I'll happily put a good word in for you.'

Her face lit up. 'Oh, miss! That's awfully kind of you. But I thought . . . Well, will you no' be looking for a staff of your own?'

I couldn't promise her a job in a household I had no desire to build – and if I somehow wormed my way out of this damn engagement, my aunt was hardly going to reward me with my own maid. Still, it would be useful to have a friend below stairs.

'I will,' I said slowly, 'but that won't be for a while yet; we're having a long engagement. You'd learn an awful lot from Mrs Greene and I'm sure she wouldn't mind me poaching you eventually.'

I hoped she would learn an awful lot *about* Mrs Greene as well, information that she would be more than happy to pass to a future employer over a cup of tea and a slice of Dundee cake. In return, I promised myself that if I were ever in a position to have my own servants, then Blackwell would be the first name on my list. I wondered how good she was at getting bloodstains out of fabric.

'Miss Gilchrist!'

Miles stood in the doorway, looking shyly pleased to see me. When I returned his smile, it was genuine – out of all his family, he was the one who had truly seemed stricken by Wilson's death, and he at least had bothered to learn her name.

'Mother said you were here. Would you care for some tea in the parlour?'

I had gathered as much information here as I was likely to, and perhaps Miles knew more than he realised.

He blushed with consternation when it became apparent

that Aurora had gone upstairs to rest and we were left unchaperoned. Quite what he thought we were likely to get up to in a room facing onto the street with an open door in broad daylight, I wasn't sure, but it didn't seem the time to mention that I had been in far more intimate situations with a man.

'H-how kind of you to ask after the servants. I'm afraid they're very shaken.'

'I don't blame them. It's hardly the kind of thing one expects, working for a family like yours.'

He nodded. 'We are all upset. To have something so horrible happen just outside our front door – and to know she was stealing from us.' He shuddered. 'It doesn't bear thinking about.'

I found myself agreeing with him. Of course, one rarely knew what really went on behind closed doors in families of quality. And yet I had come to think of Aunt Emily's house as a sort of refuge, away from the filth and secrets I had found elsewhere.

'Do you think she stole from all of you?'

He shook his head. 'I don't think so. F-Father kept everything in perfect order – the army, you know – and he'd have raised merry hell if any of his belongings had gone missing. I'm not sure I have anything worth stealing. Alisdair inherited my grandfather's signet ring and things like that – I have a rather nice set of cufflinks and a chessboard, but I don't think they'd be as easy to sell.'

Perhaps I should have felt bad that Alisdair had inherited the lion's share of the family heirlooms, especially when he stood to inherit so much more on Colonel Greene's death. Instead, one thing Miles had said had my interest well and truly piqued, and it was nothing to do with his family or the murder.

'You play chess?' Perhaps the heavy raincloud of this marriage, should I be doomed to undertake it, would have a silver lining.

He nodded, his face lighting up. 'Would you like me to fetch the set? I'm not terribly good, but I do enjoy it.'

And so I found myself seated opposite my fiancé, becoming more intimately acquainted with him than I could ever have imagined. To my surprise, we were fairly evenly matched, and with the distraction of the board he relaxed somewhat and we found ourselves talking easily. He was a cautious player but a clever one, and I realised that despite his awkward silences in company, he observed far more than I had expected.

When left to his own devices, Miles wasn't a bad conversationalist and was far happier to listen than talk, although he had nothing of substance to tell me about Wilson other than that she had been prepared to weather his mother's occasionally stormy moods.

As I swooped in to checkmate him with a rook, he smiled.

'We should start keeping a tally,' he said. 'And then when we're old and grey and too arthritic to hold a chess piece, we can add it up and see who's the winner.'

Reality came thudding down. A pleasant afternoon with a game of chess was one thing, but a lifetime? Even if both our games improved substantially – and they would have to, if we didn't want to expire from boredom – it wasn't a foundation for a marriage. Or at least not the kind of marriage I wanted.

He flushed, seeing my expression. 'I'm sorry. I know our families arranged this. I know I wouldn't have been your first choice.'

I bit my lip. 'Marriage wouldn't have been my first choice, Miles. It's nothing to do with you, not really.' I looked at him closely. 'And would I really have been yours?'

'I-I . . .' he stammered, blushing tomato red to the roots of his sandy hair. 'I can't inherit if I don't marry. A stupid clause in Father's will that he could write out but refuses to. He's so obsessed with keeping the family name going, especially when it didn't look like Frances could give Alisdair a child. She lost two babies before this pregnancy and Father always said she looked too frail. But I want to be married,' he said quickly. 'I know that isn't the fashion for men to say, but I do. I want a wife, I want a home. I want someone who looks at me the way my mother looks at my f-father.'

I couldn't help but smile. 'Why, Miles, you're quite the romantic.'

'Aren't you?'

I shivered, although the day was warm. 'I used to be. I'm afraid that now I'm just a pragmatist.'

'A good thing for a doctor,' he offered.

'It's a quality less prized in a wife.'

He sighed. 'I may not be the man you dreamed of back when you thought of romance, but I'll be a good husband, I promise. You'll learn to love me.'

Although I knew he meant well, my blood boiled at his words. 'Why do people keep saying that? Love isn't something you learn! It just happens, whether you want it to or not.'

He nodded, as though I had confirmed a suspicion he had been nursing.

'There's someone else.'

I felt a jolt pass through me, electric and awful. I had said nothing, not mentioned Merchiston's name once. Had he seen something in our interaction the night of the murder that gave us away? How could he, when all there was between us was the shared memory of one almost-kiss?

'I know there was someone in London. I-I know you're not a virgin, Sarah. My father told me. He said that it would help – at least one of us will know what we're doing.' He laughed bitterly.

So I was marrying a man more innocent than I was. The one thing designed to save me from eccentricity and immorality, and even that was unconventional.

Well, if he was being blunt, then I could be too. 'Don't

young men of good breeding typically get inducted into the amorous arts before marriage? Or do your romantic notions hold you to higher standards than mistresses and tarts?'

'Were you this forthright before your studies, or do they cover plain speaking in your lectures?' He sounded a little impressed.

'A personal failing, I'm afraid.' I smiled. 'The professors try to beat it out of me, but I'm afraid I'm incorrigible.'

'At least life will be interesting.' He sounded as though he were looking forward to our future, and I felt like the worst cad imaginable knowing that I was doing everything I could to evade it. 'But since you asked – my father took me to certain establishments, introduced me to all manner of women there.'

'That's appalling!'

My fiancé shrugged. 'I'm not sure if he was more worried that I was a simpleton or a sodomite.' He paused, looking horrified.

'I know what that means, Miles,' I sighed. 'But feel free to pretend that I don't if it makes you feel better.'

'Anyway, I had a horribly awkward few hours in an establishment off Leith Walk, where I left as unsullied as I walked in.'

My eyes widened.

'Don't look so relieved,' he muttered. 'Everything still works. I, ah, checked.'

The image that provoked would linger unwanted in my mind for some time. 'Well. That's . . . um . . . that's jolly good for you,' I said in a strangled tone.

'I've shocked you!' He looked delighted. 'The blunt and terrifying Dr Gilchrist can be shocked.'

'I'm not a doctor yet,' I reminded him. 'Not ever, if our parents have their way.'

'Like I said, I'm a romantic. And I knew I wasn't exactly the man she wanted to spend the night with, so it seemed kinder to both of us not to bother with the pretence. We talked about the weather; I paid her handsomely and never returned.'

He was kind. I thought of the men at Madame Ruby's brothel, the men who had used Lucy with little care as to whether they took her fancy. She would have been grateful for someone like Miles, a gentleman in the truest sense. A gentleman who wanted nothing more than a loving wife and a family, and I could give him neither.

He grimaced. 'I'm sure that makes me frightfully dull in your eyes.'

'What did your father say?'

'I lied. He clapped me on the back, told me I'd become a man at last and paid for a month of . . . ah . . . company up front.'

'You went back?'

'Once a week.' He grinned. 'That's how I became so good at chess – and a variety of card games with obscene names. If I do forfeit my inheritance, I suppose I could try and make my fortune at gambling.'

'And you never . . .'

'I couldn't. Not like that. Father would say it was womanish of me, but I . . . I need it to be with someone I trust. Someone I love.' He paused, and I knew what was coming next but could not stop it. 'The chap in London . . .'

'He didn't . . . I wasn't . . .'

'In love with him?'

'I thought I was, for a moment. Or that I could be. But he wasn't the man I thought he was at all. Frankly, I never want to set eyes on him again. My affections don't lie elsewhere and I'm not nursing a broken heart.'

'So the only thing I have to compete with is that.' He nodded in the direction of the university. 'I'm not sure how I stack up against a building.'

'It's more than a building. It's freedom. It's making my

own choices – making my own money! It's never having to be beholden to another person again.' I paused, wondering how much I wanted to open up to him 'If you want the truth, I'm envious. My . . . encounter was less than ideal. Honestly, I wish it had never happened and I had never met him. Please don't think I'm pining for a lost lover, because nothing could be further from the truth. But there were . . . consequences.'

'A child?' His hand hovered over mine for a moment, before tentatively resting on it. It was the nicest response I had had to my horrid story.

I shrugged, the gesture belying the deep seam of pain his question prompted. 'If there was, the poor thing thought better of being carried by such an unfit mother. I don't blame it – I wasn't particularly keen on living either.' I remembered the fall down the stairs that was never an accident, remembered my mother watching and not moving until I lay dazed in the hall. The blood the next day that could have been the remnants of my violation or just my final menses before the butchers at the asylum got hold of me. 'In any event, I can't . . . Miles, there was an operation. An ovariectomy, it's called.'

He stared blankly. Clearly his ignorance of the carnal arts extended to how babies were actually made.

'The part of me that lets me bear a child – they took it out.' Tears stung my throat. 'They took it all out. I can't give you a family, Miles. I'm sorry.'

He let go of my hand and I was unaccountably sorry for it.

'Then you're the perfect choice. A bandage of respectability for the defective son, without the risk of bringing another runt into the family litter.'

So my barren state suited both parties. Anger flared inside me. How dare our families use us to mop up their own scandals? Pair off the untouchables and then shuffle them off to some family estate in the country so that their lives would no longer be blighted by a slut and a . . . Whatever cruel name

I could conjure up, I couldn't use it, not even in the privacy of my own mind. Miles deserved more than that. Maybe I did, too.

'No wonder my family was so keen to snap you up,' he continued. 'You're everything they could have wanted. You have a family desperate to marry you off to the first man who'll have you and utterly incapable of passing on our mutual peculiarities.' His harshness took my breath away. He laughed. 'Did you really think I would have chosen you? A bluestocking who spends her days cutting up bodies? I know it must gall you, Miss High and Mighty Gilchrist, that I'm the best you could get, but my parents' choice doesn't reflect terribly well on me either.'

'Then call it off,' I said through gritted teeth. 'Say you don't want damaged goods.'

'If I do that, I lose my inheritance.'

'And if we marry, I lose everything! I've worked damn hard to get here. Do you know how many female doctors there are in Britain? One hundred. And most of them had to study at women's colleges, not darken the doors of establishments like Edinburgh. I wanted to go to the London School of Medicine for Women, you know. I wanted to stay with my family and friends and have everything I ever wanted. Instead, I'm here, at one of the best medical schools in the world. Some say it's more competitive than Oxford, but they let me in. With my lack of feminine virtue – my lack of anything that makes me truly a woman in society's eyes – I passed the examinations with flying colours. But that doesn't matter, because you need your . . . your *fucking* inheritance!' He was goggle-eyed at my profanity. 'This is what you're hitching your marital wagon to, Miles. A cursing harlot who knows more about the human anatomy – of both sexes, mind – than you ever will. And even if my mother pulls me out of university kicking and screaming – which she will if she has to – I'll still know it all. I'll have worked harder in my first year at Edinburgh than you have in your life.'

I stopped, breathing heavily and appalled at what I had said. It was true, every word, but that didn't mean it wasn't cruel.

We sat in shocked silence. To my surprise, Miles spoke first.

'I'm sorry.'

I smiled wryly. 'I was about to say the same thing.'

'I didn't mean it – not really. Just because I didn't choose you doesn't mean I'm not happy that my parents did.'

'You're a hell of a lot better than I would have expected from Aunt Emily.' He fought a smile and lost. 'I don't suppose . . .' I trailed off, wondering if what I was about to suggest was entirely proper. 'If all this goes ahead – you wouldn't teach me one of those obscene card games, would you?'

By the time Aurora came downstairs, we were helpless with laughter. She seemed bemused but relieved, and when they insisted on sending me out in the family carriage, I accepted even though I knew the sight of it would cause me to be soundly mocked by my peers.

I dashed from the carriage across the quad to where the others were waiting, then brought us all to a crashing halt like dominoes as I stared at the last person I expected to see standing amongst the grey stone buildings with the first snowflakes starting to fall.

My mother had arrived.

Chapter 8

Seeing her in the cloistered environs of the medical school was strange, as though she had been pasted on like a picture in a scrapbook, against a background where she didn't belong. My hands went to my skirts, frantically trying to brush off any trace of blood, formaldehyde or ink. I felt her eyes rake over me, taking in the brown twill coat, the poplin blouse, and the heavy leather bag in my hand bursting with textbooks and papers. She stood in the quad, a vision of London society in among the sweat and stone of Edinburgh's future professional classes. A stranger might have interpreted her curious gaze as interest, but I knew that her mind, every bit as analytical as my own, was cataloguing everything she saw and filing it away for future criticism. A future that was imminent, and involved me.

I raised my gaze to meet hers and she smiled. There was no friendly wave or movement to approach the daughter she hadn't seen in a year. I crossed the cobbles towards her, and kissed her weakly on each cheek, feeling her chilly flesh beneath my lips. It was the weather, I told myself. She must be freezing. But she felt like a marble statue – beautiful, but cold and unbending.

'Mother! We weren't expecting you until Friday. Aunt Emily said you couldn't get away.'

'What could be more important than my elder daughter's engagement?'

I felt the eyes of my fellow students watching us.

'You must be Mrs Gilchrist – how lovely to meet you! Sarah has told us so much about you.'

God bless Thornhill. She could have been at a tea party, rather than dashing between lectures. My mother took her in with a searching glance and I was relieved when she passed muster.

'Mother, this is Alison Thornhill. Of the Northumbria Thornhills. Her father—'

'Owns one of the largest cotton mills in England. A pleasure to make your acquaintance, Miss Thornhill. I met your parents at a fund-raiser several years ago. They never mentioned that their daughter had her heart set on studying medicine.'

If Alison saw Mother swallow with distaste at the mere mention of the word, she feigned obliviousness.

Mother looked around the quad, scrutinising the other girls. 'Good Lord, is that Julia Latymer lurking in the corner?'

My rival looked like a fox caught before hounds. I wondered if Julia's secrets had reached my family's ears just as mine had reached hers. Edith sank into the shadows, and much as I had no love for Julia's surly sidekick – or whatever she was – I felt sorry for her. Then again, it wasn't as though I was rushing to introduce my fiancé to people.

'Julia, my dear.' Latymer's reception was considerably warmer than mine had been, but I could still detect the note of ice in my mother's words. The Latymers were a bohemian, progressive sort – exactly the type to send their only child off to join a scandalous profession. We had had very little to do with them in London, our social circles overlapping in places like a scientific diagram – not distant enough to be strangers, but certainly not enough in common to claim a close acquaintance.

The pair exchanged stiff pleasantries until Julia was sensible enough to claim a prior engagement and fled. I had never seen her scared before, and it was an unnerving experience.

Mother glanced down at me and frowned. 'You're not wearing your engagement ring.'

'I didn't want to accidentally drop it in a corpse mid dissection,' I snapped. Why couldn't I stop myself from provoking her? Less than five minutes in her presence and we were already at war.

She huffed. 'Well, we should be off. Where's your hat? You girls really can't be running around half dressed.'

'It's a hat,' I said through gritted teeth. 'We're crossing one side of the courtyard to the other – it would take more time to put the bloody pins in!'

'Is this what this place is teaching you? Vulgarities, lack of decorum and heaven knows what else! Well, run off and fetch it. Your aunt has tea and cake waiting and I intend to have words with her about the decline in your behaviour.'

My aunt had clearly omitted to mention that I was never home in the daytime, no matter what was waiting.

I gritted my teeth. 'Mother, I have lectures all day. Every day.'

'They can hardly expect you to study when your mother is visiting! Tell them; I'm sure they'll understand.'

I briefly imagined explaining to Merchiston – or worse, Professor Williamson, whose opinion of us was already mere inches from the gutter – that I couldn't attend today's lecture because my mama was visiting. It was not a reassuring image.

'If you lassies are finished having afternoon tea on the lawn or whatever the bloody hell it is you're doing—'

Oh God. Oh no.

Merchiston trailed off as my mother turned, slowly and deliberately, like a warship facing the enemy, and locked her gaze on his.

'Forgive me, madam, I was unaware that we had a guest.'

'Professor, this is my mother. Mother, this is Professor Merchiston.'

He bowed, oozing charm I had never seen him bestow on anyone. It was an unsettling experience.

'Mrs Gilchrist, a pleasure to meet you.'

'Do you normally curse in front of ladies, Professor Mitchum?'

He didn't bother to correct her. Sensible man – where my mother was concerned, one should always pick one's battles.

'Forgive me. A momentary error. Your daughter is a fine student, Mrs Gilchrist.'

'My daughter is headstrong.'

He laughed 'Aye, I'll not argue with that.'

She gave a long, searching look around the quad. 'So you really think that this is a woman's place?'

'If I did not, I wouldnae be teaching a dozen of them.' He smiled, showing all of his teeth.

It would take more than his wolfish, dangerous charm to make my mother back down, however, and she continued her litany of criticism.

'Professor, are you not teaching your students how to comport themselves in public? There are enough doubts about the efficacy of women as physicians without introducing a hoyden to your patients.'

'Young people can be high-spirited. Rest assured, we'll have their youthful enthusiasm crushed in no time.'

He was making a joke. My mother didn't believe in jokes; she thought humour was the eighth deadly sin and that it rarely if ever had a place in polite conversation.

'Sarah, get your things. We're leaving.'

'I'm afraid I simply cannot allow that. Miss Gilchrist, lecture hall. Now. The rest of you stop lollygagging and gawping as though you were at the fairground. Scram, or I'll tell the porters you volunteered to scrub the dissection room floors!'

The onlookers dispersed, and Merchiston left us alone in what I supposed he thought was a gesture of tact. I had to bite my lip not to plead with him to stay.

I thought I would bear the brunt of her rage without an audience, but to my surprise, my mother's voice softened. 'Please, Sarah. I haven't seen you in so long.'

'You threw me out of the house! You practically had me committed, never visited me once and I was home less than a day before you had my bags packed and my train fare to Edinburgh paid. I'm sorry if you missed me, Mother, but you've had an entire year without me. You can manage until dinner.'

I had never seen my mother look so out of place before. I saw a woman at odds with the new world she found herself in, one where her rules did not apply

Even worse, I saw myself. Mrs Miles Greene, visiting her old friends, soaking up knowledge by proxy, calcified by domesticity and convention. The men might look on me with approval, an unruly woman restored to her rightful place, but the women would pity me. The one who couldn't escape, too weak to struggle free and dragged down by society to tedium and tea parties. I would be a cautionary tale for all the brilliant, independent women, and the men would take it as proof that we would always be slaves to our feminine natures.

She opened her mouth to speak. 'Don't make a scene, Mother.' I spat the words back at her that she had used a year ago, when I had left the party where I had my ill-fated encounter with Paul Beresford in near hysteria. I turned on my heel and went inside, leaving her standing there alone.

Chapter 9

If I stood three steps down from the top of the stairs, I could hear every word being spoken in the parlour without anyone seeing me. I had learned this trick in the first week of being under my aunt's roof, when I had overheard more synonyms for 'whore' than I knew existed. Eventually I had stopped listening. If my uncle had revised his opinion of me in the seven months I had been here, I didn't know about it.

'. . . positively surrounded by men whose origins I certainly don't know! Did you enquire after the characters of the male students, Emily, or did you simply blithely send my daughter off to cavort with reprobates and ne'er-do-wells?'

'Her friends are all from good families – two of them are from our circle and one of them even has a title!'

'That Thornhill girl? You can't buy breeding, not even with a fortune that size. No wonder she runs around introducing herself as Miss instead of Lady!'

Alison was aristocracy? I wasn't surprised she kept that secret – I couldn't imagine that Moira would ever let her hear the end of it, and poor Carstairs would probably try and curtsey every time she saw her. Perhaps I shouldn't have given up my habit of eavesdropping after all – what other nuggets of information about my classmates had I missed?

I felt the tension between the two women crackle throughout the house; it had been years, I realised, since I had seen the two of them in a room together. I was so used to thinking of Aunt Emily as indomitable, unbending, that to see her back down in the face of her older sister's disapproval was unsettling. I hoped that Gertie and I would never enjoy such a fractious relationship – assuming, of course, that my sister still wanted anything to do with me.

I remembered with a jolt that she had written to me; my first contact with her for a year. My mother had left the letter on my bureau. But with the desire to eavesdrop on the argument overwhelming, it had completely slipped my mind. Hang whatever complaints my mother had – I would spend the evening with a family member who actually cared for me.

My little sister's penmanship was perfect, although the letter itself was horribly misspelled, so full of digressions it was hard to follow and containing rather more exclamation points than I suspected her finishing school would have approved of. She wanted to be a bridesmaid and hoped she could visit me in my new home; she missed me terribly. She was sorry I was too busy to attend her birthday party – I had not been invited – but hoped I had had a nice Christmas and did they celebrate it differently in Scotland? It all but begged for a reply, and I wondered if any of the countless letters I had written to her in the past year had ever made it to their intended recipient. There was no mention of my studies, and I wondered if Mother had taken it upon herself to announce I was dropping them. I would be lucky if she didn't walk directly to the faculty offices and withdraw me from lectures herself.

It was so characteristically Gertie that my heart ached, but something in the slant of her pen and the flourish of her signature had changed since I last saw her. The paper smelled faintly of lilacs – was Mother permitting her to wear scent now? Childhood innocence lingered around the letter like wisps of morning fog, but already it was beginning to lift and in its place was the beginnings of a young woman I did not know. Would I be as strange to her? Did the woman in practical skirts and sensible boots, her fingers stained with ink and ammonia and her head in a textbook, hiding the dark circles under her eyes, resemble her happy, rebellious sister at all?

I no longer missed the girl I was. My mind was brimming over with new knowledge.

When I came to Edinburgh, I was weak and wasted, still unable to sleep peacefully through the night unless I was drugged. Now, I could trace the beginnings of muscles in my arms. If I ran my hands over my calves, I could feel the tautness from dashing from lecture theatre to tutorial to dissection room. Mother would have called it unladylike, but how could it be when I was more aware of my body than I had ever been in my life? She was the one who had taught me how to use it to send all those subtle messages that let our social circle know what we were thinking – the ocular calisthenics required to catch a gentleman's eye or cut him dead, the correct way to raise one's hand to acknowledge an acquaintance you didn't wish to speak to and wanted them to know you didn't. I had seen her reduce an entire dinner table to silence simply from the way she tilted her head. She had turned her body into a weapon long before I had.

At least my appetite had returned with a vengeance – Alison had relented and given me half her tongue and piccalilli sandwich the other day after I made eyes at it over my own plate of crumbs – and the colour was back in my cheeks, but whatever softness I had possessed in those months before Paul Beresford had attacked me was gone for good. In its place was something new – a confidence I had never before possessed, the kind only earned by having everything one loved ripped away. It felt like armour.

I heard footsteps ascending the stairs and quickly picked up the ring from my dressing table and slipped it back onto my finger.

There. The life I should have had, pieced back together so you could hardly see the join.

'I've spoken to your aunt, and we'll meet the Greenes this week. I'll call on Aurora tomorrow – we've exchanged letters, of course, but I'd like to see her in person. And then on Friday, they'll host a proper engagement party. I want everyone to know that my daughter is marrying into a good family.' She looked sternly at me. 'And you will marry, Sarah. I know you, I know that you're calculating a hundred and one ways to embarrass me and call it off, but for once you will do as you're told. It's for your own good, you know that.'

'I never wanted this,' I said softly. 'You wanted it for me. I'm going to be a doctor, Mother. I'm going to make my own living, my own life. Maybe I'll marry, but if I do, it will be a man of my choosing, someone who supports me in my profession.'

She snorted. 'What man will take a woman like that? A woman who wastes her marriageable years studying, who breaks off an engagement! Who isn't even—'

'A virgin?'

Mother flinched. 'There's no need to be vulgar, Sarah. Do you realise how lucky you are to have a man willing to overlook your flaws?'

I stood up straight. 'I'm not flawed.'

'Tell that to half of London. They still talk about you, you know. You're quite the cautionary tale. "Be careful how you comport yourself or you'll end up just like that dreadful Gilchrist girl, having to find a job because she can't find a husband." Well, this is our chance to prove them wrong.'

'I won't give up my studies. I won't do it!'

'Your father and I indulged this . . . this *whim* because we thought you'd come to your senses. It was never meant to be a permanent solution.'

'I don't love him.'

'You'll learn to. You're learning Latin and chemistry and God knows what at this ghastly institution; why should making a home and a family be any different?'

I didn't despise Miles. I didn't even dislike him. The more we talked, the kinder and gentler he seemed to be – there was a sense of humour buried beneath his awkward facade and I enjoyed his company, if not the reason for it. But marriage?

I thought of that first flush of desire for Paul, before he ruined everything. The way my skin prickled, hot and strange, at Gregory Merchiston's touch. The way Elisabeth and Randall looked at each other, all soft and full of longing. Even Julia and Edith had something in that odd, wild kiss I had witnessed that spoke of so much more than duty.

'Do you really mean to tell me that you never want to get married? That you want to stay alone for ever?'

'I want everything.' The words spilled out of me. 'But I can't have it, can I? I can't have a family, you made damn sure of that.'

She flinched. So that was my mother's Achilles heel – the fact that her elder daughter would never make her a grandmama. 'The doctors said it would be best. To calm your nerves and ensure that you would have no cause to regret any future . . . mistakes. We could never have foreseen—'

'I was never supposed to marry. Never supposed to resurface in society and find a ring on my finger and a man desperate to turn me into his brood mare. You're not angry with me – you're angry that your gamble didn't pay off and you're selling the Greenes a faulty bill of goods. Or are you just resentful that Aunt Emily has brought me closer to the altar than you ever did? A torn hymen, a barren womb and the first term of a medical degree under my belt and she still managed to find me a husband. Maybe it's not me who's the family failure after all.'

I had seen my mother laughing, angry, gracious. I had never seen her hurt.

'I've built a life for myself, one where I can be useful,' I said softly.

'You aren't required to be useful, Sarah! You're a young lady of good breeding, even if that rarely shows these days. The only person who need have use of you is your husband.'

'If you visited the clinic where I used to volunteer, then maybe you'd understand.'

'The falling-down cathouse in a slum? Oh, your uncle has told me all about it. Colonel Greene doesn't want a daughter-in-law who spends her time ministering to sluts and pickpockets.'

'Well I don't want him for a father-in-law, so at least we agree on something!'

I heard the crack of hand against cheek before I felt the pain.

'Ask yourself if an empty stomach and fine principles are quite the substitute for a home and a family you think they are.'

In the mirror, I saw her reflection slam the door behind her and I looked down at the diamond sparkling on my left hand. It had been formed through centuries of pressure, and even if I stamped on the blasted thing with all my might, I knew it wouldn't shatter. Well then, there was my answer.

I would shine just as brightly and be just as impossible to crush.

Chapter 10

The next morning, I stood blankly in front of my wardrobe, wondering if I owned a single dress that would meet with my mother's approval. If I chose something too plain then she'd accuse me of looking dowdy; too pretty and she'd assume I was trying to catch a man's eye. A traitorous voice in my head wondered if marriage to Miles Greene would really be worse than this.

It was cold and rainy, I was somehow in the middle of a murder investigation for the second time in my life, and if I had to stick to a palette like the Highlands in November, all grey and faded green and brown, I was going to scream. Julia might have scoffed at the idea of a sensible, intellectual woman taking pleasure in clothes, but I noticed that however mannish the cut of her jacket and skirt, they were also expertly tailored. In the end, I had Agnes dress me in a damson wool skirt and jacket with a crisp white blouse. I fastened the silver brooch Elisabeth had given me for Christmas at my throat and the maid brushed my hair until it shone before twisting it into a chignon.

My engagement ring sat on my dressing table and I sighed before putting it on. Let Mother think I was playing to her rules. In two weeks she would be gone and I would have found some way to talk Miles into breaking things off. I wondered if

I could introduce him to someone else – would Alison's cheerful manner and easy way appeal? Or perhaps he and Caroline Carstairs could find companionship in stilted conversations and awkward silences. Women married men they didn't care about every day – there must be someone of acceptable breeding who would overlook sweaty palms and shyness to claim a share of the Greene family fortune.

I was turning into Aunt Emily, I thought with a grimace, trying to matchmake at every turn. No, my best hope was that he would just see sense and call things off and weather his father's inevitable fury. Was that cruel of me? Miles was visibly terrified of the man – it hadn't escaped my attention, as we were forced closer, that he was considerably more relaxed when out of his company. But that was his affair, I told myself sternly. Mother and Aunt Emily would be no less pleased; even my own father might be moved to write a letter chiding me for my inability to keep even the blandest of men.

I didn't want to wait around for breakfast just in case Mother decided to join us for once, although I could count on the fingers of one hand the number of times I had seen her awake this early, but Aunt Emily coaxed me into taking some tea and toast, to which I added bacon and sausages – if I was going to have breakfast I might as well make it a good one – and gave me a look I had come to know well.

'I have to go to lectures. I can't just stop it all because my mama won't let me. I'm not a child.'

'Until you're married, you're under your parents' protection and mine. To all intents and purposes, Sarah, a child is exactly what you are.'

I gulped down the last of my tea and gathered my things.

'Then it's a good job I left before you had a chance to stop me, isn't it?' As retorts went, it might have been more effective if not delivered through a mouthful of Cumberland sausage, but she sighed and waved me off.

'Shut the door quietly on your way out.'

I was rather liking this new, permissive side of Aunt Emily. Apparently all it took to turn her into an ally was the introduction of an older sister who was even more disapproving of my habits.

I made it to my first lecture with time to spare, and nearly ran smack into Professor Merchiston.

'Miss Gilchrist. I wasn't sure we'd see you today.'

'My mother normally sleeps late. I didn't see the need to wake her.'

'Ah,' he grinned. 'Don't expect it to be so easy tomorrow – in my experience, you can pull the wool over a mother's eyes once and once only.'

'That sounds as if you speak from experience. You must have run her ragged.'

'The trick is not to get caught in the first place.' He frowned. 'Then again, mine was never as terrifying as yours. Has Miles met her yet? She could be just the thing you need to put him off for good. They do say women turn into their mothers.'

I thought about the woman I had come face to face with after not seeing her for a year. I hoped I would never recognise myself in her.

Two hours later, it was as though we had never spoken. Professor Merchiston stood in front of a bubbling test tube, pontificating and scrawling equations and formulae on a blackboard, and I scribbled down notes as fast as I could.

The stink of formaldehyde and ammonia made me feel dizzy. I wasn't the only one – Moira looked positively green, and it was clear that none of us could concentrate.

'What the bloody hell is wrong with you all?'

'It's the smell,' I offered. 'It's a little overpowering.'

'It's your corsets. Damn things are laced too tight. You girls will cause yourselves an injury if you're not careful.'

It wasn't until I saw Caroline Carstairs go as bright red as her hair and Alison Thornhill shaking with giggles that I realised how inured I had become to Professor Merchiston's outbursts of coarseness.

'Frankly, I don't give a damn whether you show up to my class in dresses, trousers or the finery of a sultan from the East provided you're here to work. Arrange yourselves more comfortably, if you like. I will be waiting outside in the quad when you're ready; send someone to fetch me. I won't take this out of your lecture time, but please arrive attired more practically in future.'

Within minutes, the lecture theatre became more like the dressing room of a music hall as blouses were discarded and dresses tugged off the shoulders and dropped to the waist.

'He shouldn't notice what we're wearing,' Edith scowled. 'And he certainly shouldn't draw attention to it.'

'He's a doctor, you goose,' Julia laughed. 'He's hardly going to miss the fact that some of his students are a different shape to others.'

I stood there awkwardly as everyone began to undress. If I went home with so much as a corset lace out of place, my aunt's maid would report it.

An odd expression passed across Julia's face, and I realised she thought my reluctance was because of her. She certainly seemed more comfortable than I would have been in the company of a room full of men adjusting their undergarments. My thoughts flashed to Merchiston and the night I had discovered him in the boxing ring, stripped to the waist.

On second thoughts, perhaps loosening my stays wasn't such a terrible idea.

Julia's eyes were firmly on her boots, and I realised that what I had thought was anger was really terror: that she or Edith would somehow give themselves away. No wonder she pushed everyone away with her sharp tongue.

I groaned inwardly and decided to offer an olive branch that only they would recognise.

'Latymer, give me a hand. I know you think my laces are as loose as my morals, but I still can't bloody breathe.'

'I'm trying to be nice,' she hissed angrily.

I rolled my eyes. For someone with a secret, she was terrible at deception. 'You used me as a distraction for months. I understand if you need to keep up the pretence occasionally.'

'Fair enough.' She raised her voice. 'Frankly, I'm surprised you bothered with it at all, Gilchrist. Does your fiancé mind that he's getting second-hand goods?'

Ouch. Well at least she was entering into the spirit of things. The others were watching, the atmosphere tense as they wondered whether we were about to reignite our antipathy.

'Insult me as much as you like, just loosen the bloody thing!'

'Oh, honestly,' Alison snapped. She had been off with me ever since she learned of my engagement and even our collective light mood didn't seem to have reached her. 'Some of us want to learn, not act the goat.'

Nudging Julia out of the way, she yanked my laces back into place tighter than before.

'So now you're chumming up with Julia, after the way she treated you?' she whispered in my ear.

'The way you let her treat me. Maybe she just respects me because I stood up to her.'

I couldn't tell her the truth behind my half-hearted truce with Julia and Edith. I had arrived in Edinburgh with a secret of my own that had spread like wildfire – mostly thanks to Julia – but it was the ones I kept for others that surrounded me like a wall, keeping everyone else out.

'I'll fetch the professor,' I muttered. At least there was someone in this wretched university who understood me.

The air smelled of hops from the brewery, of a city in full

flow and the sweet scent of tobacco from Merchiston's pipe. When he saw me, he blew a perfect ring of smoke and tipped his hat.

'Am I to assume that you are as decent as overeducated bluestocking wenches can possibly be, or are you luring me into a den of iniquity?'

I smiled, and there was a warmth in it I could not imagine flickering to life with my fiancé. 'I would never embarrass you by assuming you needed the assistance, Professor.'

Chapter 11

Candlelight glinted off polished silver, forks clinked off plates and conversation buzzed as sixteen people sat down for dinner in gowns and jewels that would feed the city's slums for the best part of a decade. Aurora Greene's tinkling laugh rang off the crystal chandelier and even the bubbles in the champagne seemed to sparkle.

One wouldn't think that a little over a week before, a girl had been found outside with her head bashed in. Here, life went on as normal.

'An unfortunate state of affairs,' Aurora had sighed over afternoon tea, 'but one can hardly expect the household to go into mourning over one dead servant.'

My mother had nodded approvingly as I sat in miserable silence, reflecting that along with Aunt Emily they resembled nothing more than a better-dressed version of *Macbeth*'s three witches. Instead of a cauldron, they had bone china and Darjeeling tea, but they had conjured up a feast that would have put all the kings of Scotland, murderous or otherwise, to shame. The message was clear – anything untoward that might have occurred in these refined streets had absolutely nothing to do with the Greene family themselves.

'I hope you will forgive my absence at your supper, Mrs

Greene,' my mother said. 'I was too unwell to travel alone.'

I suspected the cause of her sickness had less to do with some winter virus and more to do with the prospect of eating haggis, but it was hardly the most egregious lie any of us were telling.

'Not at all. Your presence was missed, of course, but with such a lovely young couple pledging their troth, the atmosphere was quite merry.' I concluded that either Aurora was delusional or she was describing another dinner party entirely.

'My sister speaks very highly of your family. I do hope that you find Sarah a welcome addition.'

'She's delightful, Diana. Why, I consider her a daughter already.' Aurora smiled warmly, and I was discomfited to realise that her affection for me was genuine. Another stab of guilt then, this time for the family I was deceiving.

If my mother was surprised that someone should feel so warmly towards me, at least she didn't let it show.

'She and Miles are such a sweet match,' Aunt Emily chimed in. 'I think we can look forward to a long and happy marriage.' Personally, I was looking forward to the sweet release of death.

'It was a shame that our evening was spoiled by such a tragic occurrence,' I added. From the way the awkward silence fell, you would have thought I had mentioned an embarrassing personal ailment rather than a murder.

'We are assured that the matter is in hand,' Aurora said tightly. 'We must try not to dwell on it.'

'And are such events a regular concern?'

My mother sounded positively bored, picking some imaginary fluff from her skirt and discarding it onto the floor. But the barb behind her remark was pointed, and Aurora paled.

'Not in the slightest, Mrs Gilchrist! My household only employs the most upstanding of characters. We would never have admitted someone we believed to be consorting with such unsavoury elements.'

'Let us remember that Miss Wilson was the victim here,' I pointed out. 'She can't be blamed for her own demise.'

My mother opened her mouth to correct me, and then quickly reconsidered. Checkmate, Mother. She could hardly imply that any woman touched by scandal was not unblemished without reminding the assembled company of my own past.

There was no such badinage at this party, where I was to be shown off on Miles's arm for the first time. I wasn't sure what the guests were more eager for – gossip about the macabre crime that had occurred or a chance to gawk at Miles Greene's tainted bride-to-be.

It was clear I wasn't what they expected, and it was pleasant to bathe in the compliments about my gown and figure without feeling they concealed a barb about my vanity or virtue. I wore cornflower-blue silk trimmed with white lace; a lapis lazuli brooch was fastened at my throat and the ropes of my grandmother's pearls glowed in the candlelight. The drape of fabric over bustle and corset gave my figure the illusion of curves, and hair that had looked like lank straw when I had arrived home from my lectures now shone like pale gold. The brooch brought out my eyes – I had always thought their colour insipid, hardly the kind of thing suitors would write bad poetry about, but catching my reflection in a mirror, I saw them sparkle.

In contrast to the Burns supper, which had been an intimate gathering, this dinner party boasted the cream of Edinburgh's polite society. Aside from my family and the Greenes, I didn't know a soul. Then again, neither did my mother, and yet she had taken the assembled gathering to her bosom, dispensing advice on dresses and child-rearing and matchmaking with the practised ease of someone who had known the parties involved since the nursery. She was in her element, I realised sadly. An element she had never fully inhabited even when she was parading me around parties just like this back when I was untouched by either a man's hand or the corroding influence of a university education. I knew that I had not been the daughter she wanted, but I had never truly understood that it was a loss for her too.

She caught my eye, and I found myself placing my hand on Miles's arm and giving him a brilliant smile. I felt her warning gaze melt into one of pleasure, and even the way my fiancé started and choked on his drink at the unexpected affection couldn't mar that longed-for moment of approval.

It vanished the moment another guest turned her attention to me.

'A doctor, you say?' The widowed society lady opposite me gazed over her pince-nez. 'How frightfully . . . ah . . . enterprising of you.'

The table did not fall silent, the company we were in being far too well bred for that, but there was a distinct lowering of voices, a pause between sentences and a sense that one's companions were listening to another conversation entirely.

'I think it's marvellous!' gushed her daughter, a sweet girl of nineteen and therefore practically an old maid herself. 'A woman storming the medical establishment alone, planting her flag upon the mountain of knowledge. What could be more thrilling?'

I was about to point out that I was hardly alone in my endeavour, but her mother raised an eyebrow at me. I was clearly supposed to say something, although exactly what mystified me.

'It's jolly hard work,' I offered. 'Not in the least bit glamorous.'

'And nothing at all compared to the delights of marriage and motherhood,' she pointed out.

Oh yes. That. I smiled weakly in what I hoped looked like agreement.

'Well, when you graduate I expect you to let me know the moment you open your practice. I'll be your first patient!'

The older woman frowned. 'You'll do nothing of the sort, Charlotte.'

The girl bowed her head, chastened. Once her mother's attention was elsewhere, she leaned over and whispered, 'All my friends think it's awfully daring. You must have luncheon with us and tell us all about it.'

It was the most enthusiasm I had heard about my chosen profession all night. I smiled warmly at her but she had already turned to her companion, who was expounding on the benefits of some faddish new diet or other. Whatever it was, it didn't seem to be stopping him devouring the saddle of mutton in front of him.

I had barely consumed a mouthful all evening – every time I tried, another of Aurora's guests asked me a question, ranging from the fatuous to the downright patronising. One thing no one mentioned, however, was what on earth I was doing in Edinburgh when there was a perfectly good medical school – one designed exclusively for ladies, no less! – in London. If gossip about my scandal and its resulting exile had made its way to the dining tables of Edinburgh's highest echelons, everyone was far too polite to mention it.

I glanced over at Miles, wondering how he was faring. He looked lost as one of his father's friends addressed him on the subject of hunting, and I realised that the hum of conversation and the clatter of cutlery, combined with the fact that this man was half-cut already, prevented him from following along with the discussion.

Well, I was no stranger to interrupting men's conversation. I angled myself so that Miles could see my face and made sure I spoke slowly and crisply.

'I always rather thought that shooting grouse and pheasant one must get terribly cold and damp. At least when one rides with the hunt, there's a bit more movement.'

'Ah, but that's what a wee nip of whisky is for, lass! A dram or two of Macallan and ye could be in Burma, not the Highlands! What's your poison, laddie? Are you a Scotch or a brandy man?'

The truth was, Miles turned flushed and wobbly on anything stronger than a glass or two of demi-sec, but I was damned if this blustering sot was going to know that. 'You rather enjoyed that single malt at my uncle's, didn't you, darling? Convalmore, I think you said? You must try some, Brigadier – my uncle has quite the well-stocked cellar.'

'Quite d-delicious.' If anyone noticed the grateful smile Miles shot at me, they would have dismissed it as young love. I squeezed his arm in support and turned the topic to the exploits of Brigadier Whomever-he-was in the Crimea.

We carried on in that vein, with the brigadier proffering his sage advice in increasingly slurred tones and my repeating it back as if it were the most profound thought I had ever heard, allowing Miles to follow along and contribute where he wished. If I were to face a lifetime of this, my future husband would need to find some vastly more entertaining companions.

It was with considerable relief that I allowed him to escort me through to the drawing room for post-prandial entertainment. Charlotte, the young woman who had promised to be my first patient, ran over to the piano with a delighted cry and begged the assembled company for an accompanist. Although she wrinkled her brow in seeming confusion about who to pick, no one was in the least bit surprised when the second son of a duke, who had been making eyes at her since the consommé, took his place at the keys.

Music was preferable to charades – not least because Aunt Emily without fail chose to try and act out *Martin Chuzzlewit*; at this point the main pleasure was in stubbornly refusing to acknowledge that we all knew what she was incomprehensibly miming. With music, I could pretend to listen, focusing my gaze ostentatiously on the player or singer, while actually mentally reviewing my lecture notes. Provided I tapped my foot to an approximation of the beat and remembered to clap when everyone else did, I could pass an entire evening that way and be freshly prepared for the next morning's classes.

Despite my customary reticence, I found myself enjoying it. Alisdair had an impeccable baritone that seemed to enchant every woman in the room – had he been inviting them rather than the reluctant Maud of the song into the garden, I had no doubt that the drawing room would have been completely deserted by the third verse. Even Aurora joined in with a rather alarmingly coy rendition of 'Jolly Good Luck to the Girl Who Loves a Soldier'.

Inevitably, the happy couple was called up. I was uncomfortably aware of the fact that I had neither played nor sung in public for years, although Aunt Emily made me practise several times a week and Elisabeth had once coaxed me through most of the Edinburgh students' songbook.

'"Waiting at the Church"!' one of Aurora's friends called out. I could think of more appropriate songs than one about a woman who discovered on her wedding day that her husband-to-be was already married, but our audience seemed tickled at the prospect. I took the sheet music from the pile and glanced at Miles for confirmation.

To my surprise, he played almost perfectly, and for a change his demeanour was almost relaxed.

Alisdair was frowning, and after a moment I noticed him slip away – perhaps the golden child didn't like the limelight falling on his younger brother for once. Something seemed to have happened to Miles that night; his stammer, though never entirely gone, had lessened and he moved with a confidence I had never seen before.

We finished our song to a rapturous round of applause and found ourselves called upon for an encore. Together we got through 'The Boy I Love is Up in the Gallery' – was that a tear

I saw Mother dash from her eye? – and I bobbed a cheeky curtsey before returning to my seat.

'Perhaps you should consider a career on stage rather the operating theatre, Miss Gilchrist!'

There was laughter, although I suspected as much of it was directed at the idea of me as a doctor as at the prospect of me as a music hall performer.

It was fun – silly, frivolous fun, the kind I hadn't had in over a year. If it weren't for my engagement – and Clara Wilson's recent murder – it might have been almost perfect. I could take some light-hearted ribbing about medical women and the general unsuitability of my sex to anything other than breeding and embroidery provided that when I left the party, I did so knowing I had to be up the next morning at a lecture. Even my mother was smiling, and the whole thing felt so close to how I always thought my life would turn out – tolerant if underwhelmed parents, laughter and excitement and studying – that for a moment I closed my eyes and let the sounds of the room flow over me like warm water. The music, the conversation, the laughter . . . and the harsh, irregular gasps of someone struggling for breath.

I opened my eyes to see Colonel Greene looking clammy and ill, his eyes glassy and one hand grabbing at his chest. Then he staggered and collapsed onto the rug, head narrowly missing the fireguard. By the time I had crossed the room, he was already dead.

Chapter 12

Colonel Greene had been an imposing figure in life, but in death he looked vulnerable and somehow smaller.

I knelt by his body to check for a pulse and found nothing.

'Could someone pass me a glass? An empty one.' I held it above his lips – nothing. The ragged breath I had heard him exhale was his last.

'Darling? My love, what is it?'

His eyes were glassy, staring sightlessly ahead, but Aurora took his face tenderly in her hands.

'I think he hit his head when he fell. Perhaps a concussion?' She looked at me desperately. I privately suspected he was dead before he even hit the carpet, but there was no need to tell her that, certainly not in front of an audience.

'Perhaps we should all return to the dining room and let Mrs Greene tend to her husband,' my mother said in a commanding tone. Even the vultures who had hoped for some gruesome excitement this evening found themselves following her – she would have made quite the sergeant major. 'Sarah, I'm sure Alisdair can take it from here.'

I glanced up. Wherever he had slipped off to, he had yet to return.

'Send for Professor Gregory Merchiston. If he isn't

available, get Professor Randall Chalmers.' Somewhere I found the presence of mind to scribble down their addresses – though admitting in a room full of strangers that I knew Merchiston's private address wouldn't do my reputation any favours – and hoped desperately that at least one of them was home.

'We have a family doctor,' Aurora whispered. 'Miles, tell the servants to send for Dr Hamilton.'

The assembled throng had been ushered back into the dining room and my mother took my arm.

'Sarah! Leave him alone and come with me.'

I looked up at her, this woman I loved and feared in equal measure, and it was suddenly easy to say what needed to be said.

'I'm the only person in this house with any medical training. I'm not going anywhere.'

She pursed her lips. 'I think we both know he's beyond your help.'

'But the family isn't. It's best if I stay with them until a doctor arrives.'

She shook her head sadly. 'What people will think . . .'

'They'll see a woman supporting her new family. You may not like my education, but even you have to admit it has its uses.'

She gave me a long look with an expression that on anyone else I might have called impressed and withdrew. I turned back to Colonel Greene, with his cooling skin and the beginnings of rigor mortis, and his red-eyed, disbelieving wife.

'I'm sorry, Aurora. He's gone.' She yanked her hands from mine and looked at me with pure venom.

'What do you know? You're not a doctor, just some silly little girl. Where is Dr Hamilton?'

'He's on his way,' I soothed. If she didn't want to accept it now, I wasn't going to argue with her. She had the rest of her life to come to terms with her husband's passing.

As did her sons. I looked up at Miles. He had his arms wrapped around himself as if it were his body that was rapidly decreasing in temperature rather than his father's.

'He's dead, isn't he?'

'I'm sorry, Miles.' He just stared at the corpse with an expression I couldn't read. Then he took Aurora gently by the shoulders and eased her to her feet.

'Mother, come and sit down. We'll wait for the doctor together.'

In grief, Aurora was a mess, her usual pristine facade shattered. In contrast, Miles was calm, more assured than I had ever seen him. Times like this could bring out strengths in people that even they didn't realise they had, and the family would be grateful for the younger son's composure in the difficult weeks to come.

'Father?'

The new head of the Greene family stood in the doorway, his eyes locked on the body on the ground. He was so ashen that I thought for a moment I would have a second body to deal with.

'What happened?' he rasped.

'He just collapsed. He clutched his chest, so I suspect an acute myocardial infarction.' Alisdair looked blank, and I remembered anew that this wasn't one of my lectures; this was a real man, a real family plunged into grief. 'A heart attack. It would have been very quick; he wouldn't have felt any pain.' It was a lie, but one kindly meant. I had seen the expression on the colonel's face – he had been gripped by a spasm of agony and in his last seconds I believed he knew he was about to die.

In the silence that followed, I heard footsteps, heard the front door open and close and the sound of horses' hooves striking the cobbles as the family's guests left. I hid a smile. I thought I was practical, but Mother and Aunt Emily had choreographed the evening to a close discreetly, ensuring that whatever was said about a second death in the Greene household during a party, it would be done in the same breath as admiration for the new fiancée and her family.

As the house descended into silence, Alisdair closed his father's eyes.

'Could you fetch me a sheet?' I asked Miles. 'I don't want to leave him like this.' Truth be told, I could barely stand to look at him and I wanted to prevent his family seeing his body stiffen with rigor mortis, the way his skin would fade to an ashy blue as all the blood, no longer pumping in his veins, drained to the bottom of the corpse with an ugly lividity beneath his clothes.

A light knock sounded at the drawing room door.

'Our carriage is outside.' My mother held out my coat and hat pointedly, and I didn't doubt that she was willing to dress me herself if necessary.

'I'd prefer to wait until the doctor arrives.' Propriety indicated I leave. This wasn't my family, not yet, and I certainly wasn't their doctor. But some nagging voice told me to stay and see it through. Duty, perhaps – although whether to Colonel Greene, a man I was charmed by but could never bring myself to actually like, or as a physician I couldn't say.

Unexpectedly, Miles came to my aid.

'Please, Mrs Gilchrist. If you wouldn't m-mind letting us have your daughter a little while longer.'

Even my mother couldn't refuse a grieving man the company of his fiancée. Promising to send the carriage back within the hour, she left with my aunt and uncle, and I wondered what on earth they would talk about on the journey home. Mother hadn't exactly been bowled over by Miles, but whatever he lacked in charisma he made up for in having a respectable family and being willing to take on board damaged goods. Now, with the Greenes once more the centre of all polite society gossip, his value was plummeting by the minute.

Aurora was weeping openly now, and even Alisdair was rubbing the back of his hand across his eyes. Only Miles remained impassive. I knew he hadn't been close to his father, but was he really so unmoved? I knew what it meant to have a parent disapprove of everything you did, but if Mother died, I would be inconsolable. Perhaps he simply felt numb; perhaps inwardly he was roiling with all the arguments left unsettled, the gulf between them that would never now be bridged.

'Perhaps we should move to another room,' I offered gently.

'I won't leave him,' Aurora whimpered. 'He shouldn't be alone.'

Her sons looked grim and less than pleased, but they allowed her this irrational display of grief. Alisdair poured a hefty measure of Scotch for him and his brother, and to my surprise, Miles took it with trembling hands.

A maid carried in a bedsheet to cover the late colonel's undignified state and a murmured word in her ear was all it took to bring back a pot of tea – I would have preferred strong, sweet coffee, but under the circumstances I could feign a taste for more ladylike refreshments – and we sat in silence, the only noise in the room the crackling fire and Aurora's sobs.

Suddenly the fabric shifted as the body beneath it twitched.

Aurora jumped to her feet. 'He moved! I saw it!' She went to tug back the sheet, and I pulled her away gently.

'It's not uncommon for bodies to move involuntarily after . . . What I mean to say is, you mustn't get your hopes up, Aurora.'

'Men are buried alive every day! You read about it in the newspapers. I won't have my husband locked up in the family crypt before his time just because some little chit thinks she can be a doctor!'

Alisdair knelt down with me, and together we pulled back the sheet. We were accosted by the sweet scents of recent death and stale urine – it would have happened before he hit the ground, in those final horrible moments when Colonel Greene's body left his mind's control entirely. It would get worse. Soon the muscles of the gastrointestinal tract would relax sufficiently to expel whatever waste matter was left, and neither the sound nor the smell was something I wanted to be in the room for.

No matter what Aurora might have read, the burial would not in this case be premature.

Dr Hamilton arrived after the clock in the hall struck ten, and I was grateful to be replaced as the person in the house most familiar with death and its processes. I was weary to my bones.

He was a doctor of the old school, all mutton chops and an air of condescension towards the general populace that was as unmistakable as the faint scent of Scotch he left in his wake. His face was as shiny as his medical bag and his shoes, and I wondered how long he had spent perfecting his appearance before leaving home. I knew by looking at him that he had served the Greene family faithfully and well for decades. He had probably helped deliver the boys and treated their childhood ailments and complaints until they were old enough to bring him more adult problems. And now he would see to the death of the paterfamilias.

His expression was grave as he greeted Aurora and her sons, a mere flickering glance to the covered body on the carpet enough to tell him that whatever treatment he had arrived prepared to give would not be needed.

'Miss Sarah Gilchrist, my brother's fiancée.'

Hamilton bowed in my direction, but I detected a hardening of his watery blue gaze.

He had heard of me, then – the bride-to-be who fancied she could join the august ranks of his profession. Whatever dislike he had of me, however, he shrouded in civility – I would, after all, join the list of his patients when I was married.

He knelt by the body, looked under the sheet and sighed to himself.

'Let's move him away from the fire, boys. We don't want him to overheat.'

'I thought you might prefer to see the body as it was when Colonel Greene fell, sir.'

He looked at me as though I were a dog speaking Latin. Blasted Merchiston – he'd let me forget that medical men didn't always want to hear the opinions of ladies, even if those ladies were first-year medical students themselves.

As though I hadn't opened my mouth, he turned to Aurora.

'Ladies, perhaps you might like to wait in the parlour while I examine the colonel.'

I would like nothing of the sort, but it wasn't a request. I shepherded Aurora into her parlour and murmured something about fetching her a glass of water before running back on tiptoes to press my ear against the door I had deliberately left slightly ajar.

Miles simply sat staring at the sheet that covered his father, a man who had bullied and humiliated him but who had nevertheless been family. Dr Hamilton addressed all his comments to Alisdair, and behind that I could see a lifetime of acting as though the younger son was not even in the room.

'Had he complained of any chest pains or trouble breathing since I attended him last?' he was asking.

Alisdair shrugged helplessly. 'His stomach was bothering him. And he was still getting those godawful headaches . . .'

It was as though I had been seeing everything through smeared glass, and now it was coming into focus. The way the colonel had been swallowing more frequently, and every word sounded faintly damp, as though there were too much saliva in his mouth. A stomach complaint severe enough to call the family doctor out. The way he had complained of a headache and picked at his meal. The way his body had convulsed for a few horrible moments as he collapsed . . .

That strong whiff of garlic on his breath had been from more than just the food. Merchiston had discovered arsenic under Clara Wilson's fingernails, and now I knew what she had been doing with it.

Colonel Greene had been poisoned.

Chapter 13

Voicing my suspicions to Dr Hamilton would be a pointless endeavour – he had disliked me on sight, if not before, and I could just imagine his response to my even breathing a word about murder.

Jolting across the cobbles in my uncle's carriage, I felt a twinge of embarrassment as I recalled the way I had accused Merchiston of that most grievous of crimes a few months prior. But I had been right, about the murder if not the perpetrator. And if Hamilton was a doctor worth his salt – unlikely though it was if he had genuinely missed the symptoms of arsenic poisoning on at least one visit – he would report his suspicions to the police. He would never voice them to me, but he didn't have to – I had an ally of my own.

Could I risk sending word to Merchiston now? I knew how it would look, conveying covert messages to a man late at night. I would have to catch him before lectures.

A light in the parlour caught my eye. Aunt Emily sat in front of the dying fire in her nightgown, her hair in a loose plait down her back. The firelight glinted off the strands of grey – how long had they been there? She glanced up at me and gave a faint smile.

'I told Diana I'd wait for you. Poor thing, the shock of the evening must have exhausted her. Still, on the whole I thought it went very well.'

If you set aside the part where a man keeled over and died in front of us, she had a point. Up until then, everyone had got along marvellously, and even Miles and I had formed a bond. All of which was precisely what I didn't want.

'How are you, my dear? You were very brave to stay like that, I'm sure the family appreciated it.'

I was too tired to be tactful. 'It isn't my first dead body.'

'I wouldn't mention that to your mother if I were you,' she said wryly. 'I never told her about that ghastly business with Caroline Hartigan last year. I doubt you'll want to raise it either,' she added with a warning in her voice.

I wanted to tell her that Miss Hartigan's murder had been the tip of the iceberg, that I had seen things that would turn the rest of her hair white. If I had, I think in that moment she would have comforted me. But the next day I would doubtless be locked in my room and forbidden to attend lectures or so much as mention Merchiston's name. I had thought her opprobrium about my behaviour and studies had put a wall between us, but this secret new life of mine was a crevice that seemed impassable.

'Do you want some warm milk or something to eat? Cook is still in the kitchen if you do.'

It felt rather cruel to have kept the poor woman here so late on the off-chance that I might be hungry. Then again, I was.

'Toast, perhaps? Maybe some marmalade?'

'Go upstairs. I'll send Agnes through to get you ready for bed.'

As I reached the bottom of the staircase, I heard her call quietly to me. 'Miles clearly adores you. He could make you very happy, you know.'

Miles quite liked me, but I thought adoration was overdoing

it somewhat. Still, this didn't seem the time to remind Aunt Emily that I didn't love him and didn't expect to.

The next morning, Mother was sitting at the breakfast table eating kippers. She was ready for me.

'You're up early, Sarah.' Her cheerfulness put me on guard. I had learned at an early age that it was never a positive sign – good behaviour would be rewarded by bland approval, bad by a lashing of her icy temper. Cheerful was reserved for those moments when she thought she had the upper hand and planned to exercise it.

Well, if she could act as though everything were ordinary, then so could I.

'I have a lecture at eight. I normally ride with Uncle Hugh in his carriage.'

She put her cup down slowly, eyes never leaving mine, and smiled quizzically.

'You can't mean to go to that dreadful place today of all days?'

That had been exactly what I meant to do and she knew it.

'I'm not in mourning, Mother. He wasn't my father-in-law.'

'Yet.' She bit the word off crisply. 'It wouldn't hurt to show some sympathy. We don't want the Greenes thinking better of their match, now do we? Especially since Miles stands to come into his inheritance earlier than we had expected.'

My heart leapt. Without Colonel Greene's bullying insistence, would Miles still feel the need to continue with an engagement that had been arranged for show rather than love? Mother would be furious, and God only knew what Uncle Hugh would say. But perhaps I could finally bring this hideous charade to an end.

'What if I called on Miles this afternoon once I'm finished with my lectures?' I bartered. 'I doubt the household will be up for visitors, but I'd be showing my respect without barging in on their grief.'

She looked at my navy skirt and jacket. 'I suppose you aren't completely inappropriately dressed,' she conceded. 'But for heaven's sake don't show up covered in ink and chemicals. You're supposed to be comforting your beloved, not horrifying him.' She waved a hand at me. 'Go if you must. Emily and I had arranged to call on her friends the Patersons, and Lord knows you'll find some way to cause a ruckus if we bring you.'

It took everything I had not to bound out of the house in my uncle's wake – did I detect a thawing of my mother's attitude towards my studies? Assuming that soon enough I would be off her hands, was she resigning herself to having a daughter who might be flouting society's rules but was at least doing it with her husband's permission?

I was so caught up in possibilities that it wasn't until I saw Merchiston sheltering from the rain as he smoked in one of the quad's arches that I remembered a man had died in front of me the previous evening.

'Gilchrist,' he nodded. 'You look sombre this morning.'

'Colonel Greene was murdered last night.'

He dropped his cigarette in a puddle and stared at me open-mouthed. It was rare that I could render him speechless – even at his most taciturn, he always had a clever rejoinder that was usually at someone else's expense.

'Miss Brown!' He hailed a passing chaperone, as early for our lecture as I was. 'I need to speak to Gilchrist here in private, and I'm not doing it alone. Follow us, please.'

As soon as the door was closed, and with Miss Brown studiously pretending not to be listening, he turned to me. The story would be halfway around Edinburgh by lunchtime, but there wasn't anything I could do about it.

'What do you mean, murdered? I was at the police station this morning and I didn't hear anything.'

'He collapsed at a dinner party last night. All the symptoms of arsenic poisoning.'

'Who attended him?'

'A Dr Hamilton – he's the Greenes' family physician. Practically had kittens at the thought of me even looking at the body, so I didn't try to tell him my suspicions.'

'That will be Reginald Hamilton. What he lacks in mental acuity, he makes up for in the exorbitant fees he charges.' He paused for thought. 'I'd like to take a look at those organs. If he's been poisoned—'

'Then we'll know it's murder.' I shook my head. 'It was hard enough getting Wilson's body properly examined, and she'd had her head bashed in. The Greenes will never allow it. They'll insist he died of natural causes and refuse an autopsy.'

That lunchtime, we commandeered an empty lecture hall and Randall and Elisabeth joined us – apparently for the sake of propriety but I suspected more out of curiosity.

'A man of his age, fairly robust but heavier than he ought to be at that height . . . A heart attack isn't out of the question,' Randall said.

I nodded. 'That's what I thought at first. But his symptoms are consistent, and given the residue under Clara Wilson's nails . . .'

'It's the perfect murder,' Merchiston sighed. 'He's been killed by a dead woman.' He rubbed his face, and I saw under the harsh electric light that he looked tired.

'That still doesn't tell us who killed Wilson,' I pointed out. 'And we don't know for certain that she did poison him.'

He nodded. 'Could have been the wife. Perhaps he and Wilson—'

'He didn't even know her first name!'

Merchiston gave me a condescending smile. 'He wouldn't have been the first man to bed a woman without asking her name.'

It was rare these days that I considered myself an innocent, but Merchiston had the knack of making me feel as though I had just stepped out of a nunnery.

Randall clucked in disapproval. 'It could have been gout or his heart. A once fit man gone to seed . . . It could have been any number of things. And murdering someone in a house where the police are already asking questions is a risky move.'

'Not if he knew about the murder,' I argued.

'You have a kind heart. Elisabeth would say that's what makes you a good doctor. But it's your mind that will save your patients. You once looked at a streetwalker on a slab, deduced that she had been murdered and then nearly got yourself killed trying to prove it. Don't just rely on your empathy, Sarah. Trust your brilliance. Now tell me again. Do you *think* he was murdered or are you *sure*?'

I thought of the convulsions, the waxy, clammy skin. 'I'm sure.'

'Murders usually come down to one of two things, finances or . . .' Merchiston faltered as Randall cleared his throat pointedly. 'Or passion. Perhaps Aurora tired of his philandering. Or someone needed their inheritance and decided to speed up proceedings.'

'Alisdair stands to gain the most as the elder son.'

'The colonel could have promised a tidy sum to Aurora; perhaps she decided she'd rather have the money than the man. Or maybe Miles wanted to keep you in the manner to which you are accustomed.' Merchiston grinned, but in the dim gaslight all I could see was his teeth. 'A nice collection of surgical instruments will set the lad back a pretty penny.'

'It's useless speculating,' I groaned. 'If they won't release the body for autopsy then there's no way of confirming our suspicions.'

'*Your* suspicions.'

I gave him a pointed look. 'Your eyes lit up when I said

"arsenic", Professor. You want to find out what's in his kidneys and liver every bit as much as I do.'

'I'm not his doctor,' he sighed. 'There's nothing I can do – Hamilton thinks I'm the lowest of the low, a guttersnipe who clawed his way into the higher echelons of medicine and academia. He's not wrong, but he won't take kindly to my interference. You'd better hope he smells something fishy about the whole business. Unless . . .' He paused thoughtfully. 'I'll speak to Littlejohn tomorrow morning, suggest they perform a post-mortem. Say I heard rumours or had an anonymous note delivered – either way, we'll get conclusive proof we can take to a judge.'

'And then it's out of our hands,' I sighed. The excitement fizzled out of me rapidly and I felt rather like a collapsed soufflé.

'Would it be the worst thing in the world?' Randall asked gently. 'Professor Merchiston works with the police; he's used to this sort of thing. You're a perceptive girl, Sarah, but perhaps leave this one to the professionals, aye?'

'You mean the men,' I muttered, still stinging from being called a girl, as though I were some schoolroom chit and not nearly twenty-three and studying to be a doctor. My uncle thought I was an old maid; my friend thought I was still a child.

'This isn't medicine,' he argued. 'There are perfectly good reasons why a murder investigation is no place for a young lady, no matter how worldly she may consider herself to be.'

I turned to Elisabeth. 'Are you listening to this? Your husband, alleged champion of professional women, thinks we lack the critical capability to solve murders! Do tell me, Randall – is it my smaller female brain that stands in my way? My physical constitution perhaps – I could withstand childbirth, but God forbid some ruffian spits on me. Or maybe it's my reproductive organs,' I added bitterly. Enlightened though he was, I was annoyed to see Randall grimace.

'There's no need to be vulgar, Sarah.' Elisabeth was frowning. 'Don't you have enough battles to fight?' she pleaded. 'If the colonel was murdered, Gregory will prove it.'

I lapsed into a silence that Aunt Emily would doubtless have called sulky. The grandfather clock in the hall chimed the hour and I scowled, for once reluctant to get back to my studies. As I traipsed obediently after the Chalmerses, Merchiston caught my eye and winked. It seemed that I would be assisting him after all.

Chapter 14

In life, Colonel Greene had been an imposing man whose wife and sons obeyed his every word. But in the hours between his collapse and Merchiston admitting me into the room where he lay, portly body covered by a tablecloth, any sense of his grandeur had departed.

I shivered. 'It's so strange seeing him like this. Less than twenty-four hours ago he was in full flow, telling me that women should never be taught to read, much less learn medicine. Now there's nothing left of him – not the real him.'

'*Au contraire*, Miss Gilchrist,' Merchiston said with a macabre smile. 'This is where the real Colonel Greene reveals himself.'

He yanked the tablecloth back and I flinched, not ready to see my late future father-in-law in his naked entirety. Fortunately for me, Merchiston stopped at the waist, threw me an amused look and pulled the sheet up from Colonel Greene's feet to his upper thighs. It was a little higher than I'd have liked, but I refused to look away.

'Williamson will spare your blushes in the lecture theatre, but don't expect the same courtesy on the wards,' he warned. 'There will be countless newly qualified doctors queuing up to rag the lady doctors, and the private appendages of a dead man will be the least offensive thing you're exposed to. Ahem. So to speak.'

'I don't suppose it occurred to the university faculty to teach the male students not to bully the women they'll be working with?'

'Ah, but it builds character. As they were tormented by their colleagues and professors, so will the trial by fire continue. Somehow, Gilchrist, I suspect you'll give as good as you get.'

If I ever made it as far as the wards, let alone the front of a lecture theatre, I fully intended to. It was about time some of the privileged little boys masquerading as men were given orders by a woman.

'The colonel had a lacklustre approach to personal hygiene.' Merchiston grimaced.

I shrugged. 'I suppose there wasn't time for lengthy ablutions in Afghanistan.'

'He fought in Afghanistan?'

'My uncle saved his life at the Battle of Maiwand. They were both injured and sent home.'

He frowned. 'Randall was out there for a while. I met him when he came back, traumatised and wanting nothing more to do with the battlefield.'

Elisabeth had never told me about her husband's past. I couldn't imagine the placid, easy-going Randall Chalmers in uniform.

'He never mentioned it to Colonel Greene. I didn't even know he had a military background.'

'He doesn't talk about it – not even to Elisabeth, by all accounts.' He glanced at me. 'We all have our secrets, Miss Gilchrist.'

'I'm starting to think this family has more than most.'

'And you're marrying into it. Lucky girl.'

'If it weren't for my engagement, you wouldn't be here,' I

reminded him tartly. 'And don't tell me you're doing this as a favour – any fool could see you're enjoying it.'

'So are you,' he countered. 'Your future husband may just be able to stomach a lady doctor with a genteel private practice lancing boils, but how will he feel about a pathologist who spends her days prodding at corpses?'

Could that really be my future? I had fought so hard to get this far that I could barely imagine anything past graduation. For all the time I spent protesting my right to a career, when I even tried to consider specialising I was overwhelmed by the options – and by my minuscule chances of being encouraged to do more than private practice or obstetrics. Could I really stand where Merchiston was, taking the lead on an autopsy? It wasn't as though I could cite the two – now three – murders I had investigated as proof of my suitability for such a job. I didn't even know how one went about applying – it wasn't the type of thing we had been taught at finishing school.

I was so greedy for any experience that I didn't even know how to set my sights higher than just survival, than getting those precious letters after my name – Sarah Gilchrist, MD! Anything after that was amorphous, something too hoped for to be a concrete thing. Still . . .

'If the alternative is Miles, I'd leap at the chance to lance a few boils.'

Guilt settled on my shoulders like a cloak. It was one thing complaining to Elisabeth, even Randall, but laughing about Miles to Merchiston felt wrong somehow. Perhaps it was the moment of closeness we had shared, or the way the muscles in his arms grew taut as he pushed up his shirtsleeves.

He sighed. 'I'll finish this,' he said hoarsely. 'Littlejohn will be back shortly and you shouldn't be found alone with the body.' Or with the man examining it.

But I had one last question.

'Why teach? You love this work, I can see it in your eyes.'

He shrugged. 'The money. We don't all have a business magnate for a father, you know. Anyway, it's a useful position to be in. The university opens doors a mere police surgeon could never have dreamed of. And it's not as if I'm without precedent.'

'So it was Professor Bell's influence?'

He scowled – he had mentioned that his particular blending of medicine and detection had been learned at the side of the man who had inspired Sherlock Holmes, but it was not a comparison he relished.

'I could have you expelled for sheer cheek, Gilchrist. Never forget that.'

'You didn't answer my question. If you didn't want to follow in Professor Bell's footsteps, why help the police?'

He looked away. 'Lucy,' he said quietly. 'I wanted to keep an eye on her, and that seemed the best way.' He barked out a bitter laugh. 'Not that it did a damn bit of good.'

'She would have felt safer,' I offered.

'She could have come to me. Should have, if I'd ever given her a reason to. But she saw me as her meddling older brother, too allied with the polis to trust.' He ran the back of his hand across his eyes. 'And what about you, Sarah Gilchrist? Why are you here?'

'I want to be a doctor,' I said softly. 'It's all I've ever wanted. Edinburgh was supposed to be a fresh start – the silver lining to a horrible cloud. I came here to study medicine and yet it feels as though ever since I got here I've been doing anything but.'

'Everyone struggles in their first year,' Merchiston reassured me. 'Yours weren't the worst marks. No matter what, you've always got a place in my lectures.'

He looked for a moment as though he wanted to say something else, but the clock chimed and the moment passed. Sweet as these stolen moments were, they weren't my real life and it was no use pining after something that I knew I could never have.

'You head back to the Chalmerses' now. If your aunt or mother calls and you're not there, there'll be hell to pay.'

He handed me some coins and a crumpled note or two. 'For the cab.'

'That's too much,' I protested. 'I'm going past the Meadows, not to Glasgow and back.'

He shrugged. 'A woman should have funds of her own, and you're working as hard on this as I am. It's no' a salary, but it's a start.'

As I turned to go, my pockets jingling, I realised I had my answer to the question that plagued me. Medicine would give me money, access – and there were other women out there like Lucy and Clara Wilson who had need of my services. Whatever came after graduation, I would use my education to rescue women from their fate, and avenge those I could not.

Outside, I could taste snow in the air, so crisp and cold it hurt my lungs to breathe it in. I took gulps of it like a thirsty man drinks water, relishing being outside. It was past twilight and the gas lamps dotting the Meadows were lit. The cab rattled up the Royal Mile and through Tollcross, but I barely took in the frost-rimed streets.

It felt as though my veins were running with champagne instead of blood, sparkling and fizzing. A horrible thing had occurred and I was a horrible person for being drawn to it, and yet . . . It was thrilling. I wanted to get closer – to the victim, to the crime, to the person who had committed it – and peel back the layers like an onion, find out who and how and why. It was the same excitement I felt when being led through a diagnosis – individually, the symptoms might not make sense but together they were a picture. Every element told a story – the bronchial infection that told me the patient was living in damp, squalid conditions, the mould spores under the microscope that he had breathed in from the very walls, and that I could track down to the exact street or house if I tried hard enough. The beginnings of phossy jaw told me what a woman did for a living and the sag of her stomach stretched from pregnancy could tell me how many children she had to support. No wonder our parents and guardians were so obsessed with keeping our bodies pure and blank, unreadable, when even the grime under my nails and the stains on my skirt could be analysed and interpreted.

Back at Warrender Park Crescent, in front of a roaring fire and with a plate of crumpets and honey, I waited for the results of the arsenic test. Randall had a small study stocked with medical equipment; he and Merchiston had arrived waiting to see if the hair sample I had purloined offered further fuel to the fire of our suspicions.

Despite the excitement of the day, I found myself dozing off, until a cry echoed from the study.

'Eureka!' They were out of breath, laughing like schoolboys.

'Sarah, you're a genius. I'll give you top marks for every essay from now on; I'll even get the university clerks to change your winter exam results. You spotted what Reginald Hamilton, that pompous old sot, wouldn't have seen in a thousand years. Colonel Greene was so full of arsenic he was practically shitting it.'

'Gregory!'

'Now steady on, old thing.'

I didn't care about his language, only that my suspicions had been proven right. 'Clara Wilson must have been administering it. Even after she died, it would have been working its way through his system until his heart couldn't handle it any more.'

'Then we have a powerful motive for her murder – but what about his? It's not as though she stood to gain from his death,' Merchiston pointed out.

'If I had to live with him day in and day out, I might want to poison him as well. Can you tell how it was given to him?'

'Food or drink. Some in his bath perhaps, hidden in bath salts so he'd breathe it in and there would be a clear source to blame if someone worked out what was wrong with him before he died. You wouldn't believe the rot chemists sell claiming it's medicinal – you're lucky if it's just common rock salt.'

I thought back to the long, luxuriously scented baths I enjoyed, and felt slightly queasy.

'The Greenes shared a bedroom more often than not, according to Blackwell. It would have been easy to bring the colonel a cup of tea along with Aurora's, and she takes hers so foully milky that there'd be no confusion about whose cup was whose.'

'Assuming Aurora hasn't been poisoned as well. How did she seem to you?'

Aurora Greene's company had always been something to be endured more than inspected, and I wished now that I had paid closer attention to her.

'She looks delicate but I don't think she is really. She's patron of half a dozen charitable organisations and sits on the board of more, although I don't know how much good she actually does. Wilson's death and the fact that she was stealing from her seems to have upset her more than I would have imagined. I don't get the impression that they were close – she couldn't even remember her first name – but I think she trusted her.'

I had an excuse to call on her now, though. What dutiful future daughter-in-law wouldn't want to bring comfort to a grieving widow? And if a few strands of her hair happened to find their way into my possession, it would be easy enough to test for arsenic afterwards.

'I never thought I'd say this, but it's a good thing that you're engaged to Miles,' Elisabeth said. 'If you hadn't been there, no one would even have known there was something suspicious about the colonel's death.'

Privately, I wasn't entirely sure that the sacrifice was worth it – and from the look on Merchiston's face, neither was he.

Chapter 15

I arrived at the university with half an hour to spare, even with a stop to buy a cup of tea and some toast. The extra time felt like a luxury; I seemed to spend my time rushing back and forth between my aunt's house and the medical school – or a crime scene, for that matter. And although I should by rights have had no appetite after what I had just witnessed, I found that my hunger had returned with a vengeance. At this rate, I wouldn't fit into whatever monstrosity of a wedding gown Mother and Aunt Emily were concocting for me.

Brushing the buttery crumbs from my coat, I waited outside the lecture theatre reading over my chemistry notes until the others arrived. Feeling virtuous, I was first in line as I rummaged around to hand over the attendance card that proved I was a fully matriculated, fee-paying member of the university corpus.

A card that was conspicuously absent.

'Gilchrist, move out of the way. It's a miracle you can find anything in that thing. It probably has more bacteria than the entire biology department – didn't you pull out a stale sandwich instead of your textbook the other day?'

I was barely listening as I frantically searched though my belongings. I never took the card out of the bag – as Julia pointed out, I never removed anything from it unless I absolutely had to – but there was no denying that it wasn't there.

'I'm sorry, Professor Neuwirth, I seem to have mislaid my card. I'll get a replacement tomorrow, I promise.'

'Then you may attend my class – tomorrow,' he replied in his stiff German accent.

'But you know I have it! I've presented it every day since last September.'

'Can you prove it?'

'Oh, for heaven's sake, of course she can. You've seen her! She turns in her essays, passes her exams, and she's always spilling dangerous chemicals everywhere,' Moira grumbled.

'That may be, but I cannot allow you to enter my lecture theatre without your card.'

Tears pricked behind my eyes, but I refused to shed them.

'I'll lend you my notes afterwards,' Alison whispered apologetically.

I stood helplessly in the corridor as the day began without me. I couldn't even return home – I had spent any money I could have used for cab fare on breakfast. In any case, my mother would find some way of stopping me from leaving the house again.

Lacking even the identification required to use the library, I retreated to a deserted lecture theatre, where I curled up on one of the benches and let myself collapse, hot tears spilling out.

'Miss Gilchrist!' Gregory Merchiston turned from the blackboard. I hadn't seen him there – so much for my powers of observation. 'I have twenty-five third-year students arriving in fifteen minutes.' He looked at me, taking in my distressed state. 'Such a pity that the hot-water pipe burst and the lecture is now cancelled.'

I glanced at the perfectly intact copper pipe running up the wall, and then at Merchiston as he strode over and unscrewed something, yanking the pipe off the wall and jumping back as hot water sprayed all over the floor.

'I've probably caused untold damage to the building and deprived half the faculty the privilege of washing their hands in hot water. Not to mention the deleterious effect on these poor men's education.' He glanced at me. 'Still. Needs must.'

He stuck his head into the corridor and hailed the redoubtable Miss Brown to act as chaperone, and I tried to hide my disappointment.

'Sit there, my good lady, and guard Gilchrist's virtue while I pour her a cup of tea.'

I snuffled quietly into my handkerchief while Miss Brown looked impassively on until he returned with a chipped china mug and pressed it into my hands.

'Now. Tell me what happened.'

'I forgot my attendance card.' It seemed faintly ridiculous now, certainly nothing worth ripping a hot-water pipe off the wall.

'And?'

'And . . . everything! It's all so easy for the rest of them. Even Julia and Edith. They get up every day, come to lectures and go to the library, and then go home and spend their evenings as they wish. They can study or go to a talk or the music hall or just read a novel in front of the fire. My life is dictated by other people, morning, noon and night. At every turn, someone is standing in my way. I have to go to bed early just to wake up and finish my essays before the maid comes in so she doesn't tell my aunt I'm ruining my eyesight and not getting enough sleep. I leave things at home and I can't dash back to my rooms because I live on the other side of Edinburgh. I can't go to evening lectures because my aunt has organised yet another dinner party, and all of this is luxury, because when I'm married I won't be able to do anything at all! These could be my only years of freedom and I can't even enjoy them because I'm exhausted.'

'And on top of all that, you're trying to solve a murder.'

I snorted ungracefully through my tears. 'I'm an idiot. I should be focusing all my spare energies on my studies, but I can't leave well enough alone. No wonder I barely scraped through my first term.'

'You're a capable student, Sarah. More than capable. You could be brilliant.'

'Could be. The story of my life, Professor. I could be brilliant. I could be happy. I could be at home with my parents and not the family disappointment. But I'm not.' I wiped my nose on the sleeve of my gown, much to Merchiston's amusement. 'If I were a man, I could do both. I could even marry and not worry about that holding me back.'

'At least once you're married you only have to win over one person. And he might not be as hard to convince as you think.'

'He said he admired me.'

'Then he's a clever man.' He sighed. 'I'm sorry. I'm encouraging you to neglect your studies after accusing you of not taking them seriously. I would ban you from investigating if I thought it would do any good.'

'It wouldn't.' I smiled through my tears.

There was an awkward pause. Not so long ago, on a blustery November morning, I had called him my friend. But I was an unmarried woman – at least for now – and he was my professor. Propriety, not to mention the university regulations, dictated that I shouldn't be alone with him for more than a moment outside class, even with a chaperone present. Gregory Merchiston was famous for barely tolerating his students, and yet beneath the mercurial temper and our tangled history, I knew he thought well of me. Perhaps too well.

'I'll write a note telling my colleagues that you must be admitted to lectures, unless they want to deal with me.'

I could well imagine how intimidating Merchiston must be to even the most self-aggrandising of his fellows. For all his education and brilliance, there was a roughness that no amount of authority could conceal. Even someone who hadn't witnessed him stripped to the waist and grappling with an ex-convict in an illegal Grassmarket boxing ring could see that.

I had thought him dangerous, once. In some ways I still did. It would take so little for me to cross the barrier that Miss Brown and her ilk were so desperate for us to steer clear of. And no one would ever know – my reputation might have been patched up to look as good as new, but my physical state wouldn't fool anyone, not even someone as unworldly as Miles. *Why not take advantage of that*, a little voice in my head whispered, *and take your pleasure while you can?*

No wonder we were chaperoned every minute of the day. Had I been left alone with him, I think I would have kissed him.

Had we been alone, I think he would have let me.

Chapter 16

'What in the blazes are you doing, Gregory? She's your student, a young woman engaged to be married, and you're treating her like an assistant!'

'I assure you, Randall, Sarah Gilchrist is perfectly capable of getting herself into trouble without my help.'

'Give me your word that you won't be alone with her again.'

If he did, it was too muffled for me to hear it, and I crept closer to the door.

'You have to stop this. You look exhausted, man! Get a good night's sleep, give up all that other nonsense and stick to coffee like the rest of us. Williamson commented on it the other day. You skate on thin ice as it is, and there's only so much self-administering a man can do in the name of research.'

It was easy to forget with his work for the police and his teaching that Merchiston was a man of science. Pulling late nights for research was normal in the halls of academia, but on top of a murder investigation? I was surprised he was keeping up with whatever it was he did in the privacy of his office.

I lost myself in my studies for a while. I tried to write my *materia medica* essay, but my pen jabbed through the paper so roughly that it tore in too many places to be worth turning in.

I finished a Latin translation, although it could have been Greek for all the sense it made to me. I labelled the anterior muscles of the human body from sternocleidomastoid to extensor hallicus, and every time I thought I was going to cry, I closed my eyes and made myself recite them all in order.

That night, Elisabeth's friendship – so often a source of comfort and camaraderie, not to mention far better food than my aunt's cook was capable of providing – was grating. Randall's concern felt paternalistic and Merchiston . . . Gregory Merchiston could go to hell, and I was perilously close to telling him so. I'd say it in front of a packed lecture theatre if I thought it would do any good. He had saved my life and sometimes I thought he believed I owed him for it.

The next day, I let Agnes dress my hair as prettily as she knew how. I could have done it myself – if I could stitch an incision in a man's thorax together, then I could manage a plait – but every morning she came in and it had never occurred to me to stop her.

My aunt's servants had disapproved of me when I arrived – a scandalous past and a loose-lipped uncle who never lost an opportunity to humiliate me meant that it had filtered below stairs – and my intended profession must have horrified them. And yet I had never stopped to wonder what they thought of the household's other inhabitants, or of each other.

'Do you have a sweetheart, Agnes?' The question came out awkwardly. I had mastered anatomy, Greek and the finer points of the cardiovascular system, but small talk still eluded me.

Her lips pinched tightly. 'Your aunt has no concerns about my behaviour, miss.'

Another misstep. Of course. Ladies of my station were courted; women in service would only meet other servants or tradesmen, and the slightest hint of impropriety would be enough to see them dismissed without a reference. And who in that position would have the time? When there was a household to see to and family at home to take care of, how could romance flourish? It was a lot to cram into a half-day every month.

'Forgive me – I simply realised that you've been doing my hair and dressing me for months now, and I know so little about you.'

She met my eyes in the mirror warily.

'Where did you grow up?'

'Queensferry, miss. By the Firth of Forth.' The answer was grudging, but I felt a flicker of warmth.

'I've never visited. It must be beautiful, living by the water.'

'It's fair enough, if you don't mind the smell of fish. Nothing to London, I'm sure.'

'Have you never visited with Aunt Emily?' I remembered as soon as I said it that Aunt Emily rarely travelled to London. She had come for my grandmother's funeral, but not since.

'No, miss. I'm not sure I'd care to.'

It was on the tip of my tongue to suggest that she dispense with the honorific and just call me Sarah, but I suspected that for Agnes, that might be a step too far.

Once I was dressed in the elegant but sober outfit slightly more apt than the one Agnes had laid out for me – a light rose silk that would stain if I so much as looked at a cup of tea – we set out for the Greenes', all unsure as to what we would find.

The parlour we were ushered into bore no resemblance to the room we had been in two nights before. That death had visited the house was clear before we stepped over the threshold, with the black crêpe ribbon on the door and the ever-present ticking of the clock in the hall stopped. The whole house felt suffocatingly silent and dark, the curtains closed and the mirrors covered. Somehow it even smelled like death – although that was as likely because I had been handling formaldehyde before Mother had demanded my presence and pulled me out of lectures. Not that Merchiston would complain, when it gave me a chance to find out whether Aurora was likely to follow in the footsteps of her husband.

The grieving widow herself looked almost impossibly changed. Gone was the sparkling, winsome hostess and in her place was a pallid, black-clad creature. She was wrapped tightly in a crocheted black shawl beaded with jet, the fire roaring in the grate and the curtains preventing any air from moving around the stuffy room, but she was still shivering.

She had loved him, I realised with a jolt. He had been boorish and patronising, but beneath all his army bluff and bluster there must have been a tenderness, something kept hidden from all except his wife, a side of his character that she and only she was privy to. I wondered if there was something wrong with me that I couldn't see the spark in whatever mediocre man other women swooned over. I had always privately assumed that it was pretence, that married women shared the open secret that their husbands were not the gods they believed themselves to be, but smelly, coarse mortals with insistent desires and a myopic view of the other gender.

'Thank you for coming.' Her voice was a hoarse whisper. 'Alisdair and Miles went out for a walk – they felt cooped up, I think, and there are so many errands to run.'

Aunt Emily hugged her tightly. 'You poor dear. I can't imagine what you're going through.'

'They took him away yesterday. They said . . . they suspect . . . Oh, I can't! It's too much!' She collapsed in tears, and I realised that in my eagerness to see Colonel Greene dissected, I had not given one thought as to how it would affect his widow.

Aunt Emily took the bible from her reticule. 'Perhaps this could offer some comfort?'

Mother looked irritated – had she wished she had thought

of it? Aurora just nodded, and we bowed our heads as Aunt Emily read.

I had seen death up close, and murder even closer. I had never truly encountered grief before. Had my studies – not to mention my extracurricular activities – really made me so hard? I hadn't come here to offer comfort; I had come to pry, to see if I could steal a few strands of a distraught woman's hair so I could take them away and experiment on them. For the first time, I saw my mother's point about medicine making me unwomanly.

And yet all Aurora's tears didn't bring her any closer to finding out who had murdered her husband, or who had killed her maid, a woman who had had her own family and friends and yet whose death was treated as a mere inconvenience.

'Oh, where is that wretched girl with the tea?'

I stood, relieved at a reason to escape the stultifying atmosphere and Aunt Emily's sermons. 'I'll fetch her.'

As I left, something on the antimacassar caught my eye. Glinting in the sunlight were golden hairs. Not just strands, but a clump. Aurora's hair was falling out.

In the hallway, I saw Blackwell carrying a precariously balanced tray. She looked worse than Aurora, with dark circles under her eyes and hands that had been scrubbed red raw, though the tips of her fingers were the colour of a week-old corpse.

I examined them in horror. 'Are you ill?'

'Bless you, miss. Mrs Greene didn't have any mourning dresses with her, so we've had to run out for some dye and make do until her dressmaker can come for a fitting.'

The image of Blackwell sitting at the kitchen table well into the wee hours, soaking all Aurora's pretty dresses in dye as black as pitch unsettled me. I wondered how she felt about this gross display of household mourning when her friend's death had been cause for scandal rather than grief.

My own dress was a sober slate grey, intended for university social activities that I was rarely permitted to attend, and as such had seen little use. Had the colonel been my father-in-law, I too would have carried the faint aroma of still-fresh dye. As it was, I felt positively festive in a house that had turned into a mausoleum overnight.

'I can't imagine what she must be going through.'

'And with her health too. Poor woman.' Blackwell shook her head.

'Has she been ill as well?' Aurora had certainly looked pale. With her small appetite she could never have consumed the same amount of arsenic that her husband had, but even a few grains could have made her ill.

'Her stomach's been awfully unsettled for a while now – poor Clara's murder, and now this. Her hands have come out in hives and her mouth is too sore for her to eat properly.'

I thought of Aurora sitting for hours in her parlour reading, of how fragile she had felt as I embraced her. How gingerly she moved and how warm she was to the touch; the way she kept taking to her bed for days.

She was ill, of that I was sure. But it had nothing to do with arsenic poisoning.

Back in the empty lecture theatre, I told Elisabeth and Merchiston what I suspected.

'Her hair is falling out, she's barely eating and she's feverish. Her maid says she has rashes on her hands – she thinks it's because of the upheaval over the murders, but what if it's something else?'

Merchiston raised his eyebrows.

I sighed. 'I'm a fallen woman, Professor. I know the symptoms of syphilis when I see them.'

He choked.

'My parents sent me away – for my health, they said. It was a hospital for girls from nice families who had transgressed in some way. Venereal disease wasn't uncommon; we all learned the symptoms from the doctors.' I had also learned that there were many ways a woman could transgress – so many that it was a wonder that the drawing rooms of Great Britain remained full of unblemished ladies.

Mrs Ashdown had been blemished in the most literal fashion. Her hands were pockmarked with coppery welts, her hair had fallen out so profusely that she was bald in patches. She had been wearing a wig before she came, until it had dislodged during a rubber of bridge and her deformity was revealed to her entire social circle. I was never sure if she was there because of the disease or because of her anger, at both her husband and the women she had called her friends until they had dropped her like a burning coal. But while her appearance was unsettling, her rages were terrifying. Her husband bore the brunt of it, in screaming harangues that lasted until the nurse could restrain her long enough to administer a sedative. She called him a whoremonger, a blackguard, a reprobate, ordered the porters to take him away, but he never once responded. From the moment she crossed the threshold until the moment I left, he never once visited her.

Aurora was distracted and irritable, but still composed – but what was she like behind closed doors?

'I don't suppose you kept the hair?'

I looked at him in disgust. 'I'm not sure what you think of me, Professor, but I can assure you, I don't leave clues or medical samples behind.'

He snorted as I passed him the clump of hair from my bag. 'Miles Greene is a very lucky man.'

It didn't sound as though he were joking.

'That poor woman.' Elisabeth's eyes were wide. 'To have one's husband betray you and then ruin your health – it's more than I could bear.'

'Even if her condition has progressed, it's unlikely that she has been infected for more than ten, maybe fifteen years. If it were longer, she wouldn't be in control of her faculties. Whilst syphilis can harm an unborn child, even infect it, she would have contracted it long after . . .'

'Long after Miles was conceived.' So my husband-to-be didn't have a virus lurking in his body, ready to pass on to his unsuspecting bride on our wedding night. That was something in his favour at least.

'Did Colonel Greene show any symptoms? Any lesions, particularly around the . . .' I trailed off, not sure if I was sparing Elisabeth's blushes or my own.

'None. Whoever infected Aurora, it wasn't her husband.'

I had visited the Greenes expecting to find another potential murder victim. Instead, I had found material for blackmail that could ruin Aurora's life.

Chapter 17

I was braiding my hair before bed, thinking about the handfuls of Aurora's hair I had seen and what they meant, when the door creaked open and I felt rather than saw my mother's presence. I paused, tensing out of habit. This had always been her favourite time to chastise me as a child, sitting on my bed and tugging a brush through my hair as she recited a litany of the ways I had disappointed her.

Talking back to my governess – never mind that I was right and she couldn't conjugate Latin verbs if her life depended on it – hiding novels in my bible during church, being caught on the stairs listening in on the grown-ups' conversations during dinner before I was permitted to join them, and slipping out to eavesdrop on the men after I was. There had been no end to the ways I had plagued her, and for a while her visits had been as much a staple of my night-time routine as my prayers, a complaint for every one of the hundred strokes of the brush.

At the sanatorium, some of the women had had their hair cut short or shaved. I never knew if it was part of their treatment or a punishment, but I had lived in fear of the same happening to me. That would, I think, have been the final straw, the one incontrovertible sign that my family had given up on me. Instead, I had emerged much as I went in – my hair thinner and brittle, but still there. Still long and golden like a fairy-tale princess, even if the resemblance stopped there.

She moved my hands and replaced them with her own, undoing my work and pulling the hair so tight it made my eyes water.

'Such a pretty girl,' she said softly. 'I hate to think of you wearing spectacles or getting frown lines from poring over those books. And those chemicals they make you work with can't possibly be good for your skin. You'll waste what's left of your youth in that ghastly building, and then where will you be?'

It wasn't a question that required an answer, and I didn't have one that would please her. I doubted my future patients would mind if I wore eyeglasses or had lines on my brow. But my husband would, and I knew that was what she really meant.

'We need to take you to the dressmaker,' she continued. 'Emily has you in such drab colours! I swear my sister would have you looking like a plain spinster if she could, rather than a woman in the first flush of young love. Mint green, perhaps, or a soft peach. Something light and spring-like.'

I wondered if dressing as an infatuated future bride would make me feel more like one. I doubted it, although the prospect of a wardrobe not chosen on the basis of what colours best hid formaldehyde stains did appeal. And once upon a time I had worn those colours. I had scandalised gruff old gentlemen and prim ladies with my talk of education, of never marrying, of finding a profession – but I had done it dressed in the height of fashion, still young enough and untouched enough for it to be little more than a charming oddity, my independence an endearing quirk that wouldn't last the trip down the church aisle. All the delicate pastel shades in the world couldn't bring that innocence back, and my mother's attempts just felt like papering over the cracks, her fuss and frippery designed to disguise who I was underneath like a society matron dressing like a debutante.

'Aurora clearly sees you as a good choice,' she said, and I felt a sharp stab of pleasure at her approval. 'I think she likes that you're more serious-minded. Some empty-headed young chit wouldn't do for Miles at all – he's the kind of man who needs someone to run his life for him and make sure he doesn't spend all his money on parties. But you can afford to be a little more effervescent, my dear.'

'They're in mourning, Mother.' I winced as she yanked on the braid a little too hard. 'I think I can be excused some solemnity.'

'And the last thing we need is for some gay young thing to catch his eye before they're out of mourning and you can marry. Your behaviour until then will be paramount.'

That was the only upside to this whole ghastly scenario – Aurora would not appear in society for at least a year now, meaning that any matrimonial plans were firmly on hold.

She sighed. 'Long engagements make me nervous. Your father and I had eight months, which was more than adequate for my liking.'

'Did you love Father before you married him?' I asked. I had never really considered my parents' marriage before – in my mind they were a fixed constant of the universe.

'One of us had to make a suitable match,' she replied waspishly.

'Uncle Hugh is Scottish, not illegitimate,' I pointed out. 'He has a perfectly good family name and Aunt Emily is well respected in society.' How Mother had manoeuvred me into defending Uncle Hugh I didn't know, and I found myself scowling.

She shook her head. 'Your aunt was always the giddy one,' she said. I couldn't imagine an adjective further from Aunt Emily in all her staid propriety. 'She believed in marrying for love. It was fortunate for her that your uncle has the right connections and family, or she would have faced a stark choice

– unhappiness or penury. Out of the two, the former is more easily cured. Sarah, when it comes to your marriage, my sister and I differ in one respect and one respect alone. She believes you can grow to love Miles.'

'And you don't?'

'I believe your feelings towards him are irrelevant. Acceptance, obedience and propriety are all I require from you – and believe me, my girl, it is a requirement. You are a disgraced bluestocking lacking in virginity as well as most of the social graces, and almost entirely devoid of any common sense. I'd have half a mind to disown you completely and let you take your chances on the streets if I thought you'd survive the week.'

She knew nothing about what I had survived. Not Paul, and not what came after him. She thought common sense meant marrying my attacker, not publicly accusing him. She had no idea of the world I had stumbled into, first with that horrible encounter and then when I moved to Edinburgh. The scales had fallen from my eyes, but she was still blinded by them. For all her condescension and advice, her view of the world was far more rose-tinted than mine ever would be again.

She tied the ribbon at the end of my plait and scooped up some night cream from the pot on my dressing table. It was cold to the touch and she massaged it firmly into my face, pulling at my skin.

'Your father was everything I wanted in a husband,' she said with a smile. 'Our families were friends, he was young and handsome and rich. I knew he could offer me the life I wanted – and he has.'

'But did you love him?' I repeated. 'Did he make you blush whenever he smiled at you; did you want to be in whatever room he was in? Did your heart beat faster when you imagined him kissing you?'

My mother's face grew stony. 'The only time I imagined

him kissing me was on my wedding day,' she said coldly. 'Prior to that, he didn't do more than take my arm as he accompanied me in to dinner. Your father is a gentleman. Had he attempted to do more, I would not have married him – and had I wanted him to, I would have been no fit bride for him.'

It was a grim view of romance. I wondered how much she really meant it, and how long it had taken to instil in her until she stopped questioning it.

'There are other duties a wife has to perform,' she conceded. 'I don't need to tell you what those are – nor,' she said with a warning glare in her eyes, 'do I need to remind you that they are only to take place after the wedding night. The Greenes are aware of your past history, and Emily has done an admirable job of convincing them that you are reformed. Do not make her efforts go to waste. Whatever Paul Beresford had you convinced of, such activities are for procreation and are entirely at the husband's discretion. Once you have heirs, your job will be done, your efforts will no longer be needed and it will gradually cease.'

'You must be disappointed then,' I said tersely. 'Your efforts would seem to have been rather wasted where producing me was concerned.'

She bit her lip, and I wondered if she regretted inflicting an unnecessary operation on her elder child or depriving herself of grandchildren and the status that came with them.

'It seemed kinder at the time. If we had had any idea that your . . . rehabilitation in society was going to go so well, of course we would never have taken such drastic measures. But the doctors said that your hysteria would be ameliorated, that your behaviour would calm down and we'd have no more of this nonsense about Paul Beresford or medicine . . .'

'My ambitions aren't a symptom you can cure, Mother! And it would seem that his course of treatment was ineffective.'

She wrinkled her nose as though presented with a bad

smell. 'Don't talk like that, Sarah. It isn't ladylike. I just don't understand you! Gertie is a perfectly sweet thing – tractable, excited about taking her place in the world. But you were never content. You were such a fractious child,' she said softly. 'Always crying, always hungry – we got through two wet nurses in the first four months alone. But you were a beautiful baby. And all that lovely golden hair, even when you were born. Everyone said it would darken as you got older, that your eyes wouldn't stay that pretty sky blue. But look at you – you've grown into everything I had ever hoped you would be.'

My throat tightened and I swallowed thickly. She sighed.

'On the outside, at least. You could have made such a good marriage, Sarah! Beresford would have had you if you hadn't made such a spectacle of yourself. Yes, he was a cad, but he would have grown out of it. There were half a dozen men vying for your attention, but all you cared about was your ridiculous fixation on becoming a doctor. We should have forced your hand sooner, married you off before you grew too wilful, but your father was convinced it was just a fad. All you silly girls were talking about education and emancipation, and not one of them actually went through with it aside from you. And now you have a second chance! Don't squander it, Sarah, for mark my words, there won't be a third.'

There was a threat in her words that went beyond my diminishing marriageability.

She stood to leave, and looked down at me for a long moment, her expression unreadable. 'Get some sleep. I don't want you looking tired in the morning.' She extinguished the light and disappeared into the night.

When the door closed, I suddenly felt exhausted and collapsed limply back onto the bed like a puppet whose strings had been cut. Somehow I managed to clamber into bed, pulling the sheets tightly around me. My room was warm and cosy, a dying fire in the grate and a hot brick wrapped in blankets at my feet, and yet I shook violently.

I had felt imprisoned in the sanatorium, but it was nothing to how I felt here in the bosom of my family with a gaoler I loved despite myself. Part of me – the dutiful daughter I had thought long since buried – wanted to trust her. To believe that I could be happy in the life she had planned out for me in such meticulous detail. But the woman I had become rebelled against it. I would not suffocate, walled up in a marriage of convenience arranged purely to keep the gossips at bay. I would earn my freedom and raze the whole edifice to the ground if I had to. Not today, and maybe not tomorrow, but soon.

I lay coiled like a snake biding its time. One day I would strike, I was sure of that, and when I did, there would be nothing left of the tattered ambitions my family had for me.

Chapter 18

When I arrived at Warrender Park Crescent, I was shown not into the parlour like any other guest, but into the library, where Gregory Merchiston stood, sleeves rolled up and his knuckles taped.

He looked away as I removed my jacket, leaving me clad in a starched ivory blouse and thick serge tweed skirt. I felt my mouth go dry and my heart thump beneath my ribcage, so loud I was sure he must be able to hear it.

The door closed, leaving us alone. Merchiston handed me a roll of bandages. I opened my mouth to remonstrate, but he shook his head firmly. I wrapped the gauze around my knuckles tightly, flexing my fingers to see how much movement it allowed me. Satisfied that I was prepared, I took my place standing across from him. Next to us, the fire crackled and popped, providing an excuse for the flush that stained my cheeks. Even the normally sallow professor looked positively rosy.

'Hit me,' he said softly.

I swung.

Before my fist could even connect with his face, he had my wrist captured and my arm bent behind my back. His grip was loose, but it took me by surprise.

I did the only thing I could think of, and brought my knee sharply up right below his belt.

He doubled over, swearing profusely.

The housemaid pushed open the door. She looked at me nervously. 'Should I call Mrs Chalmers?'

Grateful for her concern, I shook my head. 'No need, Flora. Professor Merchiston was simply teaching me how to fight.'

She grinned. 'I think you've got the hang of it, Miss Sarah.'

'Painful as that was,' Merchiston winced, 'it was hardly the most effective stratagem.'

'Then why are you crying?' I asked, unable to keep the smirk from my voice.

'I am not crying,' he muttered. 'My eyes are merely watering from the soot. Next time, kick your assailant sharply in the shins. It will make it harder to grab you and still produces the desired effect. Particularly if your opponent is a woman.'

We were silent then, remembering my struggle against Fiona Leadbetter, my friend and mentor who had found herself so worn down and desperate in her attempts to help women in trouble that she had turned to murder. She had lured me into her trap by charm, not force, and I doubted that all the boxing lessons in the world would have saved me had it not been for Merchiston's timely entrance. As it was, he insisted that I learn the rudiments of fighting, whether I returned to the slums or not. Knowing that violence could occur as easily in a town house as a tenement, I had accepted his offer, and so we found ourselves sparring in the privacy of Randall and Elisabeth Chalmers' library.

'Your stance is all wrong,' he grumbled. 'This is a fight, not a tea party.'

He grabbed me by my upper arms and shoved me backwards. I found myself pressed against the bookshelves, and suddenly my breath was gone. My chest tightened, and although my fists were clenched so hard my knuckles hurt, I could no more lash out than I could fly.

Sensing my distress, Merchiston let go and took a few steps back. I crumpled to the floor, not in a faint – I remained stubbornly conscious – but simply because my legs couldn't hold me up any longer.

This is what happens, a little voice in my mind said viciously. *You wanted him to touch you and he did. You invited this.*

He called Flora back. 'Hot sweet tea in the parlour, girl. And fetch Mrs Chalmers – now!'

As he stretched out a hand to pull me up, I acted purely on instinct and punched him squarely in the mouth.

'Fucking—' He bit back the rest of the curse. 'At no point in your preparation did it occur to you to take your bloody ring off, woman?'

I examined the smear of red on the stone of my engagement ring. In the firelight it glowed dangerously, more like a ruby than a diamond.

He licked the blood from his lip. It should have made him look weak, but somehow he seemed feral, dangerous, like a lesson I was incapable of learning.

He looked bewildered. 'Gilchrist, what happened?'

'Not . . . your fault,' I gasped out. 'Not you.'

He swore quietly. 'Christ. I'm sorry, I should have thought . . . I should never have grabbed you like that.'

It was the use of my surname that helped ground me in reality. Merchiston wasn't Paul, would never be Paul. I was in Elisabeth's house, my friend's house, and she would help me to my feet and hold me by the fire until I felt like myself again.

But part of me knew that I was more myself in that moment of struggle than I would ever be again. My whole life boiled down to being held in place by someone I had trusted and who meant me harm. Merchiston might not be Paul, but he still had blood on his hands and I must never entirely trust him.

When Elisabeth arrived, she found Merchiston with a bleeding mouth and me curled up on a chair in front of the fire.

'Gregory, what the bloody *hell* did you do?'

Although she was little more than five feet tall and looked like she was carved out of bone china, Elisabeth seemed ready to kill him where he stood.

My voice felt scratchy and hoarse, as though I had been screaming. 'We were boxing and I . . . I panicked.'

'I should leave,' he said, his voice raw. 'Miss Gilchrist, my sincere apologies. If you find yourself unable to attend class tomorrow, be assured I will not mark you down for it.'

Once he had gone, Elisabeth and I sat in silence for a moment.

'You're still having the dreams.' It wasn't a question.

'Not as frequently. It's just . . .' I took a deep breath and tried again. 'It's nearly a year. Since Paul . . . Everything feels sharper, like all my senses are amplified. Half the time I don't know whether I want to hit something or run away.'

She took my sore hand in hers. 'I think we have an answer to that.' She smiled gently.

I groaned. 'First I accuse him of murder, then I kick him in the unmentionables and now I act like he was trying to assault me. It's a miracle he comes round here at all.'

'I wouldn't call it a miracle,' Elisabeth said wryly. There was a twinkle in her eye I wasn't ready to see.

The room, cosy and charming as it was, suddenly seemed oppressive. I wasn't sure that home would be any better, but I wanted to leave before I fell apart completely.

'Could you call for the carriage? I'd better be getting back. We'll have luncheon together this week, I promise.'

'In that case, I have some designs from Charles Worth that you have to see,' Elisabeth said brightly. 'It's about time I bought you an engagement present – and about time you replaced that hideous hat!'

I smiled at her attempt to cheer me. But I couldn't quite shake the remnants of my fear, the way my legs had locked in place as though my entire body was siding against me with whatever Merchiston had in store for me. I had thought it was because he was a murderer, but I was beginning to suspect I was afraid just because he was a man.

'If this is the way I behave around a member of the faculty, can you imagine what will happen if they force me down the aisle? I'll have to do a lot more than just be alone with Miles.'

My fiancé seemed polite and deferential now, but on his wedding night, faced with a woman he all but owned, how would he respond to refusal?

'Not all men are like Paul, Sarah.'

'But enough of them are. Enough to make me never know when I'm safe.'

My friend paused, uncertain about how to answer my question tactfully. 'You don't . . . you're not . . . You know Miles would never hurt you, Sarah. He wouldn't hurt a fly.'

'I don't feel frightened around him,' I promised. Not overly, at least. The problem was, I could find half a dozen women in London who would have said the same thing about Paul Beresford – and the ones who would disagree knew better, in the light of my public disgrace, than to say anything.

As we went into the hall, I caught Merchiston putting on his coat and hat. I felt as though I needed to offer him an olive branch, although – or perhaps because – I knew he didn't expect it. He was my friend and I trusted him, or at least as far as I trusted anyone these days. I knew that part of my fear had come from my own desire, and I would not let it quash the sweet joy I felt in his presence.

'Could you accompany me home, Professor?' I asked tentatively. 'There's no point in us taking separate carriages, and you're practically on my way.'

He looked relieved. 'If you don't mind? I'm so sorry about

what happened – I hope you know that I would never . . . But I shouldn't have frightened you like that, I should have thought it through.'

'Thank you.' I smiled damply. Truth be told, there was something reassuring about his presence, safe even. It wasn't because of his sex, although I could hardly deny being aware of it. It was the same care and protection I felt from Elisabeth – and oddly enough, despite her prickles, Aunt Emily. The bone-deep certainty that no matter what, I had someone on my side.

Elisabeth saw us into the carriage, with a kiss pressed against my cheek and low threats of violence to Merchiston should he do anything to alarm me. If he were to give her boxing lessons as well, I suspected she would be unstoppable.

We sat in silence as the carriage rolled past the Meadows, but it was companionable rather than awkward. He knew why I had reacted as I did, and I knew he didn't – would never – judge me for it.

'It's wicked of your family to force you into a marriage with a man you don't want,' he said softly. 'After everything you've been through, how can they think this is the solution?'

I shrugged, helplessly. 'They think it will erase the past, or at least make people forget about it. All I can do is hope that we can uncover enough scandal to convince them that going through with the marriage would be worse than escaping it.'

'There is another way,' he said quietly. 'It would get you out of your aunt's house and you'd be free to study, to practise medicine – live the life you want, not the one society enforces upon you.'

'It sounds like you're talking about a miracle.'

In the dim light, his mouth twisted in a wry smile. 'I'm not sure I'd go that far.'

'So? What is this grand plan?'

'Marry me.' His voice was so low, I wondered if I had

misheard, but he carried on, words falling over themselves like rocks in an avalanche. 'It wouldn't have to be . . . I mean, my expectations of you wouldn't include all the duties a wife must perform. It would be on your terms entirely. I have a room – it's quite the nicest one in the house, really. It looks out over the garden. It could be your own private space, I wouldn't intrude. And you could have a desk in my study. Really, the house is far too large for me, and frankly, Mrs Logan has too much time on her hands. It would be good to give her someone else to chase after.

'Sarah, you would be safe in my house and you would be respected. And your family couldn't really object, could they? Their main concern is that you marry, and here I am – a husband ready to take you exactly as you are. There would be no more sneaking medical journals into bibles to preserve your pious image – you don't even have to go to church after we're married, I couldn't give a damn. No more telling your aunt that you're visiting Elisabeth when really you're running after some miscreant through the worst streets of Edinburgh. I'd be by your side, every step of the way.'

I felt unaccountably short of breath. The gaslight lancing in through the carriage windows illuminated the planes of his face, and I saw earnestness shining in his eyes.

He took my hand in both of his and rolled down my glove. I wondered if he could see the indentation left by the engagement ring, which was now stowed safely in my reticule; if he remembered that this was my second proposal of 1893 and it was only February. But as he pressed his lips to my skin, never once breaking my gaze, I couldn't even remember Miles' proposal. I couldn't remember my own name.

'I can't promise to be the husband of your dreams, Sarah. I'm irritable and solitary, and left to my own devices, my table manners are terrible. I'd rather stay inside and read than go to the opera or a party, I don't know any poetry to recite to you and I'm more likely to send you autopsy photographs than flowers. But we can be partners. We can travel – I won't cheat you out of a honeymoon, however much this is a marriage of convenience. Italy, Spain, America – wherever you want. You'll always have someone to accompany you to public talks and no one would think to turn you away if you were on my arm. Can you honestly say that Miles Greene can give you any of that?'

I could not. I could not imagine any man offering me what Gregory Merchiston promised, and not even in my wildest flights of fancy had I considered such a thing. The shackles loosened that had tightened around me ever since my uncle had informed me that I would indeed be marrying Miles if I wanted to continue having a roof over my head, and I felt dizzy with relief and possibility.

'You don't have to give me an answer now. Wait a few days. Hell, wait months if you need to. But don't walk up that aisle and throw yourself away on a man who doesn't understand you.'

The taciturn Professor Merchiston had delivered an entire speech and I had yet to say one word.

'I will,' I whispered, and realised it sounded like an acceptance I wasn't sure I could give. 'Think about it, I mean.' My thoughts flickered and jumped like the flame of a guttering candle, and although I was faced with the prospect of a happiness I had long since discarded, I couldn't summon the coherence to say the one word that would grant me all of that.

The carriage juddered to a halt, and Merchiston dropped my hand as though it had scalded him.

We were in Newington, outside his residence. I looked at the building, imagining myself living there.

'It's much closer to Elisabeth's, if you need any additional incentive,' he said hesitantly, as if he was unsure that any of his previous inducements were sufficient.

'I'll take that into consideration,' I said, smiling through tears I hadn't realised I was shedding.

'Goodnight, Sarah. Sleep on it; don't feel rushed into a decision. I need to know . . .' Here his voice broke slightly. 'I need to know you mean it.'

He leapt out of the carriage and strode the few paces to his front door without turning around. As we jolted into movement again, I watched him fumble with his keys in the lock before disappearing into the light and the warmth.

The journey home could have taken five minutes or five days. I was aware of nothing but the phantom sensation of his mouth on my skin and his words whispered hotly through the darkness.

Chapter 19

My mother's face was pinched with disapproval as she chided me over supper. I was spending too much time with my friends from the university and not enough with my fiancé. Had she known what I had really been doing, she would have had a fit of apoplexy. Not only was Miles grieving, but he was on the cusp of a substantial inheritance, one generous even for a second son. It was intended to support him in married life, but, as my mother crisply reminded me, there was no stipulation that it should be me that he married.

'A rich man has romantic prospects that a poorer one lacks. There will be plenty of women keen to overlook his . . . well, his awkwardness, now that his coffers are filled.'

'He was hardly in the workhouse before, Mother,' I pointed out. 'Colonel Greene helped him with some investments and he was quite comfortable. He was only waiting to marry before they set him up with a household of his own.'

I hoped that was true, at any rate. The thought of moving from my aunt's house into Aurora's was not an appealing one, even without a murderer on the loose.

'But now that his father is dead, everyone knows. Alisdair may be married, but there's still a Greene son who has yet to go down the aisle, even if he is engaged. Should he tire of you, there will be plenty of girls more than ready to take your place, and a dashed sight more grateful than you're acting. Send him your condolences in person, or you'll find that someone else gets there first.'

Frankly, the thought delighted me. Although I felt sorry for Miles' loss, it could be my release. All sorts of possibilities were opening up to me tonight, it seemed. There was nothing anyone could say that would dim the warm glow in my belly that Merchiston's words had sparked, although to give my mother her due, she did try.

I excused myself as early as I could, agreeing to call on Miles in the next few days, my mind awhirl.

How was it that I, the girl whose reputation had been so thoroughly ruined her family had no choice but to let her take up a university education and train for a profession, was in possession of not one potential husband but two? One whom my family approved of but who was caught in the middle of a scandal; the other enough to get me estranged from them for good but who would let me practise medicine – more than that, encourage me every step of the way.

I knew Merchiston well enough to know he didn't make promises he couldn't keep. He was a true scientist, a man who analysed things from every angle before committing to a course of action. If he suggested marriage to get me out of my engagement, it was because he thought it could work. That *we* could work.

Suddenly a whole world of possibility opened up before me – a life where I could train as a doctor and enjoy more domestic comforts than a set of rented rooms and a cat for company. Not to mention the fact that I would have access to Merchiston's extensive library and perhaps even a study of my own, or at least a desk in his. And what a boon to a private practice if I were already a settled married woman with a pharmacology specialist on hand. Surely that would make up for at least some of the prejudices against lady doctors. The filthy slate of my reputation would be wiped clean and I wouldn't even have to give up my ambition.

I wondered how Merchiston felt about cats. The thought of his companionship stretching out ahead of us for the rest of our lives warmed me, and no matter how much I relished the thought of living with his quick wit and considerable intelligence, the thought of seeing him over the breakfast table every morning pleased me in a way that had nothing to do with his medical qualifications.

Was this what women were meant to feel?

Elisabeth had once accused me of wanting a marriage that sounded more like a debating society than a romantic partnership, and it hadn't bothered me that she was right. The thought of my body – my weak, stupid female body that couldn't even bring a child into the world – wanting like this had horrified me. I had tried so hard in the wake of Paul's attack to forget it existed. I ignored all its urges – not eating unless forced, not sleeping unless drugged. And even then, it betrayed me. Images of what I had wanted – what I thought I had wanted – plagued me until I wasn't sure if my memories were even real any more, if I was the foolish slut they said I was.

The thought of a man's touch had brought bile to my throat. Until Gregory Merchiston. I had seen him stripped down to the waist, skin slick with a sheen of sweat. I had seen him charm and tease and flirt as well as glower and lecture. I had seen him kill for me and every moral fibre I possessed told me to run in the opposite direction, but I couldn't. I had fought my reactions every step of the way because surely nothing that made me feel like this could be good, but it was a battle I was losing. And now here he was, offering to cloak my need in the legitimacy of marriage, even if it was one of convenience.

Imagine the life I could live as his wife. Never having to

miss a lecture because my family wanted me home, free to spend my evenings in the library as late as I pleased. Not having newspapers hidden away from me lest my delicate female brain should be overcome with politics or international affairs. Studying *The Lancet* together in front of the fire, reading journal articles out loud to discuss them. The brush of his arm against my waist, the nearness of his body. His mouth claiming mine the way it should have done before we were interrupted all those weeks ago. My fingertips were tracing a pattern on my stomach, dangerously close to where desire pooled. This was wicked, it wasn't what he was offering, but it was what I wanted with a force that scared me.

He was no saint, that I knew, so was the offer of celibacy for my sake or his? Perhaps that magnetism that I had tried so hard to ignore was only one-sided; perhaps that not-quite kiss had been intended as a brotherly brush of my cheek. But I knew – as truly as I knew that I was meant to be a doctor, as truly as I had known anything in my life – that if we married, I would ignore his gentlemanly protestations and offer myself to him as his wife in every way.

The thought made my blood pound, and I shivered even though I wasn't cold. I cocooned myself in blankets, pressing my thighs together, not sure if I wanted to banish the feelings or lean into them, not sure even what they really were.

I wouldn't mock our nuptials by wearing virginal white – neither of us expected that of me. But I ran my hand across the lace trim of my nightgown and imagined the soft fabric of the sleeve slipping off my shoulder as I stood in front of him, daring him to stop me. The rustle of linen on wooden floorboards, the candlelight forgiving of our shared imperfections. And Gregory pressing a gentle kiss against the ugly scar on my stomach, a remnant of the operation that had robbed me of my right to bear his children. I could barely look at it in the mirror as it healed, but now I pressed my body against the fold of the blanket between my legs and the thought of his mouth against the jagged raised line was so sharp and sweet it overwhelmed me until all rational thought blurred into an aching pleasure that left me shaking.

As I drifted into sleep, lulled by languorous satiation, I felt the last vestiges of my shame dissipate and I slept deeply and dreamlessly in a way I hadn't since I was a child.

Chapter 20

'For heaven's sake, girl, stop fidgeting.'

My uncle glowered at me. The carriage jolted across the North Bridge as the pale morning light crept over the city.

'No one likes a scowling woman,' he reprimanded. 'You shouldn't have any thoughts in your head except dress fittings and what to serve at the wedding breakfast; you certainly shouldn't be sitting there memorising how many bones there are in the human body.'

'Two hundred and six,' I replied absent-mindedly. I wondered if he realised that I was in my second term and what on earth he thought I'd been learning up until now.

'Utterly useless information,' he groused. 'It won't help you run a household or raise a family.'

I supposed he would have said the same thing or worse about the obstetrics journal article I had hidden in a dull but improving novel the night before as we sat in front of the fire. God forbid women understood the processes their bodies went through before they birthed their husbands' heirs. Then again, if Uncle Hugh thought that counting bones was the pinnacle of a first-year medical education, he probably knew just as little about his own flatulent corpus. I wrinkled my nose and shuffled discreetly closer to the window.

The truth was, my mind wasn't on my studies or even on Clara Wilson's unsolved murder. A solution – perhaps the perfect solution – had been given to me last night, one that would sweep me away from a disapproving family and a pleasant but bland man whose own relatives clearly had no intention of letting me practise medicine.

Dare I marry Gregory Merchiston? Uncle Hugh and Aunt Emily would be furious if I threw over Miles for another man – but then their opinions wouldn't matter any more. I would be free . . . of them, at least. I had grown used to the idea of spinsterhood, to dismissing as a fairy tale the dream of a husband who understood my ambition and loved me for it. Was it really possible that I would be at liberty to live as I pleased? More likely, I told myself sternly, we would occupy separate rooms, separate lives, our partnership rooted in a shared love of medicine and detection than any of the warm, wicked fantasies my mind had conjured up as I tried to sleep. I felt my cheeks pinken like the dawn light outside – how on earth could I face him after that?

'That's what I like to see,' my uncle said approvingly. 'A girl daydreaming about her young man.'

I had never been so grateful to arrive at our destination. I highly doubted that Uncle Hugh would have approved of either the contents of my daydreams or the young man himself.

When I arrived at the university, the place was in uproar.

'It's Georgina Robinson and Professor Lyell!' Alison blurted out before I had even taken off my coat. 'She reads history and he teaches the Elizabethan era. Apparently they've been courting for months and yesterday they ran away to Gretna Green and she left a note in her boarding house asking them to send her things to his home in Colinton.'

'The other students are fuming,' Edith said conspiratorially.

'I'm not surprised. You'd have thought they'd at least wait

until the weekend so he didn't have to cancel his lectures.' I hoped that the levity in my voice hid the way it shook.

'Oh for heaven's sake, Gilchrist!' Julia snapped. 'Haven't you seen the way the men are looking at us? They're laughing, placing bets on which of us has set her cap at the faculty. All that time we spent proving ourselves, and Robinson has to throw it all away on some fusty academic twice her age.'

'She hasn't thrown it all away,' I tried to reason as my heart pounded deafeningly in my ears. 'At least she'll have the edge on the rest of them when it comes to how we defeated the Spanish Armada.'

Edith shook her head. 'They're saying she'll be sent down. She can't stay, not when she's married to one of the professors. She'll be accused of getting preferential treatment if she does well and of being distracted by her duties at home if she doesn't. And anyway,' she added crisply, 'it was your lot who defeated Spain. Scotland stayed well out of it.'

A minor verbal scuffle about our nations' respective military triumphs broke out, but for once no one's heart was really in it. It was as though with Georgina Robinson's marriage reality had scaled the ivory tower we had sealed ourselves away in.

Things had been tense with our male peers ever since the examination results were posted, but at least they had stayed reasonably civil. Now, the jeers had a different tenor. Overnight we had gone from bitter, sexless spinsters – not so much women as deformed lesser men – to little more than streetwalkers.

That, it turned out, was far from the worst of it. When Professor Cameron, a doughty gentleman with greying hair and a detailed – if extremely clinical – knowledge of the female reproductive system, entered the room, he did so with considerable trepidation. Glancing around, he breathed an audible sigh at the sight of the chaperones, presumably worried that without their presence we would march him to the university chaplain and marry him en masse. Chemistry was much the same, and I dreaded the thought of what Professor Williamson would say during our anatomy practical. He had never bothered to hide his opinion of opening the gates of medicine to women – 'an unmitigated disaster, but since you're all here now you might as well attempt to learn something' – and doubtless he would either be full of praise that Robinson had seen the light and withdrawn to her correct sphere, or drip some condescending bile about how her marriage proved that none of us had the intellectual fortitude to be here in the first place.

All that would be a trifle compared to what awaited me at lunchtime. Hanging back while the others headed to the refectory in search of something more substantial than the stale sandwiches their landladies packed for them, in some sort of culinary protest at where they would be eaten, I made my way towards the faculty rooms with a heavy heart.

The door was open slightly and I didn't knock, wanting to enjoy one quiet moment of just watching him before he noticed I was there. As I stepped into his office, I took a moment to breathe in the smell. Chemicals mixed with coffee, both equally acrid, and something earthier too – the salt-sweat tang of his skin. He had walked from Newington, I guessed, rather than hail a cab from the cosy house I had imagined myself occupying – and more – last night. It currently straddled the uncomfortable chasm of housing a bachelor who had once been a family man, but it felt more like a home than the tasteful elegance of the Greenes' residence, or my aunt's house, which contained more furniture than it did fondness. It could be my home, if I chose. But would it be worth the sacrifice? Could anything?

At least I could be at home in his office, I told myself.

A grinning skull sat on top of a precariously piled stack of books, and a small set of shelves beneath the window was crammed with more; on top, a taxidermied otter lounged comfortably on a copy of William A. Guy's *Principles of Forensic Medicine*. Some of the faculty displayed their books the way they hung the thick, Latin-inscribed parchment of their degree certificates, visual proof of their brilliance. Merchiston's books were tools, well thumbed, with corners turned down and scribbles in the margins. An old copy of *The Lancet* was open on a chair, its yellowing pages inscribed with *Imbecile!* in fresh black ink.

He gave me a warm smile, the kind I could be met with every morning for the rest of my life. Over the breakfast table, beside me in our bed . . . In that moment, I felt loved and I felt safe, and whatever had happened to me before we met mattered so very, very little.

'Arriving without a chaperone? Scandalous behaviour, Miss Gilchrist. I'm really quite shocked.' I had never noticed before that he had a tendency to dimple slightly when he smiled.

'If Aunt Emily knew I was here alone, you'd have another murder on your hands.'

'If your aunt knew half the things you get up to, she'd turn to strong drink. Roaming the slums alone, consorting with women of ill repute, accompanying a man to an autopsy unchaperoned . . .'

'And rejecting his offer of marriage.'

If I had truly believed that his proposal was out of sexless charity, the expression on his face told me differently. He sat very still for a moment, his grey-green gaze locked on mine with a depth of hurt exposed that I could never have imagined.

Then the spell was shattered and he turned away, shuffling papers with a hand that shook ever so slightly. Although I could no longer see his face, the tension in his rhomboid muscles spoke volumes, and I ached to reach out and soothe them, stroking from his shoulders to his spine until the rigidity subsided and he could look at me again.

'It's not you.'

'Finally seen the merits of your fiancé?'

I tried to laugh, but all that came out was an angry gush of breath. 'Hardly. It's Georgina Robinson.'

His eyes widened and he opened his mouth to speak, but although he tried to form words, they weren't coming and I realised that he had misunderstood me entirely. Evidently Julia and Edith's queer fondness for one another wasn't entirely unheard of, then.

'She studies history, or she did until she ran off with Professor Lyell. They've eloped; it's all over the quad. I don't think there's been such a scandal since they let us in.'

'Lyell? Decent chap, if a bit absent-minded. I'm surprised he even noticed her; I've seen him walk into three students in a row without realising. Still, that's nice for them,' he said with a trace of bitterness. He looked at me, confused. 'Isn't it?'

'The whole university is in uproar. They're saying she only matriculated with the hopes of bagging a husband, and two thirds of the history faculty are calling for her to be sent down for improper behaviour.'

'And the other third?'

I shrugged. 'Probably eyeing up the remaining students and trying to choose their own brides.' I winced. 'That wasn't what I meant.'

'But it's what you said. Perhaps what you thought – I can hardly blame you for having a dim view of my sex, Miss Gilchrist.'

Last night he had called me Sarah, and if I had realised it would likely be the only time he did so, I would have savoured it more. Made him say it again and again until his voice grew hoarse and his tongue numb.

Returning his attention to the stack of papers, which he reshuffled yet again – he would make rather a fine bridge partner, had I not burned all of mine – he refused to look at me. 'It's clear I overstepped my boundaries last night. I apologise, Miss Gilchrist.'

'It's something I'll treasure for the rest of my life,' I whispered. 'A kindness I couldn't possibly deserve. But no matter what I do, I risk having to give up my studies. I can get out of my engagement to Miles somehow, I know I can. But with you . . . I'm rather afraid I wouldn't want to.'

I turned to leave before he could see me cry.

'Sarah.' His voice was low, and oh, it was just as sweet as I remembered. 'I won't ask you to change your mind. You're quite right, it would be disastrous, at least now. But you must know that I didn't propose out of friendship. God knows I want to see you complete your studies and go on to a future of your own choosing, but I'm afraid my motives were less altruistic. They were selfish and they were base. I want you for you, mind and body both. You may feel free to slap me for my impertinence, but it's the truth. Even among your peers, you're like no one I've ever met before, man or woman. You're fearless and clever and a life with you would be one enriched beyond belief. I don't want to marry you to save you from a life of tedium; I want to marry you because you would save me from worse.'

I could have gone to him then. I could have cast my doubts to the wind and kissed him, dragged him to the nearest church and then back to his bed and he wouldn't have protested beyond calling for someone to take his morning lectures. But afterwards, what would happen? I couldn't continue my studies here, and were I to go elsewhere for my education, the women I left behind me would suffer in my stead. We had collectively survived our first term, proved that we were as capable as the men and more so. I had witnessed first-hand how one woman's actions could taint the others. I had already been the rotten apple who risked spoiling the whole barrel. I had worked hard not to be judged by my past, and by marrying

Gregory Merchiston, I would become the embodiment of everything society had believed about me.

What I felt for him would need very little encouragement to bloom into love. But I already knew love of a different sort, a fierce, wild longing that meant I would sacrifice anything to see it fulfilled.

My voice was thick with tears I couldn't allow myself to shed. 'It was the kindest of offers. The nicest I could possibly hope to receive. If you were to ask me in five years, my answer might be different, but now . . .'

'I understand,' he said softly. 'Please know that you will always have a place at my side, regardless of your answer.'

I pressed the most fleeting kiss on his cheek and left his office, keeping my eyes fixed straight ahead of me lest I be tempted to look back.

I was so lost in my own thoughts that I nearly walked into a woman as I entered the lecture theatre for botany. Steadying myself, I gazed up into the wide eyes of an ashen-faced Aunt Emily, looking even more out of place here than my mother had.

'It's Miles,' she said in a hoarse whisper. 'He's been arrested.'

Chapter 21

If ever there were a reason to miss two hours of botany, it was having my fiancé arrested for the murder of both his father and his maid. Damn Miles Greene! Not even at the altar and he was finding a way of blocking my path to education.

Perhaps it was the way my mind still whirled, perhaps it was that I couldn't imagine the mild-mannered Miles doing anything worth the police's attention – or mine, for that matter – but the first words out of my mouth had been 'For what?'

Aunt Emily had broken the news to me as gently as she could – which, under the circumstances, wasn't very – but if she had expected me to fall into a swoon and return home immediately she had been very much mistaken. It wasn't until after the day's lectures were concluded that I found myself once again in Gregory Merchiston's company, albeit with Elisabeth and Randall playing reluctant chaperones as we sat in the abandoned lecture theatre.

Merchiston grimaced. 'The autopsy on Colonel Greene revealed considerable arsenic poisoning over a prolonged period of time. Their fractured relationship was well known, apparently.'

'You can't honestly think he murdered his own father?'

'They weren't exactly close.'

'I'm estranged from my mother and I'm not putting arsenic in her tea! Anyway, isn't poison traditionally a woman's tool?'

'You've read the papers I gave you, then.' Merchiston's delight was painfully out of place.

'Not just that. I've come face to face with a murderer. What I saw in her eyes – I've never seen that in Miles'.'

'You didn't see it in Fiona's at first.'

'What was his motive? That he disliked his father? Half his household disliked the man. That's not a motive, that's good sense.'

'The poisoning had been going on for some time. A gradual build-up until his system simply couldn't handle it. Hence the stomach problems, vomiting, hair loss.'

'Then why not seek treatment?'

'He was a proud man who didn't want to admit he was getting older. He drank too much, ate too much and probably thought it was finally catching up with him. He was never going to live to an advanced age. If it hadn't been for Clara's death drawing our attention to the family, it would have been ruled natural causes and no one would be any the wiser.'

'Besides,' said Elisabeth, looking rather ill, 'not everyone has your encyclopedic knowledge of poisonous substances.'

'She has a good teacher.'

'Whose remit does not cover autopsies and God knows what else,' Randall warned. 'Sarah might be close to this whole sorry mess, but I'm not at all convinced that she should be involved in your investigation, Gregory.'

'I'm not involved in his investigation. He's involved in mine. My fiancé has just been arrested for a murder none of us is sure he committed. If that doesn't put me right in the middle of this—'

'You don't even like the man. You should be counting your lucky stars that you've found a way to get out of it. It's not as though anyone will expect you to marry the wretch now.'

'I might not want to marry him, but I don't want to see him hang.'

'You were all set to accuse me of murder in front of a room full of police officers with very little proof, but you're sure a man you barely know is innocent?'

'You can hardly blame me for being suspicious of you. Miles, on the other hand, wouldn't hurt a fly, let alone his father – he was terrified of the man.'

'Fear makes us do strange things. So, it seems, does love.'

'Stop acting like I have any choice in the matter. No, Miles isn't terrible. Yes, I could probably do worse. And while I don't exactly have a line of suitors waiting to save me from spinsterdom, I'm perfectly happy with that! I don't want to marry Miles. I don't want to marry anyone. What would the august Gregory Merchiston do if he were forcibly betrothed to a perfectly pleasant but drippy young woman who was accused of murder?'

'I'd think she was a damn sight more interesting than I'd assumed and proceed with caution.'

'If any woman were unfortunate enough to find herself affianced to you, I'd buy her the bloody arsenic myself!'

We lapsed into uncomfortable silence until the carriage arrived, and our farewells were muted.

Miles wasn't just an easy target for a constabulary eager to sweep a case under the carpet, I thought. His arrest was very convenient for someone, and I was determined to find out who.

I retired early, and sought refuge in my room away from my mother's frown and my uncle's temper. Sometimes it felt that this was the only place I could really breathe, and not just because Agnes had removed the whalebone trappings I wore beneath my dress.

I was brushing out my hair when the thought occurred to me – somewhere between the seventy-fourth stroke and the seventy-fifth – and I moved to the bookcase and ran my fingers across the spines of my library. Novels, all of them. The less savoury textbooks were hidden in a trunk beneath my bed, along with some of the more salacious titles. Women were taking their first steps into a new world on the page as well as in lecture halls, and when I read these books, I felt less alone. My finger alighted on what it was looking for – the dog-eared copies of the *Strand* magazine, and beautiful bound editions of the books themselves, all telling the tales of detective and faithful assistant.

Arthur Conan Doyle, too, had studied at Edinburgh, and had drawn inspiration from the same iconoclastic Professor Bell who had inducted Merchiston in the art of deduction. I had devoured these stories avidly, and now I was learning from the master himself, if only second-hand. Did my professor fancy himself Mr Holmes or Mr Watson? And where did I fit into the plot? I would not be a damsel in distress or a helpmeet, even though he could certainly do with my help. He blundered around, putting people's backs up when all it took was a light touch and a genteel manner. He would have the whole thing ruined if it were left up to him and his colleagues in the constabulary. My upbringing might have caused me to stand out in the slums, but here I fitted in; not perfectly – I had never done that – but if I was a radical eccentric, I was at least *their* radical eccentric. And a bluestocking intellectual with pretensions towards doctoring could be excused the sorts of intrusive questions that a polite society lady would never voice.

Perhaps, I realised, the strange in-betweenness of my life had some value after all.

I pulled out a blank composition book and began to take notes. This, I thought, was where I had gone wrong in investigating Lucy's death. I had mulled it over, stewed on it, but I had never thought to take a step back and make a cool analysis of the facts.

But it was no use dwelling on the past. Two people lay dead and one had been wrongfully accused. Perhaps I could atone for my mistakes by bringing the real killer to justice.

Chapter 22

The prison sat in the shadow of Calton Hill, overlooking the city. I must have passed by it a hundred times as I travelled across the North Bridge, but had paid it scant attention, preferring to gaze at the squat majesty of the castle or the craggy green-grey peak of Arthur's Seat. But there it was, less than fifteen minutes' walk from the station and the hustle and bustle of Princes Street. It somehow loomed larger than other buildings nearby, with a threatening grandeur of its own that rivalled the castle's. I knew that its south side looked out over Holyrood Park and the bottom of the Royal Mile next to a precipitous cliff edge that seemed as though it might crumble at any minute.

My carriage passed by the grand building of the North British Hotel and the General Post Office before making the gradual ascent up Regent's Road past the burial ground. I had no idea what to expect, or if they would even admit me. Miles was awaiting trial, but surely he should be allowed some privileges? He was not, despite what the police and public opinion would have me believe, a convicted murderer yet.

I was taking a risk coming here. Even Elisabeth didn't know where I was, and Alison Thornhill had taken little convincing that I had a terrible migraine and needed to go home. She said

I looked pale, and I suppose she had been right – something about entering into the lion's den, a building crammed full of the most dangerous men and women in Edinburgh, terrified me.

And yet if I was scared, with all the wickedness I had seen in my life so far, how much more frightened must Miles be?

The guard at the door gave me a searching look, and I felt horribly guilty all of a sudden. The thought of setting foot inside, perhaps never to be allowed out again, welled up inside me with mounting hysteria, and I struggled to remain composed.

'My fiancé is here awaiting trial. Could I be permitted to see him, even just for a moment?'

'Do you have an appointment?'

I shook my head, viciously pinching the inside of my wrist to bring tears to my eyes. 'I don't know how any of this works. I can't believe that he could be accused of something so awful. He's a good man, sir, I promise.'

He shook his head sadly, clearly thinking I was some poor deceived soul who had been duped by a charming smile.

'If he was that good, he wouldnae be in here, miss.'

'Please,' I begged, finding that tears sprang to my eyes unbidden now. I wasn't leaving without at least letting Miles know he had a friend who believed in his innocence. 'Is there nothing I can do?' I asked, hoping that whatever bribe he would be satisfied with was financial rather than physical. 'His name is Miles Greene. Even if you could tell him that Sarah visited, it might bring him some hope.'

He sighed. 'Wait through here, lassie. I'll see what I can do.'

I sat on a hard wooden bench in an imposing hallway. Presumably this was not the area where the resident miscreants were processed. Eventually the guard returned with a grim expression, and I realised that in the interim he must have been apprised of Miles' crimes.

'Are you sure you want to do this, hen?'

I nodded. 'I know what he's been accused of, but he's innocent. Even if . . .' My voice broke. 'Even if he's found guilty at the trial, I can't let him rot here thinking he doesn't have a soul in the world who cares about him.'

My new friend nodded. 'For your sake, I hope he's found innocent.' He and I both knew, however, that the prospect was an unlikely one.

He guided me through a maze of corridors, each one darker and more forbidding than the last. The air reeked of damp and my feet ached with the cold seeping in from the stone floors, while the clanking of the keys on the chain at his waist made me think of Jacob Marley's ghost.

We stopped at the first locked door and he glanced back at me. I nodded silently.

It was the noise that hit me first, rather than the smell. That came moments later, and turned my stomach when it did, but the noise would haunt my dreams for months to come. I thought that I had seen hopelessness in the slums of the city, that I had come face to face with the most desperate and pitiful a person could get, but the men's voices had a hollowness to them that belied whatever bravado lay in their words. These men were rats scrabbling around in a cage, biting and scratching each other because their captors were untouchable, fighting out of boredom and a need to fill their last weeks or months with whatever activity they could.

How had Miles survived even a day here? The answer came after we wound our way even deeper into the heart of the prison and it was as I had expected: he had barely survived at all.

The man in front of me was a stranger. A week of whatever passed for food here had begun to melt the puppy fat from his bones, and I could see the echoes of his brother and parents in his face. One eye was bloodshot and red-rimmed and the other was so swollen and bruised it could barely open at all.

I whirled around to face the warden. 'Has he been seen by

a doctor?'

A dry, rattling sound came from the cell. 'Now I know I'm not dreaming. Only you would walk in here and give me a diagnosis before you've even said hello.'

'The prison doctor patches them up, miss, but if the men didn't get into fights then they wouldnae need treatment. I'm sure the other fellow looks as bad.'

Somehow I doubted that.

'I think I managed to get in a hair pull,' Miles muttered. I had done worse than that scrapping with Gertie when we were children. How could this man really be the main suspect in a murder investigation?

'Can we have a moment alone?'

The warden shook his head. 'It's not safe for me to leave you.'

I turned to Miles. 'It's good to see you,' I said softly.

He tried to smile, and winced as his cut lip split open again. 'Is it? I thought you'd be delighted to be rid of me. It's no secret that you didn't exactly want this marriage.'

'Did you kill your father or Clara Wilson?'

'No, I swear to God, I never touched a hair on her head. They're saying we were lovers, that we were going to run away together until I threw her over for you. I don't think I ever said more than two sentences to her since she came to us. I've never even . . .'

He broke off, and I reddened as the recollection of exactly what Miles had never done sank in.

'They must have had some evidence, surely.'

'They found arsenic and some of Mother's jewellery among my things. I don't know how they got there, but no one will listen to me.'

'I believe you.' The relief on his face transformed it, and I saw for the first time someone I could truly care about.

'Do you have any idea who could have done this? Was there

anything suspicious you noticed in the days leading up to Wilson's death?'

His expression clouded. 'Did someone send you here to ask these questions?'

I felt a wave of remorse. He had been so delighted to have a visitor, to hear that I believed in him, and now all I wanted to do was talk about the reason he was occupying a cramped, stinking cell.

'I'm here of my own accord, Miles. I don't believe you killed Wilson or your father, and I mean to prove it.'

He looked defeated. Perhaps I was heartless, not giving him the tenderness he so clearly craved, but what I could offer was better: the possibility of freedom.

'Mother was being blackmailed. She started receiving letters that frightened her, and then some of her jewellery went missing. She always wore her garnet and pearl necklace to the opera – it was an anniversary present from Father – but the last time we went she wore her emeralds instead and flew into a rage if anyone commented on it. Father asked her to wear a sapphire and diamond set to a dinner party and she refused because it didn't go with her new dress, when I'd heard her say before that she'd had it designed specifically to go with it.'

'So that's how Wilson got the jewels.'

'Whenever I tried to talk to Mother about it, she changed the subject. Father ran a tight ship – he went through the household accounts with a fine-tooth comb, so she could hardly have used the housekeeping money – and she didn't have funds of her own.' He looked sick. 'Why didn't she tell the police about the blackmail? Surely that would exonerate me? I have my own funds; I don't need her money. I'll come into the rest of my grandfather's inheritance when we marry . . .'

He broke off. We both knew how unlikely that ceremony would be now.

I needed to change the subject – but more than that, I needed answers. 'Was it a happy marriage?'

He shrugged. 'Happy enough. Father was away a lot until he left the army – not that he ever really left. They grew closer after that.' He paused. 'You can't be implying . . .'

'Your mother has syphilis,' I said bluntly. There was no point in sheltering him from his family's secrets any more, not while he was paying for them. 'Your father didn't.'

He was quiet for a few moments, and then he smiled. There was no humour in it. 'Out of the two of them, I wouldn't have thought he'd be the faithful one.'

'You aren't surprised?' I had been, and I'd wager I knew more about the ways of the world than he did, prison or not.

'Alisdair has a taste for married women. Any illusions I might have had were shattered when I walked in on him and my mother's friend Mrs Stewart, engaged in . . . honestly, I'm still not sure what it was they were doing, but I remember it didn't look comfortable. The next night she and her husband joined us for dinner and you'd think there was no one in the world she loved more than him.'

The guard cleared his throat behind me. I couldn't stay, but I couldn't leave Miles without some reassurance.

'All we need to do is create enough doubt that the courts rule it not proven. It's a stain on your character, but better that than an early grave. And then . . .' I couldn't formally break off the engagement now. Perhaps leaving him with hope was cruel, but he had so little of it that surely I could spare some? 'Then we'll see.'

'Miss!' the guard's voice had a warning tone. 'I cannae let you stay any longer. Say your goodbyes or you'll be in the women's cells for causing a disturbance.'

Miles looked at me desperately. 'Will you visit again?'

'I won't need to,' I promised. 'The next time I see you, you'll be a free man.'

And that, I reflected as I retraced my steps to daylight and freedom, would be a problem for the future.

As I stumbled out into the early-afternoon light, even the drizzle of rain and the dark clouds promising worse on the way weren't enough to challenge the buoyancy of my spirits.

Chapter 23

Returning home from lectures the next day, my mood had lifted a little and I was resolute. I at least had new information, and Miles knew that someone believed him. But time was of the essence. Even if he could be acquitted, I was not sure he had the constitution to make it as far as the trial. I would not have his death on my conscience.

If I had known what was awaiting me, I might not have felt so sanguine. My mother sat in the parlour, gripping a note so tightly in her fingers that it had torn slightly. I recognised Aurora's handwriting, and a sinking suspicion that my previous day's adventure had not gone unnoticed settled upon me.

'Sarah, come here immediately.' Her voice was like ice, colder even than the Scottish winter outside.

I wanted to turn tail and flee in the other direction, but my body obeyed her automatically.

'I have had the most disturbing letter from Aurora Greene, alleging that you visited Miles *in prison* yesterday. Tell me that this has been a misunderstanding.'

I shook my head. 'He is still my fiancé, Mother.'

'He has been arrested on suspicion of murder. And after all your protestations, I didn't think that you would mourn the fact quite so deeply. What possessed you to go to such a place?

I truly thought you had plumbed the depths of depravity with your behaviour, first in London, then cavorting in the slums with those ghastly women who call themselves doctors – but now this. Is there any vice you cannot be drawn to? I thought you would learn your lesson here, but I see that my sister has allowed you far too much freedom.'

Across the room, I saw Aunt Emily wince and wondered if she had been the recipient of the same scolding I was to undergo.

'Aunt Emily didn't know where I was going. She would never have permitted it.'

'So you add deceit to your list of sins now? If your aunt can be duped that easily, then perhaps she is not the guardian I thought she was.'

I had complained about Aunt Emily more than my fair share of times to anyone who would listen, but I had leapt to her defence regardless. She could be strict, but I knew that she loved me. And I was wondering if I had ever felt truly loved by the woman in front of me.

'I'm sorry, Aunt Emily. I won't do it again. I just felt so bad for him . . . He can't possibly be guilty.'

She gave me a watery smile. 'I'm afraid the police think differently, dear.'

'Police! Ladies of our standing do not talk to the *police*. No, Sarah, I've made up my mind. All that nonsense last year is water under the bridge; no one will be talking about it now. I think it's better that you return home, and I've written to your father to tell him so.'

Rage and shock made me still; the thought that she could discard me like a broken doll and then pick me up again when she was bored. 'Would I be able to study there?' I fought to keep my voice level, even though I knew the answer.

'For heaven's sake, Sarah. You don't care how this has affected your family one bit, do you? I don't just mean your appalling behaviour with Mr Beresford, or those outlandish accusations you made to get yourself out of trouble. Running around going to lectures, reading textbooks. And now you're enrolled at a university. Ladies do not have professions. Our vocation is our house, our home, our children—'

'And you've made such an excellent job of that, haven't you, Mother?' I spat. 'Tell me, has Gertie forgiven you for sending me away?' The last time I had seen my little sister, she had been near hysterical with crying. No one had explained to her what I had supposedly done, simply that her beloved older sister had been wicked and would no longer be permitted to lodge under our parents' roof.

She pinched her lips together tightly. 'Gertrude understands that there are expectations placed on her. She knows that there is one way, and one way only: that a life without a husband is not one worth living.'

Somewhere at the back of my brain, the thought still terrified me. I didn't know what life as a single woman would look like. Would I be the fast, dissolute hussy of my mother's imagination, or the tragic, withered spinster of the popular press? The female doctors I had seen working at St Giles' Infirmary didn't seem like either. Yet somehow my mother made no distinction between the professional women working inside the clinic and the poor wretches walking the streets outside it.

'You're a clever girl, Sarah. You'll find that running a household is a challenge in itself, balancing the books, managing staff, keeping everything running smoothly.'

'So smoothly that even my husband doesn't know how hard I work. Don't patronise me, Mother – I know I'm clever. Don't tell me to be modest, or that my value is in my good name or whatever hideous truism you want to trot out now. Any house I keep will be mine and mine alone. Any staff I manage will be in a hospital. And if you'd wanted me to have children, you shouldn't have let those madhouse butchers carve out my ovaries.'

She looked tired. 'Sarah, what am I to do with you?'

'The same as you did when you sent me here, I imagine. Tell me how ashamed you are and leave me to fend for myself.'

'You are not the only person in this family. I have another daughter to protect, I have your father's reputation. Believe me, if he loses any more of his business investments because you've been embroiled in yet another scandal, you'll be affected as well. And it isn't just him who's feeling the strain – we'll see how welcoming your aunt and uncle are when you're leeching off them until you're old and grey.'

I had never wondered how Aunt Emily's household had absorbed the expense of a third occupant, and it had never occurred to me that her frugal spending was due to anything other than a parsimonious nature. How much trouble was Uncle Hugh's business in?

'You came here to celebrate my engagement. The first time I had set eyes on you in nearly a year, and it was because I'd suddenly been cleaned up and made respectable by some man wanting to marry me. Well, I'm not engaged any more. There's no reason for you to be here, so leave.'

Aunt Emily rose. 'Diana, please. If Sarah returns to London now with a fiancé arrested for murder, the scandal will be even worse than last time. Give it time to die down at least.'

'And you're the expert in avoiding scandal, aren't you, Emily?' Mother spat the words across the room, and for a moment they were not two grown women discussing an errant daughter, but sisters at loggerheads over something else entirely. 'My family has been subsidising your husband's business for far too long. Let Sarah do as she pleases, and heap shame on someone else's head for a change. If you think you can cope so admirably without my guidance, perhaps you will reconsider if you have to cope without my money.'

At Mother's request, I helped her pack – or rather sat while she criticised the maid's packing. A dozen day dresses were neatly folded, scent bottles carefully wrapped up, shoes stuffed with newspaper so that they would keep their shape on the journey home. And somewhere in all the paraphernalia was the telegram I had seen, discarded by the tea tray before she could hide it. *RETURN HOME IMMEDIATELY STOP DO NOT BRING S STOP YRS AFFEC PG STOP.*

So I would not be leaving Edinburgh after all. Was this my fate, to get what I wanted in the most horrible way imaginable? I was allowed to study medicine because a man had attacked me, my engagement was broken off because my fiancé was arrested for murder, and now I was permitted to stay in the city I was slowly learning to see as my home because my own father couldn't bear to lay eyes on me. What more could I have expected from a man who was too cheap to write 'yours affectionately' in full in a telegram to his wife?

The next afternoon, we stood awkwardly in the hall next to her suitcases.

'We'll accompany you to the station,' Aunt Emily said.

'Really, there's no need.'

'I insist. You can say a proper goodbye to Sarah.'

The journey felt interminably long and the station was freezing. The sisters embraced on the platform and I had never seen two women look more alike or more different. I had been haunted by my mother during my time in Edinburgh, seeing her shade in Aunt Emily: the quirk of her mouth, the way she pinched the bridge of her nose as she read, flashes of familial resemblance that cut me to the quick, remembering what I had lost. Now they only emphasised the differences between them. If Aunt Emily was a battleaxe, my mother was a scalpel – polished to a gleam and fatally sharp.

I kissed her cold cheek. 'Give my love to Gertie.'

She took my face between her hands. 'Take care of yourself,

Sarah.' It felt like a goodbye more permanent than simply seeing her off on the train.

Without looking back, she stepped into the carriage and we watched in silence as the train clattered and clanged out of the station, returning her to her one unspoiled daughter.

Back at home, rain lashed against the window and wind shook the trees in the garden. Inside, the atmosphere was no less inclement. I was alone with Aunt Emily for the first time in weeks. In all the whirl of recent events – the murders, Mother's arrival – I had barely seen her.

'Don't blame your mother. Diana . . . Well, she was doing what she thought best. If you must be angry, be angry with the right person. The operation wasn't her idea, you know. The letters she wrote to me . . . She went back and forth for weeks about whether it was the right thing to do. In the end, the doctors insisted. You were so unwell, Sarah.' Aunt Emily took my hand and pushed the sleeve of my dress up. She stroked the scar on my wrist. 'She didn't want to lose you.'

'She did,' I said hollowly.

My aunt sighed. 'Sarah, you may not think that she loves you, but your mother left me with strict instructions as to your behaviour, and what she has seen here did nothing to assuage her fears. If she thinks you are associating with criminals and lunatics, she will remove you from this house.'

'As she removed me from hers? Tell me, Aunt Emily, what will she do then when I fail to fall in line like a good little girl?'

'You thought being sent here was a punishment. Believe me, child, your uncle and I are far better than the alternative.'

The alternative, I knew, was the madhouse.

'A university education is hardly a sign of insanity!'

'It is in a woman.'

'Do *you* think I'm mad?' I asked quietly.

'I think you're wilful and wild. I wish you'd listen to me, to your mother – to anyone! I think this whole foolish enterprise of yours will end in disaster.' She sighed, and began to unpick her embroidery. 'I don't think you're mad, but it isn't my opinion that will matter in the end.'

It would be a doctor's opinion, and it wouldn't be hard to find a doctor in Edinburgh so set against women joining his profession that he would sign the papers saying that I was out of my wits to be considering it.

'If it were up to me, women wouldn't be sent away for failing to conform. We wouldn't have our most intimate areas examined by a man; we wouldn't be carved up in the name of curing our melancholy. Can you really say that medicine wouldn't be better off in the hands of women?'

Aunt Emily was silent for a long time. 'I wish I could for your sake. But I would never feel as safe as I do in the care of a man. You have your education and your fine speeches, but women are too flighty, too easily upset. Men are dependable, pragmatic. I could never fully trust someone I only saw at best as my equal.'

I was used to her lectures and criticisms, but something about her finality, the way she had tried to find the answer I wanted within herself and failed, stung so sharply it took my breath away. What came next was worse.

'If you hadn't told everyone, if you had only comported yourself with some dignity and restraint, none of this would have happened. Your father could have spoken to his father, a mutually convenient date could have been set and nobody would have been any the wiser.'

'She would have married me off to a man who took advantage of me and I'm supposed to be sorry I was too upset to be stuck with that bastard for life?'

To her credit, she didn't argue. 'Don't put her on a pedestal simply because she's a woman. We're not all angels, but we aren't all devils either. It isn't just you emancipated girls who understand that.'

I stared at her in surprise and she gave a chuckle that brought back memories of being dandled on her knee as a child. There were some ideological chasms that might never be bridged, some fights that might never be won, but she suddenly felt like more of an ally than I had ever expected.

Chapter 24

With my mother gone, I was free to spend my time focusing my attention where it was most needed: Clara Wilson's death and the murky family secrets that surrounded it. There was no way that Aurora's condition would have escaped her personal maid. She would have administered salves for the rash, set aside clumps of hair and dressed the rest so that any thinning patches were disguised. And yet Colonel Greene hadn't even been able to remember her first name, if he had ever bothered to learn it. In grander houses, the servants would have to turn to face the wall rather than make eye contact with their social superiors. The rest of the time we let ourselves forget that they had eyes and ears, that they were neither blind nor deaf. That nothing in our lives went unseen, no matter how private we thought they were.

Mrs Logan, Merchiston's redoubtable housekeeper, knew him better than I did, perhaps better than I ever would. If he was a disease, she would have studied him in all its stages, from incubation to recovery. She knew how he liked his coffee, how his breath smelled in the morning, whether he preferred jam or marmalade on his toast. Did he hang his coat up neatly when he arrived home in the evening, or toss it carelessly on a chair? Mrs Logan would know, and would be there ready to scoop it up and put it away properly, so that the next morning he would assume he had hung it up himself.

How many lazy habits did we fail to recognise because there were always servants to put things right? As an experiment, I raised my hand to my hair and tried to remember which hairpins Agnes had put it up with that morning. Was it the tortoiseshell or the mother-of-pearl? She would know – would probably have spare pins in her pocket to tidy things up as soon as I walked into the hallway tonight. I thought for a moment. Pearl, perhaps? I pulled one out. Tortoiseshell. My professors praised my attention to detail, but when it came to personal matters, someone else was the expert.

I found myself wishing I had paid more attention when Mother had forced me to watch her go through the process of hiring servants. How much did we really know about the people we invited into our homes, made privy to our most personal secrets, entrusted with the care of our children?

They took away our chamber pots, cleaned stained bedclothes, laced our stays a little looser after a few too many heavy dinners. Higgins, the maid who had taken over my care once I was out of the schoolroom and no longer needed a governess or a nursemaid, had known when my monthly cycle was due before I did. My aunt's maid was practically her spy – I knew that so much as a splash of mud on my hem would be reported back.

The night of my assault, the servants all knew within an hour of my arrival home that I had lost whatever honour I had left the house with. I wasn't foolish enough to believe that the gossip hadn't circulated below stairs: that Miss Sarah had finally gone too far and wouldn't even accept the blame for her own behaviour. It had been the footman who had been sent to fetch the doctor who had examined and then pacified me with laudanum, the maid who had brought my mother smelling salts, our driver who had driven us, me crying so hard I was sick all over my ripped gown and my mother pinch-lipped, dry-eyed and silent. And as news of my disgrace had moved from drawing room to drawing room, so too would it have happened behind the green baize door that separated our two worlds.

Just as we liked to believe that our servants were automatons, we didn't think of them as having friends. But with all those fine town houses sandwiched together in crescents that arched around private parks to which they were not admitted, surely there must be some camaraderie; surely the servants must have the same friendships and rivalries and confidences as their upstairs employers.

If Clara Wilson was involved in the blackmail, or if she was another victim, someone must have known about it. Perhaps not every detail, but if she had needed money or to make a quick escape, or if she had let slip something about Aurora's condition, then who else but a fellow servant would know?

I was stretching the limits of the Greenes' patience as it was, and my aunt's household staff had made it very clear over the past seven months what they thought of me. But if I wanted to understand the intricacies of the world that Clara belonged to, there was one other person who might help me.

I stood on the doorstep of the house in Newington for the second time in as many weeks, the sleety drizzle dripping off my umbrella and splashing into the puddles at my feet, listening to footsteps from the other side of the door.

If Mrs Logan was surprised to see me, she was too well trained to show it.

'The professor is at the university, Miss Gilchrist.' She narrowed her eyes. 'As you should be, if I'm no' mistaken.'

I winced. She was right, but somehow I didn't think that missing a botany tutorial would seriously affect my medical knowledge, unless I ever had to operate on an orchid.

'Actually, I'm here to see you. Might I come in?'

She stepped aside and let me through. When I turned automatically to the parlour, she took my arm and guided me gently through the house to the kitchen. I blushed at my mistake. She seemed so utterly in charge here that I had forgotten whose house it really was, and although I doubted Merchiston would mind if we sat there, Mrs Logan had a servant's sensibilities and would never permit it.

'Tea?' she asked, indicating the kettle on the hob. 'Or do you modern lassies prefer coffee? I'm sure the professor won't notice if I raid his private supply. And if you don't mind waiting a wee while for them to cool, there are some ginger biscuits fresh out of the oven.'

She bustled around, and in short order I was provided with a pot of delicious-smelling coffee and a plate of biscuits that looked almost as good.

'Now, Miss Gilchrist, to what do I owe the honour of you missing your lectures?' Her expression was kind but stern, and I knew that however welcoming she was, this was not a woman I would want to cross. 'Before we go any further, I should warn you that Gregory Merchiston is my employer and my friend. I'm loyal to him, and silent as the grave to boot. As I was to Isobel, his late wife – and poor Lucy, not that it did her any good.' She shook her head sadly. 'Some servants may like to gossip, but I've never been one of them. My previous employers appreciated discretion and the habit has never left me.' She caught my gaze. 'You may find yourself glad of that in time.'

I flushed. Was she picturing me as Merchiston's wife or his mistress? And what did it say about me that I wasn't sure which one I preferred?

'I would never ask you to betray a confidence,' I promised, 'but I am wondering how often that happens. I know that there's a rumour mill that goes on between households below stairs, and that servants might confide in a friend rather than someone they work with. This isn't my world, Mrs Logan, and polite enquiry will only get me so far. A man's life hangs in the balance and the only person I know who has any answers is dead. But if she had shared the details with someone . . .'

'Your fiancé's maid.'

So she knew I was engaged. I wanted to explain, defend myself, tell her I wasn't some heartless flibbertigibbet who craved the attention of men. But somehow, although I sensed her disapproval, I also felt that she understood.

'He wasn't my choice, but that doesn't mean I want to see him hang. Two people are already dead, and if I can't find the person responsible then who knows where it will end. We like to think of our homes as private spheres, but they aren't. Servants leave, or complain about their employers – if Clara Wilson had had a sweetheart or an accomplice, surely someone in her circle knew about it. I can't access that circle, but perhaps you can.'

Her greying eyebrows rose to meet her hairline. 'You want my assistance in a case, do you? Honestly, you and the professor are peas in a pod. It starts out with "Can you get the blood out of my favourite shirt, my good woman?" and ends with me in a music hall dressing room stripped down to my unmentionables armed with nothing but a prop knife.' She caught my dumbfounded gaze. 'That's a story for another time. As it happens, I have an acquaintance, a Mrs Fredericks, who runs an agency placing staff in good positions, and she makes it her business to be aware of everything her girls get up to. Celia and I have known each other . . . well, let's just say it's been a while. Long enough for me to know that the husband she still wears black for belonged to someone else entirely. She owes me a favour or two . . . I can tell her you'll be calling it in on my behalf.'

'And you think she'll speak to me?'

Mrs Logan shrugged. 'She will if she doesnae want all her fine clients to know what business she used to be in, back when she was Celia Taylor. That's the first favour she owes me.'

I was beginning to realise that Merchiston's housekeeper had as many secrets as he did.

'And the second?'

'I'm the only one living that kens who the gentleman she's in mourning for was really married to.' Her mouth gave a wry, sad twist that almost resembled a smile. 'I should do, after all. He was my husband.'

Chapter 25

The office of the hiring agency was an airy, pleasant room a short walk from Princes Street. Occupying the first floor, it was a picture of civility, from the framed photographs of demure staff to the testimonials from satisfied employers to the leather-bound copies of Mrs Beeton's *Book of Household Management* on the shelves. Although they had been dusted, I doubted that they had been opened, and suspected that their purpose was decorative as opposed to practical.

Practical was the only way to describe the woman in front of me, however, looking as though I had brought a bad smell into her office.

'Jessie Logan is no better than she ought to be. I could tell you stories that would make your hair curl – but I won't, and not just because she has nephews who are on first-name terms with the polis.'

'I suspect she could say the same thing. If she's that dreadful, I'm surprised her husband caught your eye.'

She conceded the point and smirked.

'He was handsome and I was stupid, and in any case, Jessie and I have been squabbling over each other's possessions since we were in swaddling clothes.'

The aquiline nose, the piercing blue eyes, the full mouth

that could go from smiling to severe at a moment's notice – I had seen them before, and recently. So too the salt-and-pepper hair, although Mrs Logan's was more salt these days whereas Celia Fredericks' leaned more towards pepper in a shade I suspected wasn't entirely God-given.

'You're sisters.'

'She's the elder, bossy-britches that she is. Oh, she'll deny it in public, Lord knows we were never the best of friends. But she was there for me when I needed her, even after Ruaidhri and I had our . . . indiscretion. Our brother was a bad lot and his sons are turning out the same way, but Jessie was always a good girl even when she was doing something bad.' She smirked. 'Or did you think she got her position with a doctor who solves murders for the polis on account of her cooking? She's broken more laws than you've had hot dinners, and she'd pick the lock on the Pearly Gates if that dreary lummox she mothers asked her to.'

Much as I wanted to delve into the scandalous past of Mrs Logan – and dear Lord, how I did! – I had my own investigation to focus on.

'I need information about Clara Wilson, the servant who was murdered at the Greene residence.'

'She wasnae one of my girls, but she palled around with some of them. Kept herself to herself mostly, but she seemed happy. Mrs Greene treated her well and the colonel didn't take advantage, which is more than some people can say. She always had a kind word for your young man, though I don't think she was sweet on him. You're standing by him?'

'I think he's innocent, if that's what you mean.'

'Aye, you're probably right about that. Women in service, we get a sixth sense when a man is dangerous. They can hide it from their wives, but never the women laundering their clothes. We're trained not to ask questions, so they assume we don't think about them.'

'But someone was hiding it. Someone murdered Clara. Either she was helping them blackmail an employer you say she was happy with, or they stole the jewels and made it look as if she had taken them. Did she have a sweetheart, anyone she walked out with?'

'If she did, she kept her cards close to her chest. But that's not unusual – the quality demand standards from their servants they wouldn't expect from a nun. Begging your pardon, Miss Gilchrist.'

She didn't look as though she meant it, but I agreed with her in any case.

'Do you know how she spent her days off? One of the other maids mentioned her family.'

'I heard she sent money back to them, but she always looked well turned out, so she must have kept some of it back.'

'Or she was getting it from somewhere else.'

'She was never one to act above her station, like some girls do. They'd steal from their employers soon as look at you if they thought they could get away with it. Clara liked nice things, but she never fancied herself a lady.'

'Most of her family are in service. Do you know where? If she was blackmailing Aurora Greene, she might not have been the only one.'

'I can find out. For a price.'

I met her gaze coolly. 'Would that price be not letting my aunt and her friends know that the woman they use to hire their maids used to run a brothel? I can read between the lines, *Mrs* Fredericks, and while your sister might spare your blushes about your previous employment, I have no such familial impulses.'

'Look at that – the kitten has claws. What makes a nice young lady like you want to dive around in the filth and muck, hmm? That doesn't sound like something that aunt of yours would approve of, even if it is to save your sweetheart's life.'

I was getting very tired of being on the receiving end of threats.

'He isn't my sweetheart and I'm not a nice young lady. I'm a medical student working with one of the police surgeons because a woman has been murdered and no one seemed to care until her killer targeted a man with money and connections. You can help me or you can stand in my way, but if you do the latter then know this – there will be consequences.'

A smile illuminated her features, like the sun bursting out from behind the clouds.

'I had you down for a prissy miss, looking to turn her nose up at the misfortune of others. But you're a different sort, aren't you?'

I ignored the compliment – if that was what it was – and forged on ahead. 'What do you know about Mrs Greene's health? Did she ever complain about rashes or a more . . . intimate discomfort?'

Mrs Fredericks' eyes narrowed and I wondered if I had shown my cards too early. To my surprise, she chuckled.

'So Aurora Greene has the pox. Who would have thought it? She looks as though butter wouldn't melt in her mouth, with all her charitable works and church three times a week. The colonel philandered, but what man doesn't? Nothing more than the odd discreet visit to a certain kind of establishment once in a while and the occasional tumble backstage with an opera singer. Never heard of her having a wandering eye, but she wouldn't be the first woman to tire of her husband. There are ways to avoid infection, but your class never worry about that. I've seen tarts take more care with their intimate encounters than a titled lady.'

'You seem to know a lot about the family,' I said, wondering how much she knew about mine.

'I don't keep all this knowledge to hand in case some chit of a girl with more brains than sense comes chapping at my door with questions, lassie,' she tutted.

I grinned. 'But you keep it somewhere.'

'My sister sent you and she wouldnae do that without good reason, let me tell you. There's a lassie dead and a lad accused who you claim is innocent – to me, that says that we havenae seen the last of whoever killed her, and I won't see my girls in danger. Take a seat, for heaven's sake, and I'll see what I have.'

As she moved into an adjoining room, I looked around the place. Its elegant, discreet style was fitting for someone who staffed the houses of Edinburgh's gentry, but for a woman who had once run a brothel and who had a sister in service, it was a considerable step up in the world. Celia Fredericks had built a life on knowing everything about everyone, and I had no doubt that in her first years of legitimate business, she reminded her former patrons of the fact. If she had stooped to blackmail once, why not do it again?

But somehow I couldn't see this straightforward woman, who so enjoyed the theatre of her interactions with people, hiding behind anonymous letters. Not when all it would take was the reminder of services once rendered and enjoyed, or the threat of a rumour spreading around the city faster than cholera. Her former employees may have done their best work in the dark, but this was a woman who had worked her way into the sunlight and intended to stay there.

I moved to the closed door and peered through the keyhole. It had been blocked up – quite sensibly, since I was doubtless not the only person to come nosing around. I could hear drawers being opened and papers shuffled, but little else to sate my curiosity. By the time Mrs Fredericks reappeared, I was sitting on the overstuffed horsehair sofa, seemingly admiring the decor.

She had put on spectacles in the intervening moments, and her similarity to Jessie Logan was even stronger. I cautioned myself against warming to a woman simply because she reminded me of Merchiston's housekeeper.

'There's no' a great deal I have on them. As I said, Clara Wilson was never one of my girls and she wasnae one to break a confidence.'

I slumped back in my seat, defeated. So I had made a wasted visit and missed my afternoon lectures for a wild goose chase.

'Dinnae look so disheartened, Miss Gilchrist – I said she was a close one. But families like that, they pay calls. They visit friends for an afternoon. And those friends? They have servants too. Now, let's see . . . Nothing on your young man, you'll be glad to hear. If he's ever touched a woman in his life, he went elsewhere. And nothing from the valets and footmen in case you wondered if he buttered his bread on the other side.' I stared at her blankly before comprehension dawned, and from her wicked cackle and the heat of my face I guessed that I was blushing. 'The elder brother, though . . . he's been acting like the head of the family for years. He might be the favoured son, but I placed a footman with them a wee while back who said he and his father were at loggerheads. Seems Pa wasn't ready to take a step back and Alisdair was champing at the bit to gallop forwards. Wouldnae be hard to bump the colonel off and make it look like an accident.'

It had, until I had involved myself. Had I not voiced my suspicions about his father's murder Miles might be walking free. Yet even if I had known that calling for justice would see a man imprisoned for something he didn't do, I might have done it anyway. Stubborn as I was, I would see justice done, and not only for Miles.

'As for the lady of the house, she kept herself busy. Paid calls, threw parties, endowed this charity and that almshouse with her money and other people's.'

'But she could have had a lover?'

'If she did, she was discreet. Stained sheets are hard to hide when you don't know how to wash them yourself. Of course,' she added with a filthy laugh, 'clean-up's far easier if you don't do it in a bed.'

I felt a hot flush of shame as two images fought for my attention – one a fantasy, one a memory. Merchiston's mouth against mine, the edge of his desk digging into my back. The juddering, jarring sensation of Paul Beresford inside me – and afterwards, his handkerchief offered to mop up the evidence of his pleasure and my virginity.

'Steady, lass. You've gone a bit green. Aren't you doctors supposed to have strong stomachs?'

'I'm all right,' I forced a smile. 'Just a little warm. Could I have a glass of water?'

She nodded and rang the bell before eyeing me with a penetrating stare.

'You don't like me, I can see that. You don't like what I do, what's in those files of mine. But it's my business to know what goes on in other people's houses. I'll no' send one of my girls in only to find her darkening my door six months later with a swollen belly from a master exercising his *droit de seigneur*, or beaten black and blue because some hoity-toity madam loses her temper every time her tea gets cold. I know more about the quality families in this city than they do themselves. If someone treats a girl poorly, I can make sure it doesn't happen to the next one. And my girls look out for each other. There's not a gentleman in this city whose wandering hands I don't have an eye on, and it's saved more than one young lady from ruin.'

A servant arrived with my water and I gulped it down gratefully, rinsing the bile from my mouth.

'You see everything, Mrs Fredericks. So tell me this: who killed Clara Wilson?'

She sighed heavily. 'Someone desperate. And there's plenty of those around, I can tell you.'

'If you hear anything . . .'

'I'll send a note via my sister. That master of hers helped me out of a tricky spot once before. She and I may only talk to argue, but I owe him the kind of debt that's not easy to repay.'

As I walked out onto North Castle Street, I felt the sun on my face but I couldn't shake off the shadows. My gut twisted, and I remembered the fate of the last woman I had asked for help. Ruby McAllister hadn't been so very different from Celia Fredericks, beyond not trading in her role administering the oldest profession for something less sordid. But she had given me answers when I needed them and wound up dead for it. If anything happened to Mrs Logan's sister now, it would be on my head.

Chapter 26

The sheet of paper fluttered in the breeze. It should have been innocuous, just another announcement from the powers-that-be in amongst the timetables, advertisements for public lectures and reminders that any borrowed medical equipment must be signed out, approved by a professor and returned within two days.

But it might as well have been an incendiary device.

'Congratulations, Baxter! All that swotting over books while the rest of us were out enjoying life clearly paid off.'

Baxter looked more than a little unsettled by the attention, a ruddy blush covering his cheeks, but I was sure that the two hundred pounds awarded to the student with the highest marks in first-year biology would compensate for that. Except that his hadn't been the highest marks and the Matthew Harkup prize should by rights have gone to Julia, whose name was nowhere to be seen.

Nor, for that matter, was Julia.

'She's locked herself in the cloakroom,' Alison whispered. 'She won't speak to anyone except Edith, and even she's been thrown out. I heard her cursing the entire university at one point, and I think she broke a chair.'

'She needs to calm down,' Moira grimaced. 'The last thing

any of us needs is accusations of hysteria and getting over-emotional about our work.'

If I were in Julia's position – unlikely, since a good few marks stood between us – I would have broken more than a chair. And if she had won the Harkup, fair and square though it might have been, the men would have rioted. We hadn't even been permitted to sit in the same examination room; of course our work was judged as lesser. The university might have patted itself on the back for its enlightened attitude in helping shape the modern woman who would enter the next century with a prestigious education under her belt, but it was all talk. A full term had not acclimatised the men to our presence. Even now, our cloakroom was invaded by the odd man who claimed to have forgotten its new purpose. We were constantly shuffled out of sight, only to have the small spaces we were given resented by students who had the run of the place, who didn't need to be followed around by chaperones, who were never on the receiving end of disapproving looks from professors simply for getting an answer right, and who were rewarded for worse performance.

It was clear as day that while the medical school enjoyed its reputation as a progressive institution open to all, it didn't actually want us to take up the invitation. Julia might not have needed the money, but when we would have to compete with the men for the same jobs in an environment no more welcoming than this, the prize would have been a boon.

We trooped into our next lecture, mutinous and spoiling for a fight. Luckily, Professor Williamson was on hand to put flame to touchpaper as he stood looking genuinely bemused that we were even objecting.

'As the female students benefit from smaller class numbers and therefore more individual attention, it was felt that it would be unfair not to take that into account when awarding the Harkup,' he said slowly and patiently, in a tone we hadn't heard since he had explained the skeletal structure of the body in our first week in a manner more suited to a child or a simpleton. 'Therefore Iain Baxter, who had the highest mark of any student taught in the . . . ah, *conventional* manner, took this year's prize.'

'We're only taught separately because the faculty insists!' Edith snapped. 'We learn the same things, sit the same exams and work just as hard. If you threw us in with the men, Julia would still have received the highest marks and you know it.'

'It is no use speculating on what marks Miss Latymer may or may not have received, particularly since she is absent from today's lecture.'

I had thought it would take wild horses or plague to stop Julia attending classes – none of us wanted to miss a moment of this chance we had been granted, and as a consequence the same cold had been passed around the female student body since November. Little Caroline Carstairs – herself currently stuffed up and sniffling for the fourth time – had once attended class with a vomiting bug that left us all faintly revolted and Professor Turner's shoes significantly worse for wear.

'It's her monthly,' Edith said with a sweet smile that showed nothing in her eyes and all of her teeth.

Williamson went ashen. He was more than happy to see women bleed on the operating table, and I had seen him perform a flawless hysterectomy, scooping the organ out with so delicate a touch he could have been holding a child, but the reality of us occupying his space with our messy bodily functions unsettled him to his core.

Moira nodded in sympathy; I knew for a fact that she currently had a hot brick wrapped in muslin pressed against her belly to ease her own aches. I had never expected to miss my cycle, something I had always found messy and inconvenient until it had been taken from me by doctors in the hope that it would subdue my rage against a world that treated women –

that had treated me – with such disdain. Now I felt as though there was yet another experience my peers shared that excluded me. I tried not to resent them for it – a task made easier when the faculty had provided me with such an excellent target for any pent-up emotion – but it was a relief when Williamson pulled back the sheet from the dissection table and provided us with a nice severed arm to focus on.

We were not permitted to dissect it ourselves today – he had clearly decided, probably wisely, that a gaggle of angry women should not be allowed to play with knives. Although we worked assiduously, there was a restlessness beneath the surface, a desire for rebellion, and when Julia returned to us ready for a botany lecture, no trace of her feelings evident save in reddened eyes and white knuckles, she offered the perfect outlet.

'We need a meeting,' she announced. 'We can't let them treat us like this, and if we don't fight back then that's exactly what they'll do. I propose we sit down and plan our next steps. I've asked Elisabeth Chalmers if she can find out which professors voted on the decision, and then I say we boycott their lectures.'

'And whom does that benefit exactly?' Moira asked. 'They won't reverse the decision now they've announced it, and we'll end up weeks behind, which is exactly where they want us anyway.'

'Then you come up with a better idea,' Julia snapped.

'No one's coming up with any ideas standing out in the freezing cold,' Alison groaned. 'I heard it was going to snow tonight and I plan on getting in front of the fire before that happens. After Christmas my brother John helped me smuggle a bottle of brandy from my father's cabinet by hiding it in a hatbox. I haven't had a moment to open it, but it could be just the thing for a cold night and a bad mood. Better than the glorified dust my landlady passes off as cocoa, at any rate.'

'My aunt won't even let me have cocoa,' I sighed. 'She says it excites the nerves.' Personally, I blamed a recent issue of *Cornhill* magazine, which described it as 'the undergraduette's hot beverage of choice', complete with illustrations of girls drinking the offending liquid while clearly planning some unladylike sedition such as loosening their corset laces.

'I'm surprised she doesn't just lock you away in a padded cell like a madwoman,' Alison said. It was on the tip of my tongue to confess that my family had tried just that before giving up and abandoning me to a university education. God knows what my aunt would do if I failed to come home in favour of drinking brandy from a teacup and reading the *Ladies' Enquirer*.

'I'm sorry I've been distant,' I sighed. 'I'm trying so hard to be all things to all people that I'm neglecting what I came here for in the first place.'

'An education?'

'And the company of like-minded women. If I have to listen to another complaint about how difficult it is to hire reliable servants, or someone bragging about their latest haul at a shoot, I'm going to scream.'

'So don't. Come back to our boarding house and we'll have an evening of intellectual conversation and putting the world to rights.'

I thought about Calhoun, my uncle's driver, dispatched to shuttle me from lecture theatre to doorstep every day, lest I get some foolish notion in my head about freedom. I thought about my aunt and her dressmaker and the myriad faults they would find with my figure the moment I walked through the door.

'That's a wonderful idea. I'll send Aunt Emily a note immediately.'

'Will she let you?' Alison looked doubtful.

'Not if I lie about where I'm going.' I grinned wickedly. 'Elisabeth! I have a favour to ask . . .'

That evening saw me curled up on a lumpy armchair, sipping hot cocoa liberally laced with brandy, as Julia critiqued the intellect – and physique – of the male students.

'And Barrowman! The only exams he hasn't failed are the ones where he was a patient.'

'You know, this isn't half bad,' Edith pronounced, topping up her bone-china teacup.

'Drinking alcoholic cocoa with a fallen woman?' I asked, tartly. Perhaps there was a little more brandy in this than I had realised.

'How would you know?' Julia gave Edith a lazy, teasing smile. 'Your parents never touched a drop of the demon drink.'

Edith kicked her illicit paramour. 'We weren't all raised by bohemians who drank champagne at breakfast.'

I snorted. 'Julia's parents were only bohemians by London society standards. I suspect actual bohemians would have found them rather tame.'

'How well did you know each other?' Caroline asked curiously, brandy blunting the edge of her usual shyness.

'Friends of friends. My people found the Latymers altogether too liberal for their tastes.'

'And my mother thought your mother was a prig.'

'She must be disappointed with you, then.' The words left my mouth before I could stop them. 'Moralistic lectures, temperance, and judgement that would make a preacher proud? Not exactly the Latymer way, as I recall.'

'She doesn't understand,' Julia said fiercely. Her colour was high but her knuckles were white where she gripped her cup and saucer. 'It's all very well to entertain artists and poets and degenerates when all you have to do is make sure your party is more gossip-worthy than the next. But when you're a doctor, you have to be above reproach. And when you're a lady doctor, you have to be twice as pure just to prove you haven't been corrupted by your knowledge of human anatomy.'

'Yes, all those dissected male limbs do get a girl's pulse racing,' Alison said drily. We collapsed in hysterical giggles.

'So what happens tomorrow?' Moira asked. 'Do we put our dreary cloaks of respectability on again and go back to hating Sarah for bringing down our collective moral standing?'

'Sarah doesn't care either way,' I said obstinately. 'She was perfectly happy without being inducted into your coven of judgemental witches.'

'Then leave,' Edith groaned. Julia shot her a look.

I thought about my aunt's house, the ghost of my mother's disapproval still lingering in the air, and topped up my cup.

'I'm not spending time with you. I'm spending time with the brandy.'

'Rather a lot of it, as well. Leave some for the rest of us, you drunkard.'

With everything that had happened in the past year, I was no longer certain if I believed in a glorious afterlife with angels and ambrosia, but I knew one thing: if heaven did exist, it was a room full of women arguing about politics and drinking hot cocoa.

Chapter 27

Hours later, Moira was trying to pick an argument about the suffrage movement, Carstairs had nodded off over a botany textbook, and somewhere along the line we had run out of cocoa.

'You know, it was a year ago today.' I raised my cup in a mock toast.

'It?' Alison frowned.

'*It*. The end of all my mother's hopes and dreams. In memory of my virtue, ladies.' I downed the dregs of my brandy in one gulp.

'Maybe you shouldn't drink any more.'

'That's what my mother said. Maybe I shouldn't enjoy myself quite so much, maybe I shouldn't talk endlessly about medicine to whomever would listen. Maybe I shouldn't be alone with a man in a library at a party. Well, she was right about that one.'

'Did it hurt?' Moira looked at me frankly.

'I had bruises for a week. Five fingertip-shaped marks around my thigh where he held my legs open. He bit my lip until it bled and then he licked the blood. And yes, Moira, you voyeuristic cat, it bloody hurt. I thought I was being ripped apart. I didn't even know what was happening until he started . . .' Grunting. Thrusting. I could feel his sour, liquor-laced breath on my cheek, hear him taking his pleasure through gritted teeth and injunctions to be quiet.

'Oh Lord.' I heard Julia's voice as though it were very far away. 'Alison, get that hatbox.'

I vomited profusely.

When I woke, Alison was sitting on the edge of my bed. Well, someone's bed at any rate.

'Julia gave up her bed and went in with Edith. She said you could take hers but that she was billing any damage to you.'

I winced, and then winced again because that made my head hurt.

'Was I an utter fool?'

'You were just enjoying yourself. Until, well, until you weren't.' Alison paused, uncertain of how to proceed. 'Sarah, you said something last night . . .'

Cold horror curdled inside me. I had spilled my secrets, but who else's had I told? Merchiston would never forgive me if I had spoken about Lucy – and if I had mentioned how Fiona Leadbetter had died, he would be facing a short trip to the hangman's noose. As I had survived the night in one piece – every part of me hurt enough that I could be sure of that – at least I hadn't mentioned the real reason why Julia was happy to share a bed with Edith, or how often it presumably happened.

I racked my brains, but everything was fuzzy. 'What? What did I say?'

'You were clearly in your cups . . .'

I winced, rubbing my pounding head. 'I think I was in everyone's cups.'

'True. But you had a perfectly good reason. Why didn't you ever tell me what that bastard did to you?'

I felt raw, exposed. Why had I told them? It was bad enough that they had thought me loose, immoral. Now they knew I was weak.

'Does it matter?' I asked in a small voice. 'He still did it. Took my virtue and left my good name in tatters. Everything Julia says about me is right, you know. It all happened.'

'But you didn't want it to.'

'Didn't I?' God, I must still be drunk. I felt my cheeks turn wet with tears, but I couldn't stop myself. 'He chose me. Out of all the girls at that party, all the girls in London, he did that to me. He must have seen something that made him think I'd want to . . .'

Alison hugged me tightly, and let me cry like I hadn't in months.

'Well, I don't think it counts,' she said stoutly. 'He did something to you, but he didn't take anything.'

'He took everything! My reputation, my family. My home. I'm being forced into a marriage I don't want because no one else will have me. My parents didn't want me to become a doctor like yours and Moira's did; they wanted me out of the way and off their hands. And now, thanks to Aunt Emily and the Greenes, they might actually manage it if Miles is found innocent.'

'Everyone is forced into a marriage they don't want. That's the way of the world. The only escape is to lock yourself up in a nunnery or a university.'

'Would your parents rather you married?'

'I think they've given up hoping. They think I'm batty, but they love me for it.'

I smiled. 'So do we. Now leave me alone to suffer in peace before I throw up over more of your wardrobe.'

When I awoke hours later, dehydrated but feeling slightly more robust, it was to Elisabeth Chalmers standing at the end of the bed, looking unimpressed and flicking water from a glass at my face.

'Finally!'

I scowled. 'I've seen you get giggly over one too many

glasses of champagne, Mrs Chalmers. Your judgement doesn't work on me.'

'You threw up into Alison Thornhill's hatbox!'

I paused. 'Did she remove her hat?'

'I believe she did not.'

I groaned. 'Judge away, Elisabeth. I'd spend the rest of my life in sackcloth and ashes if it meant not moving from this bed.'

'You'll have to. I'm bundling you into the carriage and dunking you into a scalding-hot bath until you stop smelling like . . . like . . . *that*.'

'Give me five minutes to make myself look vaguely presentable.'

I quickly plaited my hair and straightened my dress before scrawling an apology to Alison on the back of an aborted Biology essay.

'You look terrible.'

Julia was leaning against the door frame, studying me.

She glanced down at the note. 'Is that your idea of an apology? "Sorry about the hatbox. And the hat. Will repay you as soon as I can. PS Can I borrow your notes from today?" If I hadn't met your mother myself, I'd suspect you were raised by wolves.'

'I'll send her a proper apology on scented notepaper.'

'Don't bother. I'll rewrite it and copy your handwriting.'

'You can forge my handwriting?'

'I can forge anyone's. How else did you think I got out of being late to last week's anatomy lecture? I doubt the university chaplain could pick me out of a crowd, let alone invite me to speak to his prayer circle.'

I was starting to think that Julia Latymer had some very well-hidden depths.

She looked at me with an unreadable expression. 'You were brave last night.'

'That wasn't bravery, it was brandy.'

'Your secret made people pity you. Mine would make them hate me. And Edith! My family would be appalled, but hers would cast her out completely. You know how that feels. Please don't do that to her.'

'Isn't your family so frightfully daring?'

'On the surface. But it doesn't matter how many witty, flamboyant playwrights they have to dinner; if they found out their only child was a Sapphist, they'd be mortified. It's bad enough I'm a scholar – they think all female students are tweed-clad and monocled and have whiskers. Men of that sort have flair. Women like me are just mannish and ghastly.'

'Neither you nor Edith is mannish, and it wouldn't matter a jot if you were. You're brilliant and loyal – even if what you're being loyal to is a grudge – and Edith's mad about you, although I can't for a moment imagine why. Poor girl, she has worse taste than Carstairs with her pash on that porter who brings in the dead frogs to dissect.'

'She goes bright red and looks as though she's going to be sick! I thought it was the frogs until I saw the way she stared at him.'

'Are frogs' legs a known aphrodisiac?'

'Even if they are, I don't think their guts have quite the same effect.'

It was strange, to laugh with someone I thought I hated. Alison had once told me that the reason Julia and I drove each other mad was because we had so much in common, and I was starting to wonder if it was true.

A horrifying new thought occurred to me.

'Are we . . . friends?'

She raised her eyebrows. 'Perish the thought. If we were friends, I'd feel guilty about trouncing you in next week's chemistry test. As it is, I'm quite looking forward to it. But don't worry, she smirked. 'I promise I'll be generous in victory, Gilchrist.'

'Not if I have anything to do with it, Latymer.'

Somehow I managed to make it back to Warrender Park Crescent without losing the contents of my stomach again, and by the time I had bathed, drunk copious quantities of coffee and attired myself in one of the spare dresses I kept in Elisabeth's armoire in case of chemical spillages or the wear and tear from chasing murder suspects, I could finally face the world again. I realised that although I still felt physically dreadful, I was more at peace than I had been for quite some time – at least until I found the letter tucked into the bottom of my bag.

> *Miss Gilchrist*
>
> *It has come to my attention that your behaviour prior to commencing your studies has not been what one would expect from a doctor – and certainly not from a lady. Your illicit relations with Paul Beresford and the fact that you are no longer, shall we say,* virgo intacta, *means that you are, as you doubtless know, in breach of the morality clause you signed on matriculation. Should this be made public, your studies would be at an end. However, this could be avoided with the payment of the sum of fifty pounds delivered in cash to the address below.*

I couldn't bear to read on. My fists crumpled the paper and I thrust it back in my bag, but its presence lingered as painfully and insistently as a megrim. As the carriage swayed down North Bridge, I felt sick from more than just the brandy. I hadn't intended to open up to the others about my past, to correct their assumptions about me by dredging up a secret so painful I would have done anything to forget it. But I had, and now I was to be repaid like this. With a vile note threatening to expose me to the entire medical school unless I paid the writer a sum more than three times my monthly allowance. Clearly whoever had written it had not been present for my litany of complaints about my lack of funds, or realised how dependent I was on my relatives for even bed and board. That was why I lived with Aunt Emily and Uncle Hugh – not out of a desire for home comforts, but because even if it cost me the freedom my friends enjoyed, it came at a price I could at least afford.

Anyone could have had access to my bag the previous night. None of us had exactly been keeping track of our personal possessions – hence the ruined contents of Alison's hatbox – and it would have been easy for someone to discreetly slip out, pen the hideous thing and then slip it into my bag. But why now, when we had come to a truce? When every woman there knew that I wasn't the slut the note described, but the recipient of a drunken man's ardour and entitlement? It couldn't have been one of them. And besides, I wasn't the only one to have been blackmailed recently.

Summoning my courage, I read the letter to the end and what I found chilled my blood.

> *In addition, your unladylike curiosity around the death of COLONEL GREENE and his servant reflect poorly on you and your family. Should you cease these activities immediately, further correspondence will not be required. If, however, you fail to do so, further monies may be required.*

I banged on the carriage roof and called the driver to change direction. There had been only one person who could have had access to both my bag and the Greene household. It seemed that my trust had been betrayed after all.

Chapter 28

I could have climbed the steps to the Greenes' town house and been escorted to the drawing room to wait in comfort, but that wouldn't have given me the answer I wanted. Instead, I stamped my feet trying to ward off the cold as I waited by the kitchen door for the cook to emerge. I lurked there for nearly an hour, trying not to breathe in the stink of rotten vegetables and household refuse. I was flicking through my anatomy textbook with freezing fingers when the door finally creaked open and the hatchet-faced woman stepped into the street. I wasn't close enough for her to see me, but I was downwind. Was that Aurora's scent she was wearing? I had ascertained that Mrs Parry took a walk in the early afternoon and that, several doors down, the butler chose that same time to take his daily constitutional. I wondered what her mistress would think of a servant liberally dousing herself with expensive perfume for an illicit assignation with a man. Then again, she had bigger concerns – and so did I.

Once I was satisfied that Parry was far enough away, I slipped through the door she had left from. Sure enough, it led to the kitchen, where my latest line of enquiry sat drinking tea and darning a pair of stockings.

'Good afternoon, Blackwell.'

Had I not been standing between her and the door, I think the maid would have run the same way as her superior, but seeing the expression on my face, she seemed to collapse in on herself.

'Would you like to be shown in, Miss Gilchrist?' she asked listlessly, as though I had entered the usual way to pay a perfectly normal social call. The question was rhetorical, and we both knew it.

'It's you I've come to see,' I said, trying to make my voice sound as cheerful and confiding as possible. 'Could you spare a moment of your time? I know that with Clara Wilson gone you'll all be at sixes and sevens . . .'

Blackwell snorted. 'They cannae get a replacement for love nor money. And the tweeny left this morning, saying her father wouldn't let her stay in the house one minute longer.'

If the family was even losing the between-stairs maid, things must be worse than I realised.

'But not you?'

Blackwell shook her head fiercely. 'Whoever did that awful thing, it wasnae Master Miles. He'll be out soon enough, and he'll need a friendly face.'

I removed my coat and tossed my hat onto the table, making it clear that, unlike half the household staff, I wasn't going anywhere.

'Your confidence in him is impressive. Then again, you're good at ferreting out secrets, aren't you?' She paled and watched me like a hawk as I pulled out the letter. 'You put this in my bag, didn't you?' She nodded, eyes welling with tears. 'And the arsenic and jewellery, did you plant those in Miles' room?'

She shook her head so violently, a few hairpins tumbled out. 'I've never seen the stuff before in my life, miss, I swear! I cleaned his room good and proper, the way I always did, even though I'm doing for Mrs Greene now – Minnie, the tweeny as was, she was terrified of cleaning the men's rooms. Thought that's how you get pregnant.' She smiled wryly, and I wondered if she realised that she had just revealed her own lack of innocence in that regard. 'All I can say is that it wasnae there when I swept it that morning. The polis said it was in a drawer with his . . .' she blushed, and dropped her voice to a whisper, 'his *underthings*, but I'd put fresh laundry in there and I didnae see a thing.'

'There was nowhere else he might have kept it if he knew you were likely to be opening the drawers? No safe, nothing with a lock?'

Blackwell smiled fondly. 'He was never that cunning, miss. He kept your letters beneath his pillow, along with a miniature. I don't think it would have occurred to him to hide them anywhere else.'

My stomach roiled with guilt. Here I was, hoping that the scandal would set me free from my engagement, and the man to whom I had reluctantly pledged my troth had been keeping my letters and picture with him as he slept. As to how he had obtained the latter, I suspected Aunt Emily's hand at work.

'Do you have feelings for Master Miles, Blackwell?'

'He's nice. Gentle. There's plenty in this world who aren't.' A fact of which I was well aware. 'I may be young, but I'm no' foolish. Even the nicest gentlemen don't marry their maids, especially if they're already engaged.' She bit her lip. 'I didnae like giving you that letter, miss. Not that I read it,' she added hastily, 'but if he wanted me to slip it in your bag all secretive like, I knew it couldnae be anything good.'

I leaned forward. Now we were getting somewhere. 'Who gave you the letter?'

She shrugged helplessly. 'If I knew, I'd be straight to the polis. It's no' fair, threatening respectable people like that, no matter what foolish things they may have done.'

'You received a letter as well?'

She nodded, mouth set in a grim line. Her earlier flightiness was gone, replaced by quiet resignation.

'The blackmailer . . . he knew something about my past, something very few people here are aware of. He threatened to expose me, tell the whole university if I don't leave this whole sorry affair alone.'

'But here you are, miss.' Blackwell smiled sadly. 'It must be nice not to have to be afraid.'

I wanted to tell her that I was terrified, that part of me wanted to run back to my safe, quiet life with my textbooks and experiments, where the most dangerous thing I had to do was avoid Aunt Emily's wrath. But one of us needed to be fearless, and she had more to lose than I did.

'The secret the letter-writer threatened me with . . . When I told Miles, I thought he'd want nothing more than to be rid of me. But he was kind. He saw past all that and wanted me anyway. Lord knows why.' Miles, Merchiston – why was it that the thing that had ruined my faith in men seemed to spark the deepest sympathy and bring out the best in some of them? 'Perhaps he would have done the same for you.'

'Ladies can get away with things the rest of us can't.' By rights, she should have been bitter. But this was the way the world worked, and after running around after her employers day and night, she had no energy left to fight it. 'I've got a child, miss. A son. Leastways, I did.' She gnawed her lip, and I saw the dots of blood her teeth left behind. 'He lives with my sister out in Musselburgh. She did well for herself, married a grocer. They can't have children, but they can give him a better life than me. I'd be out on my ear if anyone knew.'

She was such a slip of a thing, it was hard to imagine her with a sweetheart, let alone carrying a child. But there were girls in the slums pregnant barely a year into their menses, and women of my own social circle younger than I was who were already celebrating wedding anniversaries. Blackwell reminded me a little of Gertie, who would be married off the moment she was out of finishing school if my mother had any say in the matter.

I had so many questions: about the father, why they hadn't married, if her son knew who she was or just saw her as a devoted aunt. But what right did I have to ask any of them? What right did the Greenes have to know that once upon a time, their housemaid had been a mother? I doubted that anyone even remembered her first name, but they would expect to know this.

I squeezed her hand. 'You must miss him horribly. I won't tell a soul, I swear.'

The tears that had been glossing her eyes finally started to fall, and I hugged her close, not caring that her apron was smudged with coal from the grate.

'If I lose this job, I've nothing to send him. My sister says he's a bright boy, he could make something of himself. We're saving to send him to school, even if all he does is take over the shop. If I cannae raise him myself, I'll do everything I can to give him a good life. That's why . . .' She broke off. 'Oh, Miss Gilchrist! That's why I sent the letter to the polis telling them to look in Master Miles' room. That letter-writer, he said if I refused, he'd have my brother-in-law's shop closed down, and then what would happen to my wee Jack? I didnae think anything would come of it, not then – I thought it was just mischief. If I'd known . . .'

'You'd have done exactly the same thing and no one would have blamed you for it. Even Master Miles,' I said, hoping I was right. The moral high ground was easy to take when one wasn't behind bars eating lukewarm gruel for every meal. 'I don't suppose you kept either of the letters?'

She shook her head. 'Threw them in the fire where they belong. You'd be wise to do the same.'

Tempting as it was, the details of my disgrace made for

useful evidence, and burning the letter wouldn't erase the truth, no matter how cathartic it might be. There would always be someone who would delight in spreading the sordid tale, whether I was a blushing bride or a qualified doctor. The only way was forwards, setting my face against the wind of public opinion, turning the handful of people who couldn't give a fig about my lost virginity into a makeshift family of my own. And even if Blackwell could have wished her shame away, I saw from the burning maternal devotion in her eyes that she wouldn't.

I pressed a note into her hand as I rose. 'Buy him a present. Spend the rest on a ribbon or some roast chestnuts; there's a seller on Princes Street. Whatever you like. And if you ever want to leave the Greenes, I'll write you a reference.'

She might have no choice. How far down the family tree did this poison spread? If news of the sorry affair came out, there could well be a household of servants with no family to look after and a second-hand stain on their characters. Blackwell might need someone to vouch for her to an employer reluctant to be tainted by leftover scandal. Not that my recommendation was likely to mean more: the would-be lady doctor with a broken engagement and her own whispers of ruin to contend with.

A sharp whiff of Esprit de Vervein and a few bars of 'A Little of What You Fancy' hummed off-key heralded the arrival of the cook – who, if her mussed hair was anything to go by, had had rather more than a little – and I hurriedly pulled on my coat and hat, as though I had only just arrived.

She started when she saw me, and I beamed my most charming smile. 'Mrs Parry, just the woman I came to see. My aunt has talked about nothing else but your *boeuf en daube* since the other night, and I thought I'd surprise her with the recipe if you can possibly be parted from it.'

Preening, the older woman was more than happy to divulge

her trade secrets, although if she really thought that the principal topic of conversation about a dinner party where one of the hosts had died was the food, her vanity knew no bounds. Still, it was a convincing pretext – and the beef had been rather nice.

She pressed a cup of tea on me, chiding Blackwell for not having offered me one, and I realised how tired I was. The remnants of my hangover, held at bay thanks to my unexpected correspondence and the freezing weather, were starting to make themselves known, and I gulped down the hot liquid gratefully. Had I not indulged in idle conversation about the weather and stayed for a second piece of shortbread, I could have made my escape and left the upstairs residents none the wiser. As it was, I still had a mouthful of sugary crumbs when Alisdair Greene descended to the kitchen, stopping dead in his tracks when he saw me.

'Miss Gilchrist! I wasn't aware you had arrived.' He shot Blackwell a dark glance. 'I do hope you were greeted properly.'

I waved the recipe for *boeuf en daube*, a meal I was already getting sick of before my aunt's cook had even prepared it. 'A domestic errand. Far too trivial for me to disturb you with, especially now . . .' I trailed off. His father had died, his brother had been arrested and there I was prattling on about French cooking.

'Believe me, Miss Gilchrist, you're a pleasant distraction.' He held out his arm. 'Allow me to escort you to more salubrious surroundings. Parry, send some more tea and biscuits. And something light for dinner; Mother doesn't have much of an appetite and I'll be eating at the hotel.'

'You aren't staying here?' The thought that Aurora had been left all alone with her grief was awful.

He shuddered. 'I've been trying to persuade Mother to leave as well, but she insists. I think it helps her feel closer to him.' He glanced at me, almost shyly. 'I'm not saying that I believe in ghosts, but this house has seen too much tragedy lately. I need to be strong for Mother, not jumping at shadows.'

The woman in question was sitting by the fire, gazing into it with a picture frame lying limply in her hands. A wedding portrait, I realised with a pang.

'I've called for some more tea, Mother,' Alisdair said softly.

She glanced up after a moment, registering her son's presence. When she saw me, what little colour she had drained from her face.

'What is she doing here?' she spat. 'You've been nothing but trouble since you came into our lives, Miss Gilchrist. I rue the day my son ever met you. I should have known better than to bring some bluestocking slut into my house.'

'Mother!' Alisdair looked shocked. 'None of this was Sarah's fault.'

'Miles was a good boy until he met you,' she said, dabbing her eyes furiously with a handkerchief. I recognised Colonel Greene's initials on the linen, and for all the spite she directed at me, my heart went out to her.

'Miles is troubled,' Alisdair said gently. 'We all love him, but he isn't . . . Well, I think we can agree that Sarah has had a lucky escape.'

'I should leave,' I said quietly. 'I can see how my presence must be distressing – to all of you.'

Out in the hall, Alisdair put his hand on my arm. 'I'm sorry about that. Mother is very upset; she didn't mean what she said.' I suspected she meant every word, but this wasn't the time to argue. 'Under the circumstances . . . Gads, this is awkward. My father and your uncle were close, and I'd hate to deprive him of the opportunity to pay his respects, but . . .'

'You would rather I didn't attend the funeral,' I surmised.

He grimaced. 'Believe me, I would be only too happy to have you with us.' He paused. 'Miss Gilchrist, on behalf of my family, please accept my sincerest apologies for all you have suffered. This should have been the happiest time of your life, and instead it has turned into a tragedy. Rest assured I will do everything in my power to ensure that you are not brushed with even the slightest taint of scandal.'

It was a little late for that, but it seemed churlish to point it out.

He took my hand in his. His thumb grazed mine – the slightest of movements, not enough to call a deliberate caress, and yet . . . If he had a point, I thought, he had better come to it quickly.

'I know Miles can't have been your first choice, even without prior knowledge of his true nature. And, unfortunately it's the case that a woman studying medicine might be off-putting to some men – many men, even. But if I can assist you in finding a suitable replacement, shall we say, then it would be my honour.'

I seized my chance.

'If only I could find a man like you, Mr Greene.'

I knew his next line before he said it.

'Please, call me Alisdair.'

He pressed something into my palm. 'My card. If you find yourself in need of a friend, I would be honoured if you would call upon me.'

On the back of the card was the name of his hotel, scrawled in black ink. It was discreet enough that I could call on him without the whole of Edinburgh watching, but expensive enough to indicate his new station in life. I had a feeling that behind its expensive and discreet doors I would find at least some of the answers I sought, providing I didn't mind sacrificing my propriety, and perhaps much more.

Chapter 29

We stood outside the dean's office, huddled together as close to the door as we could get. Edith chewed a fingernail as the sound of raised voices drifted out from the room.

'. . . simply cannot expect us to bend the rules for the sake of one student.'

'The best student. The best student in the whole damn year and you know it. The results are there, in black and white.'

The heavy oak door was designed to muffle the deep, sonorous voices of serious men. It did little to silence Julia's clear, ringing tones.

'Miss Latymer, mind your language! We will not tolerate such behaviour, especially from a lady.'

'Go to hell!'

This last was perfectly audible, because Julia had yanked open the door and stormed into the corridor with a face like thunder and suspiciously wet eyes.

'Don't cry,' Edith whispered. 'Don't give them the satisfaction of thinking that you're weak.'

'It doesn't matter,' she said in flat, defeated tones. 'They already think it. Too weak to be a doctor, too stupid to get the Harkup prize. Too bloody female to be of any use to anyone.'

She let Edith enfold her in her arms, and that was enough

for me to see how affected she was. Although they were invariably at one another's side, there was always a distance between them that was lacking in the rest of us, jostling and roughhousing as we did. Alison would elbow me, tug my arm, rest her head on my shoulder in mock exhaustion, but Julia and Edith rarely touched. Of course, I was sure that it was different behind closed doors and I felt a flush creep onto my face at the thought. But the boundaries between them in public, seemingly so necessary for keeping their secret, looked horribly lonely at times.

We retired to an empty classroom, Julia quiet but the rest of us boiling over with rage. Or most of us, at any rate.

'It's not as though you need the money,' Moira pointed out caustically.

'That isn't the point,' Alison argued. 'It's a prize for coming top of the year, not a scholarship. Julia came top, therefore it's hers by right.'

'But she doesnae need to worry about how she'll pay next term's fees, does she?'

'I'm right here,' Julia muttered crossly, wiping her eyes. 'And you're right, I don't, but neither do most of the men. It's just another reward for fitting the mould that's been created for them, and no matter what I do, I'll always break it. My money can't protect me from that, Moira. It's the one bloody way I do fit in, and I won't apologise for it.'

'Sometimes I think I should just have cut my hair, worn trousers and told everyone my name was Alexander,' Alison sighed. 'It would have been a damn sight easier.'

I looked at my friend, as soft and rounded as I was sharp and angular, with a voluptuousness that not even trousers would disguise.

'I don't think that would have worked,' I noted drily.

'Maybe she's right,' Julia said, so softly that I could barely hear her. 'If we can't be accepted for who we are, perhaps we should just pretend and hope we can convince someone.'

I didn't think she was just talking about her gender, and I realised how heavily her secret must weigh on her.

'I'd make an excellent boy; my father always told me that. I could run faster than my male cousins, I was always clever. I could have had the life I've always dreamed of, if only I had been born a boy.'

Edith squeezed her arm. 'I like you just as you are, Julia Latymer. And your patients will too, just you wait and see. Let them keep their dratted Matthew Harkup prize; you'll be covered with garlands and awards once you graduate.'

'I never thought I'd say this, but I think you're all right as you are as well,' I added, not wanting Edith's pronouncement to capture an undue amount of attention. 'I mean, you're a fearful snob and I wouldn't mind your being a fraction less judgemental, but that's not because you're a woman. It's just because you're an awful person. An awful, *brilliant* person.' The others looked on in horror, and Alison let out a shocked 'Gilchrist!'

But Julia met my eyes and, to my relief, burst out laughing, slinging her arm around my shoulders.

'Coming from an immoral slut with the best surgical technique of us all, I'll take that as a compliment.'

We marched out into the hallways of the medical school as a group, united in our anger and, perhaps, finally embracing the things that marked us out as different from our male contemporaries – though no less worthy.

And yet the injustice lingered, and as I undressed for bed that night, I thought of what a prize like that might have meant for me. My family wasn't scrimping and saving every ha'penny for my education, but my position was still precarious. All it would take was one infraction too far for me to find my fees for the term hadn't been – wouldn't be – paid. For all my lofty ideas of independence, I was entirely reliant on their goodwill, and I knew just how fragile that was.

Being welcomed back into the bosom of my family with my marriage to Miles would mean more than just having my parents acknowledge the existence of their eldest daughter once again. As it stood, I was written out of my father's will completely, and while I was hardly waiting for him to expire – not, given his total silence over the past year, that it would make a difference to our relationship – there was no denying that the prospect of an inheritance would give my future some security.

A small bequest from my grandmother was all I had guaranteed, and even that wouldn't be mine for another few years; my father was administering it until then. I knew my fees and expenses came out of it, but he had never told me how much it was and it had never occurred to me to ask. Even when I was cast out of my home, I had always been provided for, had never worried where my next meal was coming from or where I would sleep. For the past year, all I had thought about was surviving: surviving the 'treatments' at the sanatorium, surviving my exams. Surviving Fiona Leadbetter, and now surviving this wretched engagement. If I were to have a future, it would have to be planned for, and I knew that I could not rely on anyone but myself.

I needed to find out the total of my bequest, and if there was any way for me to take control of it sooner. Once I finished my studies, I would need money to support myself – my aunt and uncle had made it crystal clear that hosting a university student was one thing, but having a fully qualified doctor under their roof would be beyond the pale.

It wouldn't be enough to graduate with a degree and high marks. As a woman, the bare minimum wouldn't suffice, nor would I have a supportive family willing to give me food and lodgings while I began to make my way in the world. I could see now that preparing for a career meant so much more than simply good marks and a passion for my subject – the matter of the Harkup prize had taught me that. I needed to start planning for my future, and that meant saving whatever money I could in advance of the days when my aunt and uncle grew tired of the girlish fancies of work and independence that I stubbornly refused to grow out of.

As I removed my earrings, pretty enamel pansies that didn't dangle or get tangled up in my hair but still probably looked far too feminine for such an august institution as the University of Edinburgh, a thought occurred to me. I didn't have an extensive collection of gems, but surely there were some things I could sell if need be.

I opened my jewellery box and examined the contents. I ran my pearls through my fingers, the beads glowing a soft rose in the firelight. They were the most precious thing I owned and I couldn't bear to part with them. But much good they would do me if I were living in penury, unable to afford food and coal. As for the rest, it was all pretty but not deeply sentimental – a gold fern brooch with diamonds studded on the leaves to represent dew, a bracelet of amethysts set in silver, a strand of opals and garnets and a pair of silver filigree earrings. It wasn't much – unlike Aurora, I didn't have enough that it would be easy to dispose of a few items and have it go unnoticed. But a brooch could fall off into the street, a necklace could snap. And a pawnbroker could give me a reasonable sum that I could hide in a textbook until I needed it.

I surveyed my wardrobe, wondering what I could do without. Even if I couldn't sell the finer of my dresses – which I supposed were technically the property of Aunt Emily and Mother, who had after all paid for them in the first place – I couldn't take them with me, either. Even Julia and Alison rotated between two evening gowns on the rare occasions we had cause to wear them, and from what I had seen, their rooms had only a fraction of the space in my bedroom here.

If push came to shove and I needed to find alternative

accommodation, what would I take? Plain, serviceable skirts, smart enough for a ward round or to see patients; one evening gown for any formal events. I could sew well enough to keep them looking fresh for a couple of seasons, providing fashions didn't change too dramatically between now and 1896. I didn't need the soft kid gloves or the linen handkerchiefs. I had brought little with me from my old life – just my jewellery and bible and a few books. Somehow I had put down roots here, built a life and acquired possessions. But I knew I would throw all my worldly goods into a knapsack and carry it on my shoulder like Dick Whittington if I had to.

It could be the answer to my prayers – a gruelling road and one without the security or luxury I was accustomed to, but surely I could do it if I needed to. My fees were twenty-five pounds a year, refectory meals five pounds, and then there were textbooks on top of that. I resolved to ask Alison how much her boarding house cost; even if that proved too much, surely there were cheaper options?

And yet I had never cooked a meal or built a fire. I could open up a man's chest, remove his organs and sew it back up with the hand of a seamstress, but I had never darned a stocking or boiled an egg. Until I came to Edinburgh and began volunteering at St Giles' Infirmary, I had never swept a floor, and it wasn't until I had to manage on the meagre allowance Aunt Emily gave me every month that I had balanced a budget.

How clever it was, to keep us helpless and reliant on the social hierarchy that allegedly offered us freedom, trapped in a delicate web that held us in place. Lacking the skills to support ourselves, no wonder the security of home and hearth was so seductive.

The freedom my peers enjoyed was tantalising, but I couldn't afford to be reckless. If I could only save enough money to keep myself for a year, I could worry about the future when it arrived. I couldn't do that even keeping aside the shillings my aunt grudgingly gave me for expenses, and I couldn't wait four or five years before I had my own income.

I needed something that would horrify my family and risk my total expulsion from any safe harbour they could offer. Something that would guarantee my survival no matter what.

I needed a job.

Chapter 30

'How on earth are you planning on doing that?' Elisabeth stared at me in utter bewilderment. 'I don't even know where one would start.'

'Neither do I,' I groaned. 'It isn't exactly something they taught us at finishing school.'

'Could you ask at the university? Surely they must be able to help.'

'Somehow I suspect they won't have anything suitable. Bad enough I want to study, that I plan on practising medicine in a few years, without hoping to work now. Can you imagine Professor Williamson's expression? He'd collapse in a fit of apoplexy!'

She thought for a moment. 'I don't suppose you could chaperone? You're a little young and horribly unmarried, but if I recommended you . . .'

'They want respectable women of clear virtue,' I reminded her. 'Not lady medics engaged to a murderer whose virginity is a thing of the past.'

'Sarah, if you need money—'

'Then I shall earn it. I need a friend, not a benefactor.' I squeezed her hand. 'But if I ever show up on your doorstep with nothing more than the dress I'm wearing and a bag full of textbooks, I reserve the right to pretend I never said that.'

'Well you won't starve in this house,' she laughed, pushing another slice of cold game pie towards me. I accepted with relish, both metaphorical and literal.

When Randall arrived from his club, smelling of tobacco and whisky, he found us making increasingly elaborate plans for my future, helped in no small part by a bottle of very good sherry.

He frowned. 'Is this about the Harkup prize? I don't agree with the dean's decision, but it is final. No doubt Miss Latymer is disappointed, but at least she can still afford the fees.'

'You mean her parents can.'

He looked bewildered. 'Of course that's what I meant.'

We were all of us at the mercies of others. If Julia's family knew the true nature of her friendship with Edith, she would be as cut off and powerless as I was. Perhaps we should band together, a merry tribe of inverts and harlots, living off our wits. Or perhaps that was the fastest route to the workhouse.

'I need a source of income that doesn't depend on how pleased my family is with me on any given day,' I explained. 'I can't risk being foisted onto another man I don't love without any recourse but my own intellect. I need to know that I can support myself now, not in four or five years when I finish my studies, especially when I can't guarantee I'll make it that long.'

'There must be something you can suggest, darling.' Elisabeth gave her husband a pleading look, and I could see him begin to thaw.

'You're a first-year medical student,' he sighed. 'There's not very much your lot are qualified to do, especially not when you're . . .' He waved a hand at me, too embarrassed or apologetic to refer to my sex by name. Honestly, how did men ever practise medicine when they were so squeamish?

'You know, if Gregory is dragging you around police morgues and prisons, he should at least be compensating you for your assistance.'

It was hard to tell which of us was more horrified.

'I am not his *assistant*!'

'That's quite unacceptable!'

'I'll have you know that he's assisting me, not the other way around.'

'An unmarried woman cannot spend the majority of her time in the company of . . .' Randall trailed off and glared at me. 'Sarah, your commitment to Miles' innocence does you credit, but there are some tasks that Professor Merchiston is better able to undertake, and investigating a murder is one of them.'

I shook my head. 'I can get closer to the family than he can.'

'Just because you can doesn't mean that you should. If your aunt – or, God forbid, your mother – knew that you were putting yourself in danger like this, she'd lock you in your room and barricade the door.'

Which was why I had no intention of letting them find out about my illicit activities. And however much Randall disapproved of them, I knew he wouldn't put my studies at risk.

'Like it or not, I am involved.' I took a deep breath. 'Aurora's blackmailer is targeting me.'

'Over what?' Randall looked utterly bemused, and I realised that while I thought news of my degradation had spread far and wide, it had not reached him. Elisabeth, gem that she was, had kept my secret from the person closest to her.

Still, I didn't relish telling my story to his face. I looked at her pleadingly and she nodded.

'Later, darling,' she murmured. 'Did they write to you at home?'

'Blackwell, the maid, put the letter in my reticule. I found it yesterday.'

Elisabeth's eyes widened. 'That sweet girl is involved? How awful.'

'She had no choice. She was being blackmailed as well, but

instead of money – which she doesn't have – the writer asked her to put the letter in my bag. She has a child who lives with her sister, and if news of him got out, Aurora would dismiss her on the spot.'

'Does she have any idea who it was?'

'Not one. She's terrified, though, poor thing.'

'I really think that this is a matter for the police.'

'And then her secret becomes public and she loses her position? No. That's unacceptable, Randall, she's as much a victim as Aurora, but she has so much more to lose, and I can guarantee that the police won't care what happens to her.'

He sighed. 'At least a job would keep you out of trouble. The Royal Infirmary has been employing typewriters to type up their records. A medical background like yours would be a boon, not to mention it would give you clinical-adjacent experience.'

'I've never used one of the machines before,' I said uncertainly.

'There's one in the medical school you could practise on,' Randall offered, warming to the idea. 'It can't be that hard for a bright girl who can manage surgery and chemical equations. And I'd be more than happy to refer you to the hospital administrator.'

'And it's a woman's job, so no one can possibly complain,' I added wryly. 'Don't worry, Randall, I don't see myself as above it. I'll take in mending if I have to! I'll scrub the floors of the mortuary. While I'm dependent on my family, I'll always have to abide by their rules. Even marriage would give me more financial freedom.'

'Not in Scotland,' Elisabeth said grimly. 'Here, a husband still holds the purse strings. The money and property I brought to my marriage is mine and mine alone, but any financial decision has to have Randall's approval.'

'Which I will always give,' he said gently.

'But I wish you didn't have to!' The normally mild-mannered Elisabeth looked irate. 'I may not have a university degree, but I'm not a child or an idiot – yet in the eyes of the law, I'm both. It's ridiculous that you can countermand decisions over the land I own back in Canada, a country you've never even set foot in.'

I thought about Merchiston's proposal, and wondered if he knew what he was asking me to give up. I hadn't told Elisabeth for fear she would convince me to reconsider, but the secret was weighing on me like so many others. Tempting as the prospect was, so was my own income and the freedom that would give me, even before I qualified! It might not be much, but what it would buy me was priceless.

A flicker of warmth shot through me as a new possibility occurred to me. I could have both, if only I were willing to break society's rules. I could have my independence, my career, and Merchiston in my bed, provided he was willing to overlook the fact that it would not be a marital one. If my aunt and Aurora could use my barrenness to their own advantage, why couldn't I? Free of the one dreaded consequence of sex, why not be the woman they thought I was, the one that terrified them? I would have a job and a lover instead of a husband and a gilded cage of a home.

If my friends could hear my thoughts, they would be scandalised. Well, let them be. I was beginning to realise that the troubles I had fought to overcome might after all be my most powerful weapon. Paul Beresford, Alisdair Greene, even Gregory Merchiston all wanted me to sacrifice my propriety for their pleasure. It was time to make sacrifices for my own.

Chapter 31

I wasn't thinking about propriety when I burst into Gregory Merchiston's office the next day. But as he looked up from his task, I wished I had been.

From his haggard complexion, it looked as though the female students hadn't been the only ones partaking in the demon drink of late. I remembered the twisted parody of my friend I had met in his study, and felt a stab of guilt that my rejection had prompted another bout of overindulgence.

One shirtsleeve was rolled up, and a thick leather belt was wrapped around his forearm, the strap clenched between his teeth. The other hand held a needle. As I stared at him, he mumbled something against the leather that sounded distinctly like an obscenity.

I could see a faint trail of bruised indentations. Whatever his treatment was, it wasn't the first time he had used it.

Our eyes locked, and I could see a flicker of defiance, as though he were daring me to stop him. He pushed the syringe's plunger and I watched as the needle pierced the median basilic vein. He let out a sensuous, ragged sigh of relief, and despite the circumstances I found my own body reacting to his drug-induced pleasure. After a few moments, he looked up and gave me a wolfish grin.

'Professor, are you ill?'

He inhaled deeply, and I forced myself not to notice how his muscles shifted under the starched cotton of his shirt.

'On the contrary, Miss Gilchrist. I've never felt better.'

Gone was the lethargic slump of a man. In his place was Gregory Merchiston as I had first met him – sharp as a knife and just as dangerous. As he talked, I moved to the desk and examined the abandoned vial.

'Cocaine? Professor, I don't think—'

He waved his hand, pooh-poohing my concerns. 'You sound like Randall. He's such an old woman. You'd think he'd never touched anything stronger than weak cocoa in his life. The stories I could tell you about when he and I were undergraduates, Sarah! There was a prank with the dean's trousers and a goose . . .'

Whatever madcap japes he and Randall Chalmers had performed were lost in the annals of history as he stood abruptly and faced me.

'What are you doing here anyway? Don't you have an incarcerated fiancé to visit and a murder to solve?' He lowered his voice, eyes dark and his face so very, very close to mine. 'Or have you reconsidered your decision?'

'If I had, this would hardly be inducement to take your hand,' I snapped. 'You're forgetting, *Professor*, I know what that stuff is and what it does to you. I could give you chapter and verse on why it isn't a suitable hangover cure. Oh, don't look at me like that, your breath reeks of whisky.'

'I'm trying to help you, Sarah! Or did you forget that there's a murderer on the loose with an interest in the very family you're supposed to be marrying into?'

'The last time I checked, I was the only one doing any detective work,' I replied hotly. 'And I'm managing to do it without resorting to stimulants.'

'I can't sleep,' he said through gritted teeth. 'And when I do,

I can barely open my eyes. Tell me, what bloody use am I to you as professor or partner if I'm bleary-eyed and stifling a yawn?'

'Then get some rest,' I said softly, laying my hand on his arm and rubbing the bruised area gently with my thumb, resisting the urge to kiss it better. 'Let someone else take over your lectures today and let Mrs Logan fuss over you.'

'Is that your diagnosis, *Doctor* Gilchrist?'

I found myself returning his smile as I unrolled his shirtsleeve and fastened his cufflink back into the buttonhole. I could have induced him to work off his cocaine-induced agitation somewhere other than the university, if Randall Chalmers hadn't burst in at that point.

'Gregory, do you have an écraseur I can borrow? I'm covering McLeod's surgical lecture and I need to talk some fourth years through a tumour removal.'

He stopped short at the sight of a jacketless Merchiston standing rather too close for decency to an unaccompanied woman.

'Sarah, you need to leave. Now. This is completely inappropriate.' He turned to Merchiston. 'For heaven's sake, Gregory. We've spoken about this. It could damage both of your reputations.'

I stood in the hallway, mind whirling. Oh, it wasn't unusual for doctors to self-medicate, and what he was using was commonly prescribed – my father had taken some in a small dose for toothache once, and had been unimpressed when I stole the packet to read the label. But at eight o'clock in the morning, injected straight into the vein – that wasn't medicine. Anger surged up inside me. Did he really think *I* was sleeping? My fiancé had been arrested, I was in the middle of a murder investigation, I had turned down a proposal from the only man I could really see myself married to and I had an anatomy practical in half an hour. If I was managing perfectly well on strong black coffee, so could he.

When Randall emerged, he sighed when he saw me standing there.

'I had hoped – foolishly, I know – that you had left.' He looked stern. 'He's not in a state to receive visitors now, and even if he were, I don't have to remind you that you are not permitted to be alone with him.' He ran a hand through his hair. 'God knows I wouldn't have wanted Elisabeth to see this.'

'Has he been like this before?'

'Not for years. There was a . . . bad patch when Isobel and William died. I thought we'd seen the last of it, especially when he was so worried about Lucy. He wanted to be a good example for her when she finally came back into the fold.'

But she would never return. He had thrown himself into this case – and, I suspected, partly into his proposal to me – in an effort to outrun the tidal wave of grief that he had to know he would never escape. And when it looked as though it would come crashing down around him, he turned to whisky or fighting or cocaine.

'He's drinking to forget his sorrows and injecting cocaine to stay alert,' I said softly. 'And I've seen the bruises. He's been at the boxing ring.'

'Gregory's always had a self-destructive streak,' Randall admitted. 'That wilful defiance that Lucy had – it's in him too. He can keep it chained up most of the time, but he's had a bloody few months.' He shook his head. 'You shouldn't be here. People are going to start arriving soon and there'll be talk if you're found loitering in corridors. Elisabeth is downstairs. Go and join her.'

I resented being scolded like a naughty child, but I forced a smile onto my face and went to find my best friend.

'I can't stop thinking about poor Blackwell.' She frowned. 'Do you think there's some way I could discreetly send money to her sister and child?'

I squeezed her arm. 'Has anyone ever told you that you're entirely too good?'

She pulled a face. 'I am not. But separating a mother from her child just because she's unmarried, that's wicked. I can't imagine the pain that poor girl must be in . . .' She trailed off, and I hugged her again. Despite wishing for it more than anything in the world, Elisabeth was yet to be a mother. There had been a moment over Christmas that she'd hoped, but just as quickly those hopes had been dashed. 'Who would blackmail the poor girl over one mistake?'

'A lot of people,' I said grimly. 'The world is hardly kind to unwed mothers. If it hadn't been for her sister, the child would probably have ended up in the workhouse.'

Elisabeth shivered. 'Well, I hope we catch whoever's behind these ghastly events soon. Alisdair knows more than he's letting on, I'm sure.'

'That's what I intend to find out.'

She frowned. 'Why do I get the impression that you're about to do something completely reckless?'

'He asked me to call on him at his hotel,' I whispered.

Her eyes widened with shock. 'Did you tell him that would be completely inappropriate, and slap him for good measure?'

'Not exactly,' I confessed.

'Sarah, no man invites a woman to call on him at his hotel with innocent motivation. He's a blackguard! He's a rake! He's—'

'Any number of synonyms for "cad", I know. But he likes me. He might reveal more than he realises if I question him. He's like a flower that blooms under women's attention.'

'The kind of attention he'll want from you is not the kind you'll want to provide,' she warned.

I shuddered. I didn't like the weight of his gaze on me but I'd be damned if I let that stop me. I wouldn't be some wilting creature jumping at shadows any more. If I had to beard the lion in his den, so be it.

'I'm going after lectures. I've told Aunt Emily I'm dining at yours again, and I will come over the moment I'm done. If I'm not there by six, send Randall to find me.'

'And what good will that do?' she demanded. 'By six o'clock, you could be murdered, or . . . or . . .'

'I know,' I said softly. 'And believe me, I don't want to risk my life or the tattered remains of my virtue either. That's why I have a plan.'

Elisabeth looked resigned, as though she already knew that whatever my plan was, it was risky if not downright dangerous.

'Can you cover for me at luncheon?' I said. 'I need to slip out and buy some arsenic.'

Chapter 32

If I had wondered why the heir to the Greene fortune wasn't staying somewhere more ostentatious, the North British Hotel perhaps, with its view of the castle and proximity to restaurants and music halls, my questions would have been answered as I swept into the lobby of the Carew, an unaccompanied woman asking to meet with a man, and not a single eyebrow was raised. I was ushered into a private parlour, small but richly furnished. The dark green velvet settee would not, I thought, accommodate two people who wished to keep a respectable amount of distance from one another. Then again, respectable wasn't what I had in mind.

Without my having to ask, a glass of champagne was set next to me. I glanced at the clock on the mantelpiece in case I had somehow dreamed half the day away, but it was still a little past two in the afternoon. In London society, this would be cause for a raised eyebrow or two; in Edinburgh, it was unheard of. I shifted uncomfortably in my seat, wishing I had chosen a more practical outfit – or at least a less exposing one.

The dress was a rich burgundy with a matching cape trimmed with mink, cinched so tightly that my ribs ached. I was uncomfortably aware of the way it put my embonpoint on display, pushed up and out like lamb's livers on a serving platter. My gloves stuck to my palms. I wished I had brought my medical bag. Without it, I felt curiously unprotected. But Alisdair needed to believe that I wanted him, and I had to remind him that I was a woman, not a doctor.

Once I was finished, Gregory Merchiston would never know the details of what I had done to aid our investigation, but he would be in my debt until the end of time and I would make sure he knew it. Had he known I was here, intending to flirt my way into finding proof, he would have stopped me. It was simpler – if a little riskier – for no one to know where I was.

The door creaked, and I willed myself not to startle; to look like a woman of the world instead of a trembling girl.

Alisdair smiled warmly and crossed to take my hands in his.

'Miss Gilchrist!'

He peeled my glove off tenderly, turned my hand over and pressed a warm kiss to the centre of my palm. Despite the situation – despite the man – something low down inside me gave a jolt of pleasure. It was enough to make me want to slap him.

'Mr Greene!' My blushes at least were not feigned, although I tried to look coy rather than furious.

'I was hoping you'd call. I wasn't sure that you would.' How could such a notorious rogue look like a shy schoolboy, flustered at his first kiss? I could see how some women would find it endearing, distracting enough to miss the predatory glint in his eye.

'I shouldn't be here,' I whispered hoarsely.

'But you are. I knew from the moment I met you that you were different. An educated woman, so knowledgeable about the human body and its mysteries . . . I must admit, I envy your patients.' He came to stand before me, his hands heavy on my shoulders, moving with a gentle and unwanted caress. 'What a crime it would have been, sentencing you to a life with a man who could never truly appreciate you.'

He traced my jawline with his fingertip.

'I was going through my father's papers when I stumbled across the most interesting reference to your good self and an incident in London with a certain gentleman.' He flashed me a wolfish grin. 'I won't insult your reputation by asking if you know which gentleman I'm referring to.'

I felt the floor lurch beneath me as though we were on a ship. I had to concentrate. The details of my shame were not important now. I could relive it a thousand times later if I had to, but for now, Alisdair was my only concern. He wasn't wearing the expression of someone who had discovered that his sister-in-law-to-be was a harlot, an unvirtuous cuckoo in the nest. It was the expression of a man who had invited a woman to his hotel and thought he was getting far more than afternoon tea.

Before I realised he was moving, his mouth was on my neck, hot and wet. He took my gasp of surprise as arousal, and groaned against my skin. I wanted nothing more than to turn in his arms, raise my knee and repeat that move that had brought tears to Merchiston's eyes.

Instead, I pulled back as far as I dared while still giving him the impression I found his attentions pleasing instead of revolting.

'Won't someone come in?'

'I tip generously.' His mouth returned to my neck. 'We won't be disturbed.'

I glanced to the door. 'It doesn't seem very private.'

He chuckled. 'You little minx. You don't have to feign modesty, you know. If you want me to take you to bed, then all you have to do is ask.' His mouth brushed mine and I could feel his teeth against my lower lip.

I couldn't say no, not if I wanted to find whatever he was so eager to keep hidden.

'You're married,' I murmured, hoping the trembling of my

voice sounded like desire rather than revulsion. 'I'm engaged to your brother!'

'I was under the impression that engagement had been called off, unless you're desperate enough to flout your family's wishes, not to mention becoming a widow before your wedding night.' He smiled, but all I could see was teeth. 'Some would say that's the best part of a wedding.' I wondered if his wife felt the same way. 'There's a discreet staircase; we won't be seen.'

He pulled a handle hidden on the side of a bookshelf and it swung open, revealing a passage. Honestly, it was like a Gothic novel written by a lecher.

I ascended the stairs after him, until he stopped suddenly to press me up against the wall, kissing me feverishly as he left me in no doubt whatsoever of his physical affection for me. Panic gripped me, coupled with the increasing likelihood of my being sick all over him if he didn't stop. I was going to have to distract him with whatever means I had at my disposal if I was to avoid giving myself to a man with a touch like an octopus – omnipresent and disgustingly damp.

'Not here,' I gasped into his mouth, in an effort to stop him putting his tongue in mine.

He pulled me up to a narrow door that led into a large, well-appointed bedroom. There was a desk, a bureau, a wardrobe and a cabinet – but all I could see was the bed that dominated the room. I sat down on it tentatively.

'Could I have something to drink?' I asked.

'Nervous?'

I nodded, and he smiled as he poured me a glass from the decanter on the table.

I took a large gulp and choked. Gin.

'Perhaps some water?' There was a jug on the bureau with two glasses, and I poured with shaking hands.

Alisdair stuck his head out of the main door and yelled at a passing footman to bring a bottle of Moët. 'As chilled as you can get it.'

When he returned, I was at the window, gazing out onto the street.

'Quite the view.' Somehow, I didn't think he meant the street outside.

I felt his arms encircling my waist and my muscles turned to lead. I reached to hand him a glass of water as I sipped from mine, and he took a long gulp.

'You're enough to make a good dog break his leash, Miss Gilchrist.'

I smiled coyly. 'Under the circumstances, I think you can call me Sarah.'

His hand went to the hem of my skirt and I felt it lifting. What was I doing? What in this blasted investigation mattered so much that I was willing to put myself through this again? I braced myself for whatever came next.

Instead, Alisdair pulled away. 'Forgive me.' He made a dash for the water closet, and the sound of vomiting echoed through the closed door.

I glanced around the room. How blurry the boundaries between right and wrong seemed in pursuit of justice. Was this what Fiona had thought? That the end justified the means so utterly that the oath she had taken – the one I yearned to take – no longer mattered?

I rummaged through the desk drawers as silently and quickly as I could, coming up with a half-empty bottle of cologne and what on closer inspection looked like one of the sponges I had seen prostitutes soak with vinegar and insert inside . . . I dropped it quickly and moved on to the next drawer. It was empty, save for one envelope – and the name on the envelope was my own.

I ripped it open and scanned the contents.

Miss Gilchrist

I observed you entering the CAREW HOTEL on the night of 26th Feb., 1893, to meet with Mr ALISDAIR GREENE. You were seen going to his rooms and emerging some time later looking dishevelled. Hotel staff report hearing noises of a carnal nature emanating from behind the door of the room, and a device known to prevent conception was found in the bedside cabinet, believed to be left behind by you.

Given your existing reputation (I refer to your illicit consummation with PAUL BERESFORD in the Jan. of 1892 at his house in Robinson Crescent), I have reason to believe that should this become public, it would end both your engagement and your future plans. In order to assist with keeping this matter quiet, I require the sum of £500 to be placed in an envelope and left behind the bar at the SPECKLED FROG in Haymarket. Should you fail to do so, I will be unable to prevent the news of your assignation from becoming public.

Yours,
A Friend

Bile rose in my throat. Alisdair had been confident of his chances with me, then. Of course I had given him reason to believe that he had caught my eye, but the idea that he would have bedded me and then blackmailed me over it made me feel ill. So much for not wanting to taint me with scandal. I shoved the letter in my pocket and opened the other drawers. They were full of unpaid bills and creditors' letters, and I realised that the blind eye the hotel staff turned to female visitors wasn't the only reason Alisdair had chosen this over the considerably more expensive North British Hotel. He had no money, and with his inheritance taking too long to materialise, he had resorted to extorting his family. With his father barely cold in his grave and the will not yet read, it seemed he couldn't wait long enough to inherit.

Beneath the letters was a locked box. Sending up a silent prayer of thanks for Merchiston's extracurricular tuition, I used one of my hairpins to catch the mechanism and force it open. The contents glittered in the candlelight. A diamond bracelet, a grey pearl choker, a sapphire ring: all items Aurora had reported missing. And beneath them, an emerald earring to match the one found on Clara Wilson's body. She had been his accomplice then, or more likely his stooge. And then she had been his victim.

I heard the sound of running water and closed the drawer. With any luck, by the time Alisdair found the box unlocked I would be on my way to the police station.

When he returned, he looked pale and clammy.

'Miss Gilchrist, forgive me. I am unwell.'

'Such a difficult time. I'm only sorry I couldn't be of more solace.' I rested my hand on his. It was easier to touch him knowing that he was incapacitated, but I had to suppress a shiver, knowing now what those hands were capable of.

He smiled weakly. 'Perhaps another time. Given my new-found responsibilities, I will be visiting Edinburgh more often. Perhaps I could call on you?' It should have been a polite question, but I knew what he wanted and his next words made it painfully clear. 'It must be so hard, cooped up here away from real society. Oh, my mother is loyal to her dressmaker, but since when was Scotland the height of fashion? If you would permit it, I'd be happy to send you any fabrics or patterns.' He smiled, and for the first time since I met him, it reached his eyes. I realised that this was a real seduction, at least for one of us. 'Or some ghastly textbooks, if you'd prefer.'

Be his mistress, then. A wife with none of the benefits legitimacy would lend to the proceedings, his whore without the limited protection of Ruby McAllister and her ilk. I was tired of having my compliance bought. I wanted something to trade for a change.

I stood, dusting down my dress and trying to stop myself from shaking. It was over, and I had got what I had come for even if Alisdair hadn't.

I watched in horror as the vial slipped from the folds of my skirts across the floor, the glass splintering and the arsenic powder spilling out over the floor. Alisdair watched it with dawning realisation.

'You put something in my drink. You mad bitch! I should have you locked up.'

'If you call the police, I'll show them what I found in your rooms. If the blackmail letters don't convince them, your mother's stolen jewellery will.'

'They were a gift for my wife. Mother must have been confused.'

'You killed Clara Wilson. Why? Did she grow tired of your threats? She may have dosed your father with arsenic, but his death is on your hands.'

'Breathe a word of this and I'll tell everyone I had you anyway. I'll say you came to me offering your services as my mistress before my brother was even arrested.'

'Arrested for a crime you committed,' I spat. 'And I'd rather be thought a whore than a murderer.'

He leaned heavily against the bed and pulled something from beneath his pillow. I thought that he meant to bribe me, but the object he drew out was intended to threaten – and worse.

I didn't look away from the barrel of the gun as I grabbed hold of the cord that would summon a servant. 'Put that down or I'll tell the entire hotel you tried to rape me.'

He laughed, but I saw a flicker of doubt in his eyes. 'Yes, that's rather your modus operandi, isn't it, Miss Gilchrist? Tell me, what did Paul Beresford do to warrant such an accusation?'

The shock of seeing the gun had driven all thoughts of the scalpel hidden in my dress from my mind, but somehow I found myself with the cold steel in my hand. The flat of the blade pressed lightly against his carotid artery, but it would take a fraction of a movement to pierce the skin.

The only sound in the room was Alisdair's shallow, terrified breath. He shook like a leaf, but I was still as stone.

In that moment, I could have done it. It wouldn't have solved anything. Any sense of satisfaction would have been fleeting, and then all I would have had would be a blood-soaked dress and the corpse of a man who was almost my brother-in-law. Had Alisdair recovered more swiftly from the arsenic's effects, I would not have left his room untouched. Then, he would have deserved it. Then, I might not have been able to still my hand.

Chapter 33

The City Chambers stood back from the cramped Royal Mile, which wound its way from the castle to Holyrood Palace, opposite St Giles' Cathedral in all its Gothic splendour. I wondered if the saint himself extended his influence to the police station his church faced, or if the beggars, madmen and outcasts he patronised were left to their own devices once they were in front of Edinburgh's constabulary.

Although it was late afternoon, the station was already full of the inebriated and the immoral and it was impossible to tell who was the criminal and who the victim. I pushed past the people waiting, much to their annoyance, but I didn't have time to waste.

'Mind yersel'! I've been waiting ten minutes to see the polis after this witch snatched my bag!'

'Haud yer wheesht, you daft besom. That was my bag and you're the thief!'

I reached the desk unimpeded once the drunken women's attentions were turned back on each other. From the look of the bag itself, it was far more expensive than either could afford, and I suspected that whoever's possession it had been originally was long gone.

'My name is Miss Sarah Gilchrist and I need to speak to

your superior immediately. Alisdair Greene has confessed to murdering his mother's maid and letting his brother take the blame for it.'

My hair was falling down and my skirt was soaked with rain, mud and heaven knew what else, but my accent and the fabric of my coat were enough for the harried constable on duty to overlook my dishevelled appearance. In a moment, he was on his feet ushering me into a side room.

'A lady to see you, Detective Inspector Murdoch. Says she has information about the Greene case.'

The detective looked up from his papers and my heart sank as I recognised the man sitting ready to take my statement. He raised an eyebrow.

'Another murder to report, miss?'

I had tried and failed to convince him once before of a crime that had taken place, and his refusal to act had nearly cost me my life.

'Alisdair Greene is the man you're looking for. He killed Clara Wilson and I believe he was responsible for the murder of his father. He blackmailed his mother for money and was trying to blackmail me as well – see for yourself.'

I handed Murdoch the evidence I had purloined and the letter I had received and realised too late what they implicated me in.

A salacious grin spread across his face as he read the filth that had come out of Alisdair's pen.

'Lovers' tiff, was it?'

'None of what he says there is true! He thought he could seduce me, but—'

'He didn't catch your fancy?'

'He repulses me,' I said, disgust making my lip curl. 'Detective Inspector, he was furious! He threatened to kill me like he'd killed Wilson. Even if she was stealing Aurora Greene's jewellery the night she died, he'd been extorting his mother for months. He has mountains of unpaid debts and a child on the way – he's desperate.'

Desperate enough to make him kill again if this idiot man couldn't see reason.

'That's quite the tale you're spinning, lassie.'

I wasn't some silly little girl jumping at shadows. Had I been a man, they would have listened. But all they saw was my sex, and that was enough to dismiss me.

'With respect, sir, I'm not some overwrought, hysterical female, and I'm a damn sight more reliable than some of your other visitors today. I'm studying at the University of Edinburgh. I'm a medical student, among the top in my class. You have to listen to me! If you speak to Professor Gregory Merchiston, he'll vouch for me.'

'Oh ho! You're the lassie he brought into the morgue. Tell me,' he smirked and ran his tongue over yellowing teeth, 'did you find the bodies . . . stimulating?'

I bit my tongue so hard I tasted the metallic tang of blood. I would not rise to his bait. It would take very little for him to have me escorted off the premises, and I had to make him see. I had escaped a killer's knife once before; I did not relish the thought of facing Alisdair alone unless I absolutely had to. But my faith in the man standing before me was dwindling by the minute, and part of me knew that when I left the station I would not be returning home safe in the knowledge that they would apprehend the murderer.

Murdoch frowned and looked at the letters again.

'Gilchrist, you say? Not the same wee lassie engaged to the murderer?'

Oh God. They were never going to believe me, and if I didn't make it to the Greene residence in time, Alisdair would have his mother convinced I was a lunatic or a slut – if she was even still alive by the time I got there. Thoughts of forged suicide notes, of one too many swigs from the laudanum bottle or the sharp edges of embroidery scissors pressed against wrists crowded my mind.

'Miles didn't do it,' I insisted. 'Alisdair Greene confessed – he has a motive! Miles wouldn't hurt a fly. Ask any of the servants – they'll vouch for him even if his family won't. His brother has killed at least once, and I believe he'll do it again.'

Murdoch sighed. I could see his dilemma – he might not believe me, but he had no more wish to see a murderer stalking the streets of Edinburgh than I did. And yet they had their man, apprehended and facing the gallows.

'I can see you're distressed, Miss Gilchrist. But you see, I've no proof he even wrote these letters you're waving about. For all I know, you could have written them yourself – you're a smart lassie; I'm sure copying someone's handwriting is no difficulty. Maybe you were hoping to start your married life with a nice inheritance, or maybe you'd just do anything to save your beloved from the hangman's noose. Either way, you're no' exactly what we call in the trade a reliable witness. Stick to playing at doctor and keep your legs closed, that's my advice.'

On the other side of the office wall, a scuffle broke out. I heard the sound of swearing and the smack-crunch of fist against face. I sorely wished I had the nerve to strike the man in front of me, but instead I seethed silently, forced to see myself through his eyes. A hysterical woman babbling about a murder that had been satisfactorily solved, trying to clear her fiancé's name by spinning whatever outlandish story she could. A woman in a dress designed to catch men's eyes, confessing to having been in a man's hotel room. He could have had me arrested for prostitution and no one would have batted an eyelid.

No matter what I said, the police were never going to listen to me. Even if I convinced one of them, it would be like chipping away at a glacier. I tore a sheet of paper from my notebook and hastily scribbled a note to Merchiston. Let them think it was some sweetheart's love note so long as they delivered it.

'Can you make sure Professor Merchiston gets this? Please, you don't have to believe me, you don't even have to listen to me, just make sure he reads it.'

'Sure he'll want to hear from you when he kens you've been running around with other men?'

I had endured too much today already. If he didn't think that I was a lady, I saw no reason to behave like one. I spat in his face and ran in the direction of the New Town like the devil himself was at my heels. There was only one other person who might listen to me, but I would have to reach her soon – and even then it might be too late.

It was a little past four o'clock, but already the night was drawing in. Gas lamps illuminated the New Town, with its smart Georgian buildings and well-kept gardens, and the sky was fading to a bruised purplish-black. When I had left Alisdair's hotel, it had been daylight.

As I mounted the steps to the Greene residence, I felt strange, detached, as though I were watching myself from a distance.

I could walk away from this. I had done all I could, alerted the relevant authorities and given them what proof I had. I might feel guilt over not being able to save Miles, but I wouldn't truly grieve him, and surely his scandal would taint me sufficiently that Aunt Emily would abandon all hope of marrying me off. The Greenes were not my family and now they never would be. Walking into that house as good as signed my death warrant – even if Aurora believed me over her own flesh and blood, Alisdair was strong.

And abandoning her now would make me so very, very weak. Fuelled by a stubbornness and an anger I hadn't felt since I paced the Cowgate slums in pursuit of Lucy's killer, I took the door knocker in my hand and slammed it back against the wood. Let him know I was coming. Let him be afraid.

Blackwell answered the door, and behind her I saw a familiar coat and hat. He was already here.

'Mrs Greene, where is she?'

'In her room, miss, but she's not at home to visitors.'

I wasn't going to let etiquette stop me from saving her life, if it wasn't already too late.

As I burst into her room, Aurora let out a shriek of alarm. Alisdair put his arm around her possessively and glared at me.

'I've spoken to the police. They're on their way.' A lie, but it might keep us both alive. Aurora whimpered.

'It was an accident,' Alisdair said softly. 'Nobody's fault. The police can't blame her for that, can they?'

In her son's arms, Aurora started to sob.

'I shouldn't have helped dispose of the . . . of Wilson, but what was I supposed to do? Mother was hysterical – she'd only meant to frighten the girl off. And really, Wilson was the real criminal. Blackmail! She knew exactly what she was doing.'

'Then why blame Miles? Your own son, Aurora!'

'Someone had to be found responsible. God knows I love my brother, but he's never been the sharpest, and it isn't as though the two of you would have had children. That's one of the qualities that endeared you to us, in fact.'

Alisdair smiled as though he had paid me a compliment rather than remind me of my barrenness. But it didn't reach his eyes.

'What happened, Aurora?' I asked gently. 'If it was really an accident, you won't be arrested.'

'That horrid girl,' she whispered hoarsely. 'I found her leaving a note. Ghastly little poison-pen letters, threatening to stir up trouble that was well in the past.'

'Aurora, she didn't die of the blow to the head. She was suffocated.'

I had a picture of it now. Aurora frantically calling Alisdair in, the motionless body of Clara Wilson on the floor. Him promising he would take care of it, smuggling her out in the dead of night only to realise that she was still alive.

Perhaps she had regained consciousness, or perhaps he had felt the flutter of her faint pulse, the warmth of her breath on his skin. Either way, it had been his hand that extinguished the life from a woman whose only crimes were ones he had manipulated her into committing. His hand that had pressed against her mouth, fingers pinching her nose so that no air could enter her nostrils.

For the first time, Alisdair looked uncertain. 'You're lying. Or if she did suffocate, it was because I'd put her face down. That must have been it.'

Aurora let out a broken cry.

'I helped perform the autopsy,' I said coldly. Aurora might not have killed her maid, but she thought she had and she would have let her younger son swing for it.

'What kind of woman are you?' Alisdair asked in disgust. 'What kind of ghoulish, unnatural—'

'Fine words coming from the man who smothered the life out of a woman he had forced to commit a crime. Tell me, Aurora, how much jewellery have you had to give away to pay off your blackmailer? And how much was found with Wilson's body?'

'I . . . I don't understand.'

'This afternoon, I found some of your necklaces in your son's hotel room. Along with a blackmail letter addressed to me, trying to extort money in exchange for his silence about the affair that he somewhat overconfidently assumed we would have.' The look I levelled at Alisdair was full of all the revulsion and contempt I held for him, and I was satisfied to see him quail slightly. 'Before I left to report him to the police, he threatened to kill me like he'd killed Wilson – and,

I presume, he would have let someone else take the blame again.'

'I told you, my mother gave me that jewellery as a gift for my wife.' Sweat was beading his upper lip, and for the first time I realised that his charisma lay not in his looks but in his confidence. Without it, he was nothing but a pathetic excuse for a criminal. He turned to Aurora. 'Tell her!'

She closed her eyes, and I saw a tear slip through her lashes and fall down her cheek. I felt sorry for her, in a way. I knew what it was like to feel backed into a corner.

'If you needed money, why not just ask for it?'

'I tried,' he said through gritted teeth. 'I asked Father time and time again, but he said that I had made a rod for my own back and had to fix the situation myself, like a man.' He snorted. 'As though that puffed-up old duffer knew what being a man was any more.'

'Your father was a good man. He was a soldier. A hero.'

'And he died twitching on the floor and shitting himself at one of your bloody dinner parties,' he snarled. 'All because the pathetic bastard was too cheap to pay off a couple of creditors. He was wasting my inheritance on celebrating the marriage of my idiot brother and his bluestocking bride when I needed it! I'll make a better head of the family than Father did, I promise. Just the two of us, without him holding the purse strings and lecturing you about every charity you support.'

Was she tempted in that moment? There was a far-off gaze in her blue eyes that I couldn't read, and I could see every muscle in her body tense, from the rigidness of her shoulders to the way her knuckles clenched bone white around the base of the candlestick.

I jumped back as soon as she moved, but she wasn't aiming at me.

The candlestick cracked against Alisdair's skull, and I heard a howl of pain – but not from him. He lay motionless, slumped back against the bed as a tiny trickle of blood seeped down onto the coverlet.

Aurora stared down at him, her chest heaving with sobs and her face lit up as if with some divine light.

The curtains were on fire.

The flames spread quickly, hot against my cheeks. I yanked her up and away from them, searching fruitlessly for so much as a glass of water I could douse them with. It was spreading too fast, the heat a physical presence that sent me reeling. But I wasn't going to die in here, and neither was she.

As we stumbled into the hallway, she swayed and I saw her legs give way beneath her in a dead faint. She was smaller and slighter than me, but it was still a struggle to scoop her up and carry her downstairs as I screamed for help.

Blackwell came running.

'Mrs Greene's room is on fire and it's spreading fast. How many servants are home? You need to get them all out, as fast as you can.'

She nodded, and banged her fist on the dinner gong with all her might, shouting for her companions. As I dragged Aurora out of the front door and into the street below, her house and all her beautiful things – her fabrics, her dresses, the miniatures of her sons, and Alisdair himself – were curling into ash and smoke.

What happened next I can recall only in fragments. The clanging of the fire engine bells and the clatter of the horses' hooves on the cobbles. The shouts as the neighbouring houses began to evacuate in panic. And Gregory Merchiston, miraculously there, holding me in his arms and promising never to let me go.

Chapter 34

The weather was mild. Winter was giving way to spring, and outside I could see snowdrops scattered across the garden. Pale afternoon sunlight shone through the window, making Miles' mousy hair, recovering from the assault of the prison barber's blade, glint with strands of gold.

We sat in my aunt's parlour, pale amber tea untouched in china teacups in front of us, as though we were any other young couple with our lives ahead of us. As though he didn't have a bruise healing in yellows and browns on his jaw, as though my voice wasn't still hoarse from the smoke I had inhaled the day I confronted his mother with Alisdair's crimes. Aunt Emily had left us unchaperoned for once, and I couldn't blame her for not wanting to witness the conversation that was about to take place.

Miles looked better than he had in prison – a week of proper food had filled out his hollow cheeks and the dark circles under his eyes had begun to fade. And yet he wasn't the man he had been before, either. I had thought he would have emerged a wreck, a shadow of his former self, and it was true that there was a solemnity about him now that I had not seen in the early days of our courtship. It was as though the weight of his family's expectations, the unbridgeable divide between younger son and elder, had kept him small and scared. In the end, it was that difference that had saved him; where Alisdair's confidence had hardened into arrogance, Miles' self-consciousness had made him a gentler sort of man, one who listened rather than held forth like his father had done.

He still blushed when he met my gaze, he still stammered when he spoke. But there was a gravitas to him now, and when he stumbled over his words he did so calmly, as though what he had to say was important, and the world could damn well wait until he managed to say it.

I realised what my mother saw when she looked at me now – a stranger in her daughter's skin, changed by experiences she could never comprehend. Broken once, but stronger in the places where I had been put back together. Miles was already growing into the position he had unexpectedly inherited, and I was growing too – into whom I wasn't sure, but I knew I liked her.

This was the stuff fairy tales were made of – the unassuming but kind boy revealed to be the heir to vast wealth asking for the maiden's hand after she had assisted him along his journey. The entire Greene fortune could be at my disposal if I simply said the word, and with that money would come respectability. I would never have to worry about my reputation again.

And then these new wings of mine would be clipped once more. A cage was still a cage, even when you could see daylight through the bars.

He knew my answer before I gave it, but he sat there patiently as I forced the words out.

'I can't. I'm so sorry. You of all people deserve happiness, but I can't give you that. I don't want to marry – not you, not now. Maybe I never will.'

He took my hands in his. They were softer than mine, even after everything he had been through. There were calluses beneath my second and fourth fingers from gripping a scalpel, the raised blister of a burn on the heel of my other palm, and the skin was rough from scrubbing with carbolic soap. His skin felt like the echo of the girl I once was, cosseted and protected from the world right up until the moment I wasn't.

'I could give you an easy life.'

Accepting his proposal would not give me that softness back. I twisted the ring he had given me off my finger and placed it on the table, sparkling where it caught the light. It was such a little thing, really, and yet I felt as though a great weight had been lifted off my shoulders.

'I don't think I want easy,' I said. 'I don't think I know how.'

He nodded, and I felt the promise of the future I was supposed to want crumble into ash.

'Perhaps it's for the best,' he said, in a voice that only shook slightly. 'With my new position . . . I have family responsibilities that will take time to resolve.'

I thought of Aurora's unconscious body as Merchiston and I had carried her in a makeshift stretcher to the police carriage; of the gutted rooms and the acrid smell of smoke that still lingered in the New Town. The servants had escaped only because most of them had been given the evening off by Alisdair on his arrival; it would have been easier for him to dispose of my body, and perhaps Aurora's too, if there were no witnesses.

There had been little left of Alisdair by the time the firefighters had arrived from Lauriston Place, and if a post-mortem had picked up on the crack in his skull, then the professor had not seen the need to bring it to anyone's attention but my own. Aurora had confirmed my statement in monosyllables, clearing her younger son's name, but I had not seen her since.

'My mother is unwell,' Miles said. 'The death of my brother so close to losing my father took its toll on her nerves and she is recuperating in the countryside. It's a private hospital,' he continued. 'The effect on her nerves . . . The doctors aren't sure that she'll ever fully recover. They say she blames herself for everything that happened.'

He met my gaze steadily, as though daring me to challenge his version of events. He was a far better man than I had ever given him credit for. Aurora had thought herself a murderer and been prepared to let her child hang for it, and their future relationship would be forever tainted.

'You think I'm weak.'

'I think you're kind. Far, far kinder than I could ever be.' I thought of my own mother, safely back in London now and out of my life perhaps for ever.

'She couldn't survive prison.'

Privately, I wasn't sure how much longer Miles would have been able to survive, and wouldn't that have been a perfect end? The Greene family name spared even the stigma of the gallows and the whole incident swept under the carpet with all their other secrets. Perhaps it was best that they were getting a fresh start with a new heir, their collective past nothing but ashes.

'Will you keep the house?'

'I couldn't sell it even if I wanted to. Even before the fire, a house that had seen two murders would be a millstone around my neck. And I was happy there, for the most part.' His lips twisted in a wry smile shot through with sadness. 'I loved my father, you know. He was bluff and strict, but he only ever wanted the best for me. And Alisdair – he was my protector. My best friend. He was the captain of our pirate ship when we were boys, and at school he thrashed any bully who so much as called me names. He was going to be best man at our wedding. We talked about you like gossiping schoolgirls – he liked you, you know. Thought you'd bring me out of my shell.'

I couldn't reconcile these tales of fraternal support with the man who had framed his brother for murder and tried to seduce his fiancée. But I was comforted that at least some of Miles' illusions about his family remained intact. He would grieve for the people he thought his mother and brother were, and I knew how fiercely he would need to cling to those happy memories.

'I've told Frances she can have the place if she wants. Alisdair left her drowning in debt and she has a child on the way who will grow up without a father.' He shook his head. 'I should have seen how desperate he was.'

'You couldn't have known what he was going to do.'

'You did.'

'I ask too many questions and make a nuisance of myself. You've had a lucky escape, really.'

He smiled sadly. 'Which brings me to my next point. I stand to inherit a considerable sum of money, and I've looked at my father's business records. It seems that on our marriage, he was planning to invest in your uncle's brewery. I would like to honour that commitment. If it hadn't been for you . . .'

I swallowed thickly. I had rejected his offer of marriage and I knew that my family would never forgive me for walking away from him and everything that he represented. But while my uncle would never understand female emancipation, he did understand money. Miles had bought my freedom, at least for a time, and I would always be grateful for that.

I pressed a kiss to his cheek.

'Find someone who loves you. Find someone who thinks you're the most wonderful man in the world.'

I let him hold me for a moment, willing my pulse to race, my cheeks to flush. It would be so much easier if I loved him.

'I would have made you a terrible wife, Miles, but I can be a good friend if you ever need one.'

'As can I. You deserve to be happy too,' he said softly.

I thought of my calluses and burns, of the long hours spent in cold lecture theatres and of the way I had coaxed Clara Wilson's body to give up its secrets. I thought of a future filled not with a husband and children, but with colleagues and patients, and I felt a shiver, giddy with the promise of a future of my own devising.

'I am.'

Chapter 35

I pushed open the heavy door, my nerves fluttering with anticipation about what I would find behind it.

'Ah, Gilchrist.' Professor Turner nodded without looking up. 'We're on hearts today. Take a look at this beauty.' He waved a jar of formaldehyde in my general direction, and I gazed fascinated at the lump of dark flesh swimming around in the viscous yellowish liquid.

'It doesn't look like much, does it?' he asked rhetorically. I had made the mistake, in my first week, of attempting to answer one of these questions, but he had simply talked over me as if I had made no response at all. In fact, I sometimes suspected him of a slight deafness – not that it mattered, since he was more interested in the work of my hands rather than any opinion I could offer.

I took the jar from him, and gave it an experimental slosh.

'The poets say that all of human emotion originates here,' Turner said conversationally. 'In reality, it is far more important than that. Love is a paltry thing in comparison to circulation.'

I was willing to agree with him there.

'We hear such sensationalist rubbish from the popular press, and even some of my own colleagues. But, Miss Gilchrist, always remember this: the heart is nothing but a cog in a sophisticated machine. And when something breaks down, as I am told machinery parts so often do, everything grinds to a halt. Terminally, in the case of the poor chap who owned this one. Now, if you would be so good as to remove your gloves?'

I peeled them off and handed them to my unsmiling companion.

'Open the jar and scoop the fellow out then, Miss Gilchrist.' This was a test, I realised. Would I swoon in horror, or wince at the feeling of the preserved muscle against my fingers? I was determined to do neither of those things, but nevertheless I couldn't stop myself from taking a deep breath before removing the lid and plunging my hand into the freezing liquid.

The heart was soft as silk and cool to the touch – they had to be kept in the cold to prevent them stinking up the place, I supposed – and heavier, far heavier than I had expected. I turned it over in my hands, tracing the blue veins gently with a fingertip.

'One thing the poets have right,' Turner said softly, 'is that in this organ lies all the mysteries of human existence. Why don't we open it up and have a look, hmm?'

I placed it on the table reverently. He handed me a small, sharp scalpel and I hesitated for a moment.

'It seems almost a shame,' I murmured. 'It's quite beautiful in its way.'

'Don't get sentimental, Gilchrist. Make the first incision and stop wasting both our time and that of the good lady over there.'

Elisabeth, absorbed in reading *Lady Audley's Secret* for the third time, didn't look as though she were in a rush to go anywhere.

I pressed down with the blade, then harder, and felt it sink into the purplish muscle.

'Right in half, if you please,' my tutor said briskly. With a swift, decisive motion, I cleaved the heart in two as though it were an apple, and stared in fascination.

'And so the heart gives up its secrets at last.' Turner smiled. 'Now look at the left side and tell me what you see.'

The diagrams in my books had not prepared me for the reality of the thing – the papery skin of tissue that fluttered against the light touch of my breath had looked so much more substantial when rendered in pen and ink, and the pulmonary artery was, in its way, quite beautiful. I described it all in wonderment, and when I picked up its mirror image, I realised that I too was smiling.

'Feel, Miss Gilchrist, the weight of it. It is far sturdier than those poets would have you believe. Next time you fear that your heart is broken, take comfort in the fact that it takes a great deal to really damage it.'

His voice was wistful, and a little sad, and I wondered what had occurred in his past to make him remind his students – and perhaps himself – of the imperturbability of the organ.

I bisected the halves again, and repeated my task of describing what I saw. Eventually, when Professor Turner was satisfied, he set me to sketching the heart and labelling the attendant parts. He nodded at my work.

'You've a good and steady hand, Miss Gilchrist. Let me know when it comes time for you to choose a specialty. If you can keep your head in a crisis, we might make a surgeon of you one day.' I flushed with pleasure, and handed him the sheet of paper. He shook his head. 'Keep it. In fact, frame it, and when you think you've lost your heart, remember exactly what it is you're losing.'

I nodded mutely. I would have pressed his hand with mine had it not been an appalling breach of etiquette to be so familiar with one's tutor. I settled for a grateful smile and an effusive 'Thank you, Professor,' before traipsing off to two torturous hours of botany, where the stamens and pollen sacs that I sketched failed entirely to make my blood pound the way that the heavy weight of human muscle had.

Not for the first time, I wondered if I was entirely normal, but I realised this had ceased to bother me. My heart beat rhythmically and securely beneath my ribcage, but I knew that it was no longer entirely my own.

It was still light when I emerged from the lecture theatre, and I felt a sense of freedom, of possibility that I had not felt in the longest time. More than a year had now passed since the fateful encounter with Paul Beresford that had so altered the course of my life, and in that time I had carved out a new path for myself. I had lost so much – family, friends, even myself for a while. But what I had gained was worth so much more.

'Miss Gilchrist? Could I have a word?' Gregory Merchiston stood squinting into the sunlight, and it was all I could do not to run to him.

We had not been alone since I stumbled out of the burning building, soot-stained and carrying Aurora Greene, to find him arriving with cavalry in tow. Even then, in the hubbub that followed, he was able to do little more than check me for injuries, mumbling thanks to a God I didn't even know he believed in for keeping me safe.

My aunt had kept me off lectures for a week before either her sympathy or her patience ran out and she dispatched me to the university with a barely concealed sigh of relief. Although my broken engagement must have rankled, my close brush with death had frightened her into silence, and even Uncle Hugh was uncharacteristically mute. Miles' investment in his company must have softened that blow, otherwise I was sure he'd have been happy to see me burned to a crisp and out of his house for good.

My classmates hailed me as a heroine, and someone – I suspected Alison – had torn out the page from the *Edinburgh Evening News* about the fire and pinned it to every noticeboard in the medical school. *DARING RESCUE BY LADY MEDICAL STUDENT*, it shouted in a bold font, and I felt an odd mix of pride and embarrassment. At least my aunt and uncle didn't subscribe to the *Evening News*, although the headline could hardly have escaped my uncle's attention. Well-brought-up young ladies weren't supposed to find their names plastered over the front page of a daily newspaper, and was it really necessary for them to call me a 'charming young undergraduette'? I had been damp with sweat and reeking of smoke, and the only person who could possibly have found me attractive in that state was standing before me now.

'The lady of the hour,' he teased. 'Do you have any more heroic acts to carry out today, or could I give you the assignments and reading you missed?'

My heart thumped in my chest as I followed him back into the building. My uncle's carriage could wait. Elisabeth trotted at my heels, although I had no doubt that she would find a way to make herself absent. True to form, when the door closed behind us, she had excused herself to powder her nose.

Alone, Merchiston looked almost shy, but my boldness made up for it. I kissed him fiercely, feeling him gasp into my mouth and return the kiss with an ardour that matched my own. Out in the corridor, students were talking and professors were arguing with them and there was nothing but an unlocked door standing between us and total ruin, but I didn't care. I had faced down murderers, escaped from a burning building and saved a man from the gallows. I might still have been a woman with a scandalous past, but in that moment I had never felt stronger or more untouchable.

'Marry me,' he murmured against my skin, pulling me closer against him. 'Forget that boy. Even if he lets you practise medicine, he'll never make you happy.'

'I'm not marrying Miles.'

I had never expected to see such unfettered joy on Gregory

Merchiston's face, and it killed me to be the one to dash it.

I wanted the man in front of me, but I wanted a room like this of my very own more. Georgina Robinson and her ill-timed elopement had taught me that I couldn't have both, not right now. If I wanted a future where I had patients and a plaque with my name on, as well as a husband to go home to at the end of a long day on the hospital wards, I would have to build it myself.

'I'm not marrying anyone,' I told him, extricating himself from his embrace even though every fibre of my being wanted nothing more than to stay in his arms, press closer and not leave until we were both thoroughly sated. 'Not now, at least.'

He swallowed hard, fighting to collect himself.

'I know. That was unfair of me. I just keep thinking about arriving at that house to see the smoke and wondering if you had managed to escape.' He drew a ragged breath. 'I wanted to give you something.'

He handed me a small, square package that was far too heavy and large to contain jewellery, but whatever it was, it came from him and it was just as precious in my eyes.

'Don't open it here. And you might want to hide it from your aunt – and Elisabeth.'

My eyebrows rose as I wondered what on earth he had given me that I needed to keep a secret, and I felt a warm flush wash over my body.

'It's nothing scandalous,' he said quickly, reading my reaction. 'But I think you'll find it useful.'

I didn't care what it was, although I knew my curiosity would get the better of me sooner or later. I didn't want to waste these few precious moments of privacy when I had him all to myself. I allowed my hand to drift across the planes of his face, tracing the stubbled line of his jaw. I had sketched him once, in the course of another investigation, and it had embarrassed me then that I was able to draw him from memory.

Now his face, his body were the source of my most private imaginings, and I would not feel shame for it.

'Do you think I don't know that most women would jump at a chance like this?' I murmured. 'I'm honoured that the great and grand Gregory Merchiston wants my hand in marriage.'

'I'm not great or grand, Sarah. I'm a doctor from a poor family who somehow convinced the elitist bastards here that I was worth moulding in their image.'

I had seen what a good family name and money could turn men into, and I had no use for it.

'I'm not going to be your wife. I'm going to be your equal, maybe even your superior. And one day I'll come to you with a proposal from one of the most respected forensic surgeons in Edinburgh, and you can accept it if you still want me.'

Most men would have laughed in my face. But the slow smile that spread across Merchiston's features held no mockery; only pride and the tenderest affection. I wondered for a moment if I really had done the right thing by rejecting his proposal.

He gave me the lightest of kisses, his mouth smiling against mine, and I realised as we pulled apart that while he wasn't my first kiss, he was the first one – and maybe the only one – that mattered.

'Four thousand words on the structure and use of formaldehyde with particular reference to its use in preserving the liver. On my desk by Monday, if you please.' I looked at him, bemused. 'Well, if I have to wait for you to graduate and begin your glittering career, we'd better get started.'

I felt unaccountably warm inside, as if I had just drunk some of his precious whisky. He believed in me. He didn't dismiss my ambitions, grandiose as they were; he supported them. And not only that, he had given me extra work to do.

'You know, some girls prefer flowers, Professor Merchiston,' I teased.

He shrugged. 'Then let them have all the bouquets they desire. You and I are motivated by something entirely different – even though preserved organs don't smell quite as nice as roses.'

'Oh, I don't know.' I smiled, resting my cheek against the rough tweed of his jacket and breathing in the smell of tobacco and sweat – and yes, formaldehyde. 'I think they have their charms.'

Tempting as it would have been to stay like that all afternoon, I had work to do. As I strode out of the medical school and across Middle Meadow Walk, the trees with their budding, unfurling leaves casting shadows across my path, I felt lighter and more free than I had in years, giddy with anticipation that had surprisingly little to do with the man I had just left behind and everything to do with the building in front of me.

The Remington typewriter was a cumbersome machine, and I stabbed awkwardly at the keys until I produced the name of the hospital – the Royal Infirmary of Edinburgh. As I stared at the initial fruits of my labour, I felt goose bumps prickle across my skin. Here I sat, in one of the most august hospitals in Britain, in gainful employment. It wasn't surgery, but it was closer than I had come to breaking through the myriad invisible barriers that stood in my way. Even in this small office, I could smell the disinfectant. If I listened carefully, I could hear the sounds of the hospital in action – doctors issuing orders, nurses obeying them and patients audibly praying that nothing would get lost in translation.

The hospital in all its red-brick, chloroform-scented glory only stood on the other side of the Walk from the medical school, but there were days when it might as well have been on the moon for all the chance I thought I had of practising medicine behind its walls. The typewriter felt like my Trojan horse – now that they had admitted me past the locked gates, there would be no getting rid of me.

Chapter 36

As I pushed open the door of my uncle's house, I revelled in how tired I felt. Ladies, as Aunt Emily was forever reminding me, weren't meant to exert themselves. But I had tried to be the girl they all wanted, sweet and simpering, and it had exhausted me more than I could have imagined.

'Sarah?'

Aunt Emily's summons had been getting friendlier of late, and any concerns that my aborted engagement would drive yet another wedge between us seemed to be unfounded. For all she scolded and interfered, she did it out of love, a love that had been markedly absent from her sister.

She sat by the fire, lamps burning brightly to ward off the dark and the cold and whatever lay in wait there. I wanted to go to her, to pretend for a moment that I was still the chubby little girl she had dandled on her knee, whose scrapes and scratches she had kissed better. That she was still the woman who could protect me. For a moment I was overcome with a fierce love for this rigid, resolute woman. She might not have known it, but our roles were reversed now – she couldn't or wouldn't see the evils that the world held, far worse than a torn skirt or a ruined reputation, than education or spinsterhood. I would do everything in my power to ensure that she never learned.

'The son of a family friend is moving to Edinburgh from Aberdeen. He's a lawyer and according to his mother has considerable suffragist sympathies.' She said the word as though it were a rash – an unpleasant condition, but easily overlooked. 'I thought we might invite him for dinner once he's settled.'

I struggled to keep a smile out of my voice. 'Perhaps. I'm going up to change, Aunt Emily. I look a fright.'

I ran up the stairs before she could elucidate further on the charms of this new prospect – legal, political and otherwise. She would never change, still so determined to bring me the kind of happiness she thought I deserved, still so incapable of realising that it would be more of a prison than a happy ending. I felt the weight of Merchiston's gift in my reticule, and wondered what she would have said had she known I had turned down not one proposal, but two.

Gregory Merchiston was nothing like the men she had in mind for me – no title, no respectable family lineage, no fortune. He didn't want me at home in the parlour, embroidering baby clothes and accepting visitors. His was a life that required a very different mate, a life soaked in blood and whisky, where a needle and thread would be used to stitch up the ragged edges of skin, rather than fine linen.

Did I want to be that mate? To be something more than a sleuthing partner or protégée, to have more than a sweet stolen kiss that awoke parts of me that had frozen over ever since Paul Beresford had taken more than I willingly gave? Did I want to erase that painful part of my past and give myself to this man?

I did. Oh God, I did.

But it wasn't enough.

Perhaps there was something wrong with me. Perhaps I was damaged, unnatural. Even Julia and Edith, so happily ensconced in a Sapphic love affair I couldn't quite fathom even now, looked to more than medicine to fill their lives. I had spent so long carving out my small space in the world, and I didn't know if I was ready to share it – or myself. Gregory Merchiston was still a man, enlightened though he seemed to be, and he might be willing to overlook behaviour in a friend that he couldn't countenance in a wife. Could he really accept that there was something else that made my pulse race, my breath catch? Even if I could take the risk, could he really marry me knowing that my heart was only half his and that the rest belonged – and would always belong – to medicine?

I kicked off my boots as Agnes drew me a bath, and began to pull off the tailored fawn wool suit that had, in the intervening hours between breakfast and dinner, become covered in ink and chemicals and something I decided was better off unidentified. It felt as though I was taking off my armour, and grateful though I would be to sink my aching muscles into the hot, rose-scented water, I wished I could keep it on just a little while longer. Let Sarah Gilchrist, medical student, sit down for dinner, and to hell with what Uncle Hugh thought.

The severe style suited me, I thought, catching sight of my reflection as I unbuttoned the collar of the crisp white blouse that had been starched into such stiffness that it still held its shape even as I tossed it into the pile on the floor. The swathes of silk and lace that my aunt would drape me in – even the pistachio-green taffeta that Agnes had laid out for me to change into for dinner – felt like a costume now. I couldn't run in those soft kid shoes and I would barely be able to breathe, much less eat, in a corset laced as tightly as it would have to be for me to fit into the dress. Part of me wanted to be able to lose myself in those pleasures again – I could dress as plainly as I wanted for lectures, but that didn't mean I couldn't luxuriate in colours and patterns and fabrics each evening. But when I looked at my wardrobe, all I could see was the tiny sets of clothes Aunt Emily had given me for my doll one Christmas.

These were outfits I could be shown off in, admired, posed in, insofar as my corset would allow it.

For a moment, when I felt the heat of the fire on my face, it wasn't the one that burned merrily in the grate but the raging inferno that had blazed its way through one of Edinburgh's finest town houses. I felt that same snarl of heat and rage in my veins and I wondered what Aunt Emily would do if she came up here to find all my frills and furbelows in a pile of smouldering ash. Lock me up for good, probably, in the same genteel facility that now housed Aurora Greene.

Pushing thoughts of arson aside, I placed the dress back none too gently with all the other pretty things I found myself outgrowing, and instead picked out a plain poplin gown of dark forest green. Aunt Emily had been reluctant to buy it, but I had persuaded her that I needed something sober to wear to public lectures, and she had paid the modiste with a weary sigh. Somehow I doubted that even her young lawyer with all his calls for female advancement would be won over by me in this – although I remembered the heat in Merchiston's grey eyes when he saw me smoothing the fabric down over my hips over dinner with the Chalmerses.

With a broken engagement behind me and years of study ahead of me, there could be no more room for meek acquiescence. I felt the mould my family was trying to force me into splinter and crack around me, no longer able to contain the woman I was becoming.

A woman who accepted presents from a gentleman who had made his intentions very clear, no less. As Agnes closed the door behind her with a quick curtsey, I pulled the package out of my bag and ripped the paper off in haste, like a child with a birthday present. What I uncovered took my breath away.

The mother-of-pearl glowed softly in the firelight. I ran my fingers over the smooth handle, but it was the dark metal of the gun's barrel that held me enraptured. A strange gift to give the object of your affections, but then Merchiston was a strange man. It was the promise I had been looking for, that he would help my future endeavours, not hinder them.

A small box of bullets lay nestled next to the gun, and I picked it up to read the message scrawled on it in black ink by a familiar hand.

To S. G. – for when I can't be there. All my fondest regards, G. M.

I knelt before the carved wooden box my mother had given me for my trousseau and placed the weapon beneath the filmy softness of the petticoats that would have layered beneath my wedding dress.

I might need them one day. But something told me I would need the pistol sooner.

Acknowledgements

The fact that these acknowledgements feel like they need to be twice as long as the one for *The Wages of Sin* is a testament of the amazing support structure I've found since then. This has a lot to do with Scotland's overwhelming dedication to literature, from Nicola Sturgeon's constant promotion of reading to Creative Scotland's terrific funding team (I miss you all, but I don't miss the terrible office coffee) and of course the incredible individuals who make up the literary scene in Scotland, especially the Woolf Pack. I always wanted to be able to thank a fabulous group of writers with a catchy name in my acknowledgements, and now I can! Particular thanks must also go to Angie Crawford of Waterstones in Scotland, Blackwells in Edinburgh, Mairi and the team (especially Artemis!) at Lighthouse Books and Julie at Golden Hare. I'm insanely honoured to have you selling my books.

None of this would have been possible without:

My wife Lola – I admit my choice of music at our engagement party was inappropriate but hey, at least no one got murdered!

My incredible agent Laura Macdougall, for putting up with me. Words can't express how grateful I am for your support, which is ironic under the circumstances.

Imogen Taylor, editor extraordinaire, who I'm convinced can make a book better just by looking at it.

The rest of the team at Headline/Tinder Press, especially Amy Perkins – you all rock and I feel so lucky to have you in my corner (and on my social media feeds).

I write about families of choice and families of blood and am immeasurably lucky that mine happen to be one and the same. Dad, you're my best friend and staunchest supporter and I hope this finally sets your mind at rest re: why I was asking about syphilis.

Meg Kissack, friend and coach extraordinaire. I literally could not have done this without you and I wasn't kidding when I said I'm hiring you for every book in the future. You saw me through the most gruelling part of the process and made it fun again.

Islay Bell-Webb who inspires me by just being in the same room – please move up to Edinburgh so you can do it more often.

Deanna Raybourn – my best decision was wandering into Waterstones in Covent Garden to shelter from the rain and walking smack into a table holding *Silent in the Grave*. You are everything I would have imagined from that first sentence and a wonderful friend to boot, even if all your heroes do knock me a few places back down the Kinsey Scale.

Ruth, you are the Christina Yang to my Meredith Grey – smarter, more together and with better hair and always on hand with exactly what I need to hear.

Ali Trotta, who keeps me sane on the regular by letting me send her screenshots of my to-do lists.

Karen Burrows – at this point, you know more about me than anyone else and I'm afraid of what you'll make public if I don't include you. Friendship, like corsets, is a two person job. I'm very glad that friend is you.

Historical fiction relies so heavily on other people's

research, so special thanks must go to Alison Mould, Matthew Sweet, Kathryn Harkup and of course Elaine Thomas.

The bulk of this and every Sarah Gilchrist book was written at Elephants and Bagels, who said I could have a free bagel if I mentioned them here. I was going to anyway, but since you asked I'll have smoked salmon and cream cheese on spinach with extra pepper.

And lastly, to Franklin, Orlando, Nora and Collins – I could have written this a lot faster if you hadn't spent so much time lying on the laptop, but it wouldn't have been as fun. I know you can't read this because you're cats, but I hope you enjoy lying on, gnawing and generally destroying this book as much as you did the first.